two is a lie

TANGLED LIES

PAM GODWIN

Cover Artist: Okay Creations
Interior Designer: Pam Godwin
Editor: Lesa Godwin, Godwin Proofing

Visit www.pamgodwin.com

disclaimer

The books in the TANGLED LIES series
are not stand-alones.

They must be read in order.
One is a Promise
Two is a Lie
Three is a War

one

Spineless.

Bloodless.

The early morning fog constricts me with ghost-like arms. The milky pall drapes over my backyard, swallowing the weak light of sunrise and contorting my sense of reality.

This moment, this entanglement of two distinct parts of my life, can't be happening.

The vibrating silhouette of my past paces a few feet away, staring at me like an ethereal presence.

Cole. My first love. My greatest loss.

My second chance stands beside me, his expression as naked as his upper body, chilling in the cold mist.

Trace. He's supposed to be my new beginning. My future.

Dark hair versus blond, brown eyes clashing with blue, Cole and Trace couldn't look more different from each other. But the emotions coiling their postures and tightening their faces are the same. Pain, fear, desperation, and most of all, unbridled rancor. The anger between them is so potent it crackles the air.

I hug my waist tightly, shaking in my attempt to stifle the tears.

Cole's alive.

Trace knew there was a chance he'd come back.

And they look like they're seconds from killing each other.

My entire body is a heartbeat, pulsing heavily, painfully, flaring every cell and nerve ending. I think it's my muscles twitching or maybe overworked blood vessels. I think I'm in shock.

They watch me as if waiting for me to do something. Send them away? Have a nervous breakdown? Stab them with a sharp object? Any of those things are possible. But first, I need to pull my shit together and demand some answers.

The questions pile up in my throat, some screaming louder than others. Why did Cole disappear for over four years? And why didn't Trace tell me he knew Cole or that they were best friends? Why didn't he tell me Cole might come back?

"I need you to put aside your animosity for each other and give me the truth." I pace the driveway alongside my house, my breaths huffing in white clouds as I try to gather my thoughts. Circling back, I stop in front of Trace. "If you've been watching over me since Cole left, you knew how badly I—" My voice cracks, and I clear my throat. "You knew I was hurting. Why didn't you tell me there was a chance he was alive?"

"There are a lot reasons why I couldn't." Trace wipes the blood from his lip where Cole punched him. "First and foremost, it would've endangered your life."

"What does that even mean?" My mind jumps to CIA, special forces, or some secret organization within the government.

"It's classified." Cole inclines his head away from me, depriving me of eye contact and closing himself off. "The less you know, the safer you are."

"The less I know…" I echo in a hollow voice. "Do you have any idea what it's like to *not know?* When you stopped calling and emailing, it gutted me. Then a stranger showed up at my door and told me you died in an explosion." My breaths quicken, chopping up my words. "The pain is indescribable, Cole. I wanted to die a thousand times over." I angrily swipe at the moisture on my cheeks and turn to Trace. "And *you* didn't tell me shit."

"I had no concrete information." Trace's scowl deepens. "I was operating on assumptions and—"

"But you knew there was a chance, and that chance—"

"Could've brought you more pain." He leans toward me, all rock-jawed and blazing eyes. "Let's say I broke protocol and told you he could've been alive. It would've raised your hopes, and you would've waited and waited." He straightens and squares his shoulders. "What if I was wrong? If he never showed up, what then? It would've made things so much harder for you. I couldn't bear it."

"Because you wanted her for yourself," Cole

seethes, launching toward Trace.

"Stop!" I dart forward, pulse racing.

Cole spins away and plunges his fingers in his hair.

"If you hit him again, we're done." I press a hand against my throat, fighting for every painful breath. "Understand?"

With his back to me, Cole tenses. Then he drops his head and nods.

"He's right," Trace says, low and scratchy. "When I watched over you the first year he left, I became enamored. Obsessed. I wanted you, irrationally and hopelessly. Then I watched you mourn him for the next two years, and I still wanted you. But I had no intentions of pursuing you. You know this, Danni, given the lengths I went to push you away."

"You wouldn't have had to push her away," Cole roars, "if you hadn't made contact in the first fucking place!"

The thunder of his voice is loud enough to rattle my bones and bring all my neighbors outside.

The moment I have that thought, Virginia calls out from the rear of her house next door. "Danni?"

"Everything's fine, Virginia." Squinting at Cole, I whisper, "What am I supposed to tell her? How do I explain your reappearance?"

What do I tell my sister, my parents, and everyone else in my life? Maybe he won't be around long enough to say anything. I press the heel of my hand against the pang in my chest.

"I have a cover story." Cole grabs his duffel bag from the driveway and strides toward my back door. "For now, just…don't say anything."

When he slips inside my house, I approach the

short metal fence between the backyards and bend over it to see Virginia.

"What's all that ruckus?" She stands in her doorway, wearing a flowery robe and house slippers, her white hair rolled in pink curlers.

"It was me." Trace leans beside me and braces his forearms on the fence. "Good morning, Virginia."

"Don't *good morning* me, young man." A cane appears in her hand and she points it at him. "I know that wasn't you hollering."

Fuck. She can't see shit, but her hearing is better than mine on most days.

"He has a cold." I grab Trace's hand and pull him away from the fence. "I'm taking him inside before it gets worse."

"Hm, well…" Suspicion creaks through her voice. "Make sure he drinks hot tea and gargles salt water."

"Got it." I release Trace's hand and head toward the back door.

As I reach it, he hooks an arm around my waist and pulls my back to his chest. "I'm not letting you go."

My heart pounds, and I compulsively slide my fingers over his against my hip. I love him so fucking much, but that love feels trampled and wounded beneath a thousand unanswered questions.

"It killed me to watch you grieve for two years." He rests his forehead against the back of my head. "But I couldn't give you hope without knowing with absolute certainty he was coming back. I *needed* to see you heal."

Warmth fills my chest, expanding my ribs. His constant concern for me is one of the countless reasons I fell in love with him. But… "You proposed to me, knowing he might come back. What did you think would happen?"

"Proposal or no proposal, there was no stopping what was happening between us." He turns me in his arms and cradles my face in his hands. "The day you told me you loved me changed everything."

Our eyes connect and fasten. Whenever I tumble into that blue gaze, it doesn't matter where I've been or how far I have to go, because this is the moment, the bright spark of belonging and grace, that's worth fighting for.

I don't understand the enigma of love, only that it holds me hostage, cares for and worships me, abandons and breaks me, and always lures me back for more. I'm greedy for it. For *him*.

"I feel deceived, Trace. By both of you." I grit my teeth. "I don't know what to think about your omissions and secrets. And Cole better have a damn good reason for disappearing, for letting me believe he was dead all this time."

"He'll have the best reason of all." His voice is gruff, dejected, as his attention drifts over my shoulder at the closed door behind me. "Protecting you is the *only* reason he would've stayed away."

I step back, anxious to go inside and get answers, but Trace tightens his grip on my jaw.

"I'm not giving up on us." He bends his knees, putting us at eye level. "I will never *ever* walk away from you."

I can only nod. His declaration both thrills and terrifies me.

Since Cole didn't die, does that mean I'm engaged to two men? What if I can't forgive either of them? What if I lose them both in the end?

My heartbeat quickens, stomping through my veins. What am I going to do?

Deep breath. Cole owes me a lot of answers. He left me for over four years, and it's going to take a *saving children from a burning building* type of excuse to abolish everything he put me through.

When I open the back door, he's not in the dance studio. I'm trembling with anxiety by the time I reach the kitchen. I still don't see him, but he's here somewhere. In my house, in the home we shared, where we made so many memories together. I met him right outside the front door. Kissed him goodbye on the porch. Mourned him for years within these walls. My mind is having a helluva time accepting his resurrection.

I pause at the coffee maker, desperately needing caffeine for the impending conversation.

"I dropped my mug on the driveway," I say numbly.

"I'll clean it up later." Trace removes three cups from the cabinet.

"Cole drinks his—"

"The same way you do." His expression empties, matching the detachment in his tone. "Cream, no sugar."

"Don't do that." I touch the stiff muscles in his forearm. "I hated that cold mask when I met you. I don't want to see it ever again."

"I'm struggling to hold myself together, Danni." He grips the edge of the sink and stares out the kitchen window. "At some point over the last six months, I convinced myself he was dead, hoping with everything inside me you wouldn't be put in the position you're in now."

By position, he means decision. The choice he demanded I make two months ago.

If Cole was in this room right now, where would I fall? Would you shove me aside to get to him?

At the time, I chose Trace. He was my future. But that was before I knew a future with Cole was still possible.

"I'm going to make the coffee." Trace straightens and focuses on the task. "So you can have a few minutes to talk to him alone. I know you need that, and I trust you."

His tone is soft with sincerity, not a hint of warning or conjecture. He's trying to make this easier, for my sake.

"Thank you." Lingering behind him, I ache to press a kiss to the bare skin on his spine, but I'm conflicted.

I don't know what's going to happen to us, and I can't let myself get bowled over by longing, dread, and all the other things I'm feeling right now.

In the hallway, I peek into the dining room, expecting to find Cole with his motorcycle where he left it all those years ago. But he's not there, so I head to my bedroom and pause on the threshold.

He stands in the doorway of my closet with his back to me. The lift of his shoulders, the sound of his exhales, and the intoxication of his living, breathing presence catapults me into the one emotion I hadn't let myself feel yet.

Happiness.

I linger in the moment, savoring the soul-deep elation curling through my insides. No matter what happens or what he's done, I will forever be grateful for his life.

Raising a hand, he touches the hangers that once held his clothes. His fingers trail along the crisp shoulders of suit jackets and collared shirts that belong to another man. His posture tenses, and a tremor shakes down his spine.

"Your things are boxed up in the basement." I slip into the tiny room, circle the bed, and stop within arm's reach behind him. "I didn't get rid of anything."

He stiffens, and his hands lift to palm the doorframe on either side of his head, as if seeking the support to stay upright.

With a stomach full of nerves, I ghost my fingers over the back of his t-shirt, taking in the protruding ridges of his ribs. "Why are you so thin?"

"I've been separated from my heart for four and a half years."

The fierce wound inside me cries out, begging to be soothed. "I've been here, Cole. Where have *you* been?"

"Hiding." A ragged breath shudders through him. "I was being watched. Everything I did was monitored, tracked, and recorded. I can't—" He drops his hands, fisting them at his sides. "That's all I can tell you."

"You have to give me more than that. Something I can grab onto. Who was watching you? Please, Cole. Talk to me."

He whirls toward me and wraps his arms around my back, giving me a glimpse of his damp, bloodshot eyes before he buries his face in my neck. "Tell me I haven't lost you."

two

Tell me I haven't lost you.

Cole's plea whispers through me, igniting an ache in my throat.

"Be very careful what you ask of me." I push against his chest, breaking his embrace. "*I* lost *you*. I moved on. It took me years. Years of unimaginable heartache—"

"I don't have to imagine it. I lived it!" He paces through the room, panting and gripping the back of his neck. "I would never move on from you. You're it for me. My beginning. My end. My fucking forever. If you died, even if I saw your lifeless body with my own eyes, I wouldn't move on. And I sure as hell wouldn't marry someone else."

The raw, unrestrained pain in his words punches

me straight through the heart, and I gasp.

"Clearly, you don't share my feelings." He glares at the ring on my hand.

I share his feelings in every way, and guilt stabs me anew. I never saw his body. I just blindly believed he was gone. Should I have questioned more? Dug harder?

A sob rises up, threading my voice. "I didn't—"

Something blurs in my periphery. Before I can blink, Cole is slammed against the wall, choking in the shackle of Trace's hand.

"*Never* talk to her that way again." Trace shoves harder against Cole's throat, punctuating his point. "She's suffered enough."

The thick concentration of testosterone clots the air and locks my joints. Though I've seen Trace attack a man once before, I'm immobilized by the calmness in his movements. He strikes, neutralizes, and commands, without showing a single sign of being winded or agitated.

Cole grips the fist around his throat and closes his eyes. His body slumps, and an anguished sound escapes him.

"I'm so sorry, Danni," he whispers, seeking me with unguarded misery in his gaze.

I share that feeling deeply, because despite the lies and unanswered questions, I love him. But that doesn't mean I can walk away from Trace.

When I nod my acceptance of Cole's apology, Trace releases him and steps back.

Cole sags against the wall, tucking his chin and gripping his knees. I've never seen him look so defeated and shattered.

The instinct to go to him urges my legs to move,

but I fight it. I can't choose sides until I've heard the truth. Not that I'm capable of choosing. My heart wants both. But my damn heart got me into this mess. I need to use my brain to find a way out.

Trace hands me a mug of coffee from the dresser and kisses the top of my head.

"Thank you." I turn to Cole and gesture at the other two mugs. "He brought you a cup."

As Trace steps into the closet and pulls on a t-shirt, Cole trudges toward the dresser and stares at the mugs with a slack expression.

"I can't drink coffee," he says, lifting it to his lips, "without thinking about the morning we met."

My smile trembles, and my insides cave in. Will this ever stop hurting? I can't see how. There's no resolution that brings both of them happiness, and that's what I need. I need them to be happy again.

Dressed in a collared shirt and jeans, Trace emerges from the closet and sits on the edge of the bed, hands clasped between his spread knees, head tilted down. I can't see his face, but I know those glacial eyes are angled toward Cole, scowling as intensely as his mouth beneath the mantle of his brow.

My bedroom isn't big enough for the three of us, and as the seconds tick by, the space grows smaller, tighter, pressing against my chest. Unbidden, my foot taps, drawing attention to my churning nerves.

We should move into the living room or somewhere with more space. But there isn't a room in my house large enough to contain this.

I kick off my fuzzy slippers and climb onto the bed. With my back against the headboard, I chew my thumbnail, fidget with the pull strings on my hoodie, sip the coffee, and wait for someone to speak.

The silence endures.

Awkward, pregnant, miserable goddamn silence.

I draw a steeling breath and search Cole's eyes. "What are you going to do, Cole?"

"I'm going to fight for you." His jaw flexes, and he sets down the mug.

"Fight for me? All I see is you glaring at your colleague, best friend, or whatever Trace is to you. Meanwhile, I'm sitting here in the fucking dark without a clue as to where you've been or what you do for a living."

He stares at me for a long moment, his Adam's apple bouncing. "I can't tell you, Danni." A tortured whisper.

My blood heats. "I don't know you."

"Yes, you do." He sucks in a harsh breath and slams a fist against his palm. "You know me better than anyone."

"I don't even recognize you."

Where are his tattoos? And he always kept his brown hair clipped high and tight. Now it's long enough to run my fingers through, at least an inch around his ears and thicker on top. His jawline's still square, but narrower. His entire face seems drawn, emaciated, sharpening the angles of his cheekbones. He's a beautiful man, even now, but he looks so different. *Unhealthy.*

"You look like shit," Trace mutters. "Does anyone know you're stateside?"

"Just my handler." Cole meets his eyes. "I assume the house is clean?"

"Spotless," Trace says.

What the hell?

"You're obviously not talking about housekeeping." I gesture at the dirty laundry all over the floor. "What does spotless mean?"

They continue to glare at each other. But this is more than a silent sparring match. They're sharing some kind of a wordless conversation I'm not privy to.

I was being watched. Everything I did was monitored, tracked, and recorded.

Is the house clean?

"Does your job put me in danger?" A chill drips down my spine as I think about how careless I've been with my safety. "Is that why you're both always on me about locking my doors? And what do you mean by *is the house clean?* Is there a chance it was bugged?"

"Locking your doors is common sense." Trace glances at me over his shoulder, his expression stone-cold. "And no. No one knows about your connection to Cole."

"Except my handler." Cole relentlessly rakes a hand through his hair. "He's the man who came here three years ago."

"Robert Wright." My neck goes taut against the memory. "He's the one who told me you were dead."

"Not his real name, but yes." Cole looks at Trace. "He's the only person who has access to my whereabouts."

"Can you trust him?" I wrap an arm around my waist, hating the paranoid thoughts they're putting in my head.

"Yes."

"Did he tell you about his visit with me?" My voice

croaks as I relive the gutting horror of that day.

I don't hear the door shut, don't feel the couch beneath me, don't taste the tears flooding my face. The agony is all-consuming, crippling my body, twisting me into something unrecognizable, and spiraling me into a shapeless, hopeless place.

"No. He wouldn't tell me anything about you." Cole inhales deeply. "He thought it was best that I focus on staying alive."

Cole was in danger. Life-threatening danger that forced him into hiding, and I had no idea.

"Before you left, I specifically asked if your safety was a concern, and you *laughed* at me when you told me no."

He stares at his feet, unable to meet my eyes.

"Were you even in Iraq?" I ask.

The liar pins his lying lips and doesn't look at me. Maybe Trace can shed some light.

"You said you used to work together?" I wave a hand between them. "Is that how you became best friends?"

"Yes." Trace slides a knee onto the mattress as he shifts to face me. "I used to be his handler."

"You keep using that term." I finish off the coffee and set the mug on the nightstand. "I don't know what *handler* means, because I don't know what Cole does for a living."

"I'm bound by the same secrecy agreement as Cole, but I'll try to explain…" Trace strokes his chin, as if carefully choosing his words. "Here's an analogy. The handler of a weapon controls how the weapon approaches a target and decides when and where to aim."

A weapon. He said it was an analogy, but he chose that example for a reason. He wants me to understand the severity of Cole's job.

"Okay, so you were Cole's handler, and you called the shots." I study Trace's unreadable expression. "And Cole is what? Some kind of assassin?"

"No." Cole drags a hand down his face. "Don't dig, Danni."

"Do you kill people?"

He closes his eyes and breathes deeply, refusing to answer.

I bristle with frustration and turn to Trace. "Are you retired from this handler job?"

"Yes."

"You're not employed by the government or whoever Cole works for?"

"Correct. I'm completely severed from that business. I own the casino and work for myself."

"But it's okay for you to know about Cole's job and not me?" I feel like I'm pulling teeth to collect tiny pieces of a convoluted puzzle.

"Since I was intimately involved in his prior jobs, I knew…things." Trace's mouth bounces between a flat line and a frown. "But I know nothing about his last mission."

"Except you knew there was a chance he survived it."

"I knew Cole wouldn't have been stationed at an oil terminal, therefore, I knew he didn't die in an explosion." Trace rubs his brow. "What I didn't know was if the story about the explosion was a cover for his actual death."

"Bullshit." Cole clenches his jaw. "You know how hard it is to kill me. I'm fucking trained—"

"No one's impossible to kill." Trace lifts his head, glaring at Cole. "You went on that mission knowing your heart wasn't in it. You were preoccupied, unfocused. Frankly, I'm surprised you survived."

"What's he talking about?" I ask Cole, my stomach twisting into knots.

Cole scrapes a hand over the back of his head, frowning at Trace. "My job doesn't allow for personal distractions. We don't have relationships or attachments or—"

"Girlfriends? I was a distraction?" My voice is thin, pitted with alarm.

"No," he says heatedly. "You're the reason I fought so damn hard to stay alive. When I met you, I knew I'd have to complete this last job and that I'd survive it—*for you*—then I could quit." His timbre drops to a tormented whisper. "The job should've only taken a year. A year, and I would've been back with you, married, and maybe even planning a family."

His gaze falls to the ring on my finger, and he clenches his hands. The agony lining his expression is gut-wrenching, and my stomach cramps in sympathy.

Had he returned within a year as planned, we'd be together. I would've been oblivious about the true nature of his job, and Trace would've never made contact with me. Maybe that's the way it was supposed to be, but the pang in my chest disagrees.

My relationship with Trace undoubtedly made Cole's homecoming a clusterfuck. I would've still been furious and resentful with Cole, but I would've eventually forgiven him for being gone and let it go.

Because I love him.

But Trace is here, and no part of me regrets meeting him or falling in love with him. How could I? He was here for me when Cole wasn't. He showed me how to smile, hope, and love again.

Maybe this is the hand of fate at play, but it's too early to know if it's a curse or a blessing. The only thing that's certain is the inescapable decision looming in the future.

Dread builds in the back of my throat. It feels as though I have two hearts, and I'm waiting for someone to tell me I have to rip one out and hand it over.

And it's going to hurt like hell.

three

Every time I hear Cole's gravelly timbre or find his warm brown eyes watching me, I'm overcome with the instinctual need to wrap my arms around his neck. I ache for the familiar scent of him clinging to my body, for the fever of his passion to delete the distance between us and make me forget the past four years.

Then I look at Trace, the gorgeous man I woke next to this morning, and shame burns through me. I'm not a cheater. Even if Trace weren't here, staring at me with the kind of devotion that makes my heart twist, I wouldn't break my promise to be faithful to him.

But didn't I make the same vow to Cole?

If I'm with one of them, am I cheating on the other one?

Sinking beneath the horror of that thought, I slouch

against the headboard and tuck my knees to my chest.

Trace told me Cole would have a good reason for disappearing for so long, and while I know I've only heard a snippet of the full story, I can't begrudge Cole for the godawful choices he had to make. If he returned when he promised or contacted me in any way, it would've endangered me. I don't understand the threat, but I trust that he did what he had to do. He kept me safe and suffered greatly for it.

Trace, on the other hand, stole his best friend's girl. On the surface, it doesn't get more douchey than that. But I know him. My gut tells me his motivations are more selfless than they seem.

I regard him for a moment, itching to brush the disheveled blond strands away from his forehead. "Why did you retire from this James Bond job and not Cole?"

"Danni," Cole groans. "Don't call it that."

"What the hell am I supposed to call it? You're not telling me anything."

"When my parents died," Trace says, ignoring Cole. "They left me a sizable inheritance."

I nod, already aware of this.

"I didn't have a relationship with them." Sitting at the foot of the bed, Trace stares at his empty hands. "Part of our falling out had to do with my career choice. They wanted me to run a corporate empire. I wanted to…do something else. When I lost them both abruptly—"

"How?"

"Car accident." He draws his arms closer to his body, his expression moody. "When they died, I didn't need to work. But it wasn't just about the inheritance. My perspective on life changed, including the risks I was taking with my job."

There's more to that story, but I don't interrupt as he continues.

"I wasn't married to the job, so it was easy for me to not renew the contract. Cole's position, however, is different." His gaze flicks to Cole and returns to me. "Men in his line of work don't retire. They're born to do it and undergo years of rigorous specialized training in preparation for it. They breathe, live, and die for the job."

"Unless something extraordinary comes along," Cole murmurs from across the room. "*Someone* worth giving it all up for." He lifts his head and looks me directly in the eyes. "I meant what I said to you before I left. I already started the termination paperwork. I'm not renewing my contract."

I press a fist against my mouth as a mixture of joy and dread hijacks my breaths. "If you're retiring, why can't you tell me what happened to you?"

"You already know I work for a Federal agency." Cole approaches the bed and kneels beside it, resting his forearms next to my hip. "I can't tell you more than that. A spill relating to trade secrets, processes, operations, or style of work could cause irreparable damage to the national security of the country. It could result in loss of life."

The air whooshes from my lungs. *Jesus*. What's he involved in? Is he Delta Force? Some kind of SEAL team badass? A CIA operative? My knowledge of secret government shit is limited to movies and TV shows.

"He's leaving out another reason." Trace glances from me to Cole before giving me firm eye contact. "Neither of us want to go to prison."

"What?" My scalp tingles. "You would go to

prison for telling me what you do?"

"Yes." Cole props his elbows on the mattress and steeples his fingers against his lips. "We worked for an entity that doesn't exist, doing things that never happen and fighting wars no one will ever hear about. If we talked, it would be a criminal—"

"I would never say anything." I snap my spine straight.

"You would if you were interrogated. There are many ways to glean information. Ways far more sophisticated than lie detector tests." Cole frowns. "Our nation's enemies are even more creative, especially in their methods of torture."

"Torture?" A bud of fear bursts inside me. "You said I'm not connected to you, that I'm not in danger—"

"Something went very wrong with this last job." His eyes cut to Trace and back to me. "I was forced into hiding for three years, had to change my appearance, assume another alias, and stay far, far away from you. You're safe because I followed protocol and will continue to do so."

I expect Trace to rebuke Cole's unbelievable story, but as his head lowers, his mouth sets in sullen affirmation.

"Someone wanted you dead." Saying it out loud doesn't help it sink in.

"Lots of someones. It's the nature of the job." Cole's brown eyes lose focus as he stares at the mattress between us. "I couldn't risk looking you up, not even to see an updated picture of you online. I couldn't contact Trace, because my connection to him could've led someone back to you. When I…" His nostrils flare. "When I ran into trouble, I severed communication with you and Trace and disappeared. I had all my tattoos removed, wore colored contacts and glasses, shaved my head, and grew a beard. That man, the identity I assumed for three years…" He blinks and meets my eyes. "You wouldn't have recognized him."

I wilt against the mattress, reeling at the desolation in his words. "Are you still hiding?"

"I don't exist. The world I was embedded in is only aware of my fake identities, and I didn't come home until every threat against my life was eliminated."

Hiding…fake identities…threats…eliminated…

My eyes feel hot and gummy, and I suspect the tears have only just begun. "Is your real name Cole Hartman?"

"Yes, baby." He grips my hand and squeezes. "I've only ever lied to you about the job, and I'm so fucking sorry. I didn't have a choice."

There are so many questions pounding in my head I can't spit them out fast enough. "If you operated under different identities, what was the purpose of the fake explosion? Why couldn't you have just disappeared and left it at that?"

"I needed you to believe I was dead…for your own protection."

"But you said I was safe."

"You were. You *are*." His fingers weave around mine. "It was just another layer of security. I wasn't taking any chances with you."

My throat works through a tight swallow. "*Another* layer of security?"

"I was the first layer." Trace glances at my hand where it tangles with Cole's. "If something happened to me or if someone targeted you without me knowing, they would've seen you grieving, completely in the dark and unaware of Cole's true whereabouts."

"I thought you were watching me to keep me from dating?" I pull my hand from Cole's grip and narrow my eyes at Trace.

"That, too." Trace bends forward, resting his forearms on his thighs.

Trace succeeded in keeping men out of my bed. He kept everyone away except himself. We're all thinking it, and it feels gossamer-fragile writhing and tangling around us.

I'm in love with the man Cole entrusted to protect me.

Trace proposed to his best friend's fiancé.

I'm engaged to two men.

The unspoken thoughts gather between us like black clouds, charging the air and pricking my skin with icy darts of electricity. I hold my breath, hoping the storm will pass. But it's swelling, tensing Trace's posture, and shortening Cole's breaths. This time, the storm wins.

"I trusted you." Cole explodes to his feet, knocking the nightstand against the wall in his sudden fury. "If I'd known you'd move in on her, that you'd put your fucking dick in her—"

"Cole!" I surge to my knees on the bed and ball my hands. "That's not how it was!"

"I've never hated anyone as much as I hate you." He bares his teeth at Trace. "Why her? She's my goddamn life. My entire fucking world." Cole stabs a shaky finger in my direction without moving his focus from Trace. "You know what she means to me. You could've had anyone. Why did you have to go after her?"

"You know why." Trace looks at Cole with

compassion in his eyes and temerity in his scowl. "You know exactly how accidental love is, especially when it comes to her. There was no premeditation. No deceptive planning. Loving her is a privilege, one I don't deserve, but it was never a choice."

Love isn't a choice.

Those were my words to Trace only a couple months ago, and a sad smile pulls at my mouth.

Cole slowly blows out a breath, and his entire body seems to sag with the release of air.

"Cole." I scoot over on the bed, making room for him. "Please, sit down."

He toes off his shoes and lowers beside me with his back to the headboard, watching me warily.

I swivel to face him, sitting cross-legged and keeping Trace's position at the foot of the bed in my line of sight. I need to see both of them as I talk through this.

"I need to tell you things." I hold my hands out to Cole, palms up, and look into his eyes. "Some of it, you're not going to like. But I need to say it, get it all out in the open."

He doesn't hesitate to lean toward me and slide his fingers over mine. "I'm listening."

Trace rests a fist beneath his chin, intently focused on me. If he has a problem with Cole holding my hands, he's keeping his jealousy reined in.

I give him a grateful look and return to Cole. "Six months ago, I started dating. My sister set me up with a guy. I didn't know him, didn't really care who he was. I hadn't so much as kissed a man in three years, and I needed… I just really needed to move forward with my life. So I kissed this guy. He groped me—"

Cole's hands clench tightly around mine, and his molars saw side to side.

"Sleeping with him was a possibil—" I squeak at another painful squeeze of his grip.

"Shit." He relaxes his fingers around mine, adjusting his hold to stroke his thumbs over my knuckles. "Go on."

"I was lonely, Cole." My voice trembles, and the backs of my eyes burn. "You were dead, and I…I missed you so much. I thought, maybe, if I put myself out there again, if I spent the night with someone, I wouldn't hurt so badly." Tears sneak into my words, breaking up the syllables. "I started thinking I was sick, you know. Like I had an addiction to grief and heartache, because I couldn't pull myself out of it and—"

"Danni." Cole cups my face, lifting my chin to look at me. "I get it, baby. I couldn't eat, couldn't sleep, couldn't fucking breathe without you. You don't have to explain it. I felt every mile and second that separated us, and I'm so goddamn sorry."

"Did you…um…?" I grip his wrist and swallow. And swallow again. "Did you seek comfort…?"

"With another woman?" His eyes widen. "God, no." Then louder. "*No.*"

My heart thuds wildly. "It's been four and a half years since you…you…had sex?"

"You're the only one." He searches my face, his expression earnest.

Why do I suddenly feel so cold? I shouldn't be stunned by this. Cole is unwavering in his loyalty to me. I just…I hadn't let myself hope.

He was faithful.

And I wasn't.

As the realization settles in my chest, my lungs work harder. My breaths become shallow, and I gulp for air.

I wasn't faithful to him. I wasn't faithful.

Sweat beads on my skin. Shadows blot my vision. Oh God, I can't breathe.

Trace moves in my periphery, and his hand clutches my arm. "Danni?"

"Give her space." Cole brushes the hair from my face. "Breathe, baby. Deep breaths."

"I'm good." I push him back, wheezing as I try to keep the sobs from escaping. "Just give me a minute."

"This isn't your fault." Cole leans away, but doesn't go far.

"None of this is your fault." Trace hovers beside me, the heat of his body a comforting presence.

"I know." I pull in a deep breath, and another. "But I feel this…this overwhelming shame, like I betrayed you. Like I'm betraying both of you."

Cole reaches for me. "You're not—"

"I love him, Cole." I grab Trace's hand while holding Cole's wretched gaze. "I love him *fiercely,* and that's not all." I turn to Trace. "When I look at Cole, all the longing and devotion I felt for him comes rushing back. My feelings for him haven't faded. Not at all."

A muscle bounces in Trace's jaw, and his eyes shutter.

"So yeah…" I sniff and glare at the bedding. "I feel confused and helpless and so goddamn guilty. I know this isn't my fault. It's yours. Both of you." I lower my voice. "Which means you probably feel a lot worse than I do."

Their postures are mirrored—tense shoulders, bowed spines, heads down, and hands fisted. This sucks, but I haven't said everything I need to say, so I power forward.

"The night I started dating, Trace showed up and chased that guy away. That's how we met, and it wasn't a friendly introduction." With Trace's hand still curled around mine, I pull it against my lips, breathing across his knuckles. "He bought Bissara—"

"The restaurant you dance at?" Cole's head shoots up as he glances between us.

"Yeah. He really caught me off guard with that." I tell Cole about the employment contract, my ridiculous counteroffer, and the obscene salary I'm earning as a result.

Trace tilts his chin. "Hiring you was the easiest way to watch you discreetly."

"The cameras in the casino," I say with realization. "And you were such a dick about making me work there five days a week."

He hired me so he could watch over me and keep me under his roof? That's crazy. And sweet in a stalkerish way.

As memories of the past six months bubble up, I talk through them for Cole's benefit, explaining how contentious and hateful my relationship with Trace was in the beginning. I skip over the intimate interactions while punctuating Trace's dictate on anti-sex, anti-dating, and anti-anything between us.

"He's the only man who turned my head after you died." I watch Cole's brooding expression. "I swore I wouldn't pursue him, because he was adamant about his disinterest in me. But I couldn't ignore the way he made me feel when he wasn't being an asshole."

A smile twitches my lips, and I catch a glimmer of light in Trace's eyes.

"It'd been so long since I felt happiness." Tendrils of warmth unfurl inside me. "Trace made me want to try again."

Cole squeezes his eyes shut, and with a heavy sigh, he looks at Trace. "Thank you for that. For being there for her."

Given Cole's strained expression, it took a lot for him to say that.

"You're welcome," Trace says softly. "But she's not lying. I was cruel to her, and I deeply regret it."

I hold his hand beneath my chin, thinking back to all his hurtful insults and painful rejections. "I understand now why you treated me the way you did."

Cole was his best friend. He wasn't supposed to fall in love with me.

I continue to describe Trace's behavior to Cole, detailing how Trace repeatedly pushed me away. Then I broach the incident with Marlo and the devastation that followed—the guy I picked up at the bar, the blow job I gave in the car, and the punch Trace delivered in my driveway.

"Jesus Christ." Cole scrubs a hand down his face and glares at Trace. "You pretended to fuck another woman? That was your solution? Not only did you hurt Danni, you drove her straight into the arms of a stranger!"

"What would you have done?" Trace leans toward him, his throat turning crimson. "I was desperate and torn and at a complete and total loss. I loved her and couldn't tell her. And she loved me. I couldn't say *no* to her anymore. You don't know what that's like, Cole, because you've never had to hide your feelings from her."

Cole clasps his hands together behind his neck, his shoulders curling inward. "You forgave him for cheating, Danni?"

"We weren't technically together, so yeah, I eventually forgave him." I need to put everything on the table, and there's no easy way to say this part, so I just spit it out. "That night, Trace and I had sex for the first time."

A pained noise crawls from Cole's chest.

"It was angry and bitter and full of so much resentment." I pull Trace's hand against my breast, certain he can feel my heart banging. "He left me right after…" I peer over at Trace. "You left me because of Cole. You were shocked, spooked…"

"Sick with guilt." His fingers curl around mine, his eyes stark. "Because of Cole. But also because I caused you so much pain. I've never felt as stricken and worthless as I did that night."

"You slept in my driveway."

He nods.

"And took a beating from Virginia's cane the next morning." I scrape my teeth against my lip.

Trace gives me another nod.

"You shouldn't have made contact with her," Cole whispers.

"*You* shouldn't have ever gotten involved with her." Trace looms over him, scowling. "Your job forbids relationships, because it endangers the people you're close to. But you ignored that mandate and moved in with her. You got engaged to her. Then you fucking left her."

"I left her under *your* protection. The one person I trusted."

"And I kept her safe." Trace's lips pinch, his eyes taking on a lethal glint.

"Yeah." Cole sneers. "I know exactly how you—"

"Shut up! *Jesus.*" I feel like I'm drowning in turmoil with no salvation in sight. "Trace, the moment Cole and I met, our future was sealed. We were *involved* instantly. Going our separate ways wasn't an option. And Cole…" I reach out and nudge Cole's chin up. "Six months ago, I made the decision to move on from you. Whether it was with Trace or some other guy, I was going to find a lover. So your prevention plan with Trace was fucked from the get-go." I squint at him. "Surely, you realize it's better that I ended up with someone you trusted to protect me instead of some stranger you didn't know?"

The tension in Cole's face remains, but softens. He knows I'm right.

"Something I don't understand…" I cock my head. "If you and Trace were best friends, why didn't I meet him before you left?"

"I couldn't explain our relationship without a lot of questions." Cole's forehead crinkles.

"You could've made up a story and evaded my questions. You seem to be good at that."

He winces. "I had to lie to you about my job. I didn't want any more bullshit between us. Introducing him to you would've been an ongoing deception to maintain, because our friendship was founded in the work we did together. It would've been lies breeding more lies. I couldn't do that to you."

"Okay, I get that. Kind of." My chest rises on a deep breath. "Did you talk to him when we were together?"

Cole nods as Trace says, "We were in constant contact. He told me everything."

Everything? Before Trace and I made our relationship official, the sight of my engagement ring upset him. His reaction makes sense now. The ring was a persistent reminder that I belonged to his best friend.

But he also reacted to the piercing on my labium. The night in my dressing room, when he touched it, he immediately withdrew. That's when I found him in the casino bar with the brunette on his lap. It's like he knew I got the piercing because of Cole.

"Did you tell him about my piercing?" I ask Cole.

His gaze flashes to Trace and holds. "Yes."

My shoulders droop as I consider the ramifications. "You were close enough to share intimate details about our relationship. And I didn't even know you had a best friend."

"Danni." Cole rests a hand on my knee. "I'm sor—"

"No more apologies. I just need… I need to think about this. All of it." I look down at Cole's touch, his golden skin contrasting Trace's paler hand interlaced with mine. "I still can't believe you're alive."

The gravity of that floats between us, waiting to be plucked and processed. What now? Where will Cole live? This was his home. But it's Trace's home, too. Do I send them both packing and return to my isolation? My chest hurts at the thought.

I'm nowhere near ready to make decisions and

formalize action plans. The aftershock of Cole's reappearance is still shaking the foundation of my very soul. I need to let the disturbance settle and see where my feelings fall.

"Do you still have the dress?" The caution in Cole's voice lifts my head.

"The wedding dress?"

He nods.

My stomach tumbles. I never showed him the gown, because he wasn't supposed to see it until our wedding day.

"I have it," I whisper.

"I want to see it."

four

A broken heart undergoes varying degrees of pain, from a smarting sting to crippling desolation. I thought enduring it alone was the darkest level of hell. But as I watch Cole crouch beside the boxes in the basement and remove the wedding dress, I stagger beneath the combined weight of our torment.

With his back to me and his head angled down, he gently touches the crumpled white fabric. His spine bows through heavy gasps as he lifts the neglected thing and tries to straighten the wrinkles.

The sound of his strangled breaths slams my lungs together. His shoulders fall, pulling mine down with him. His knees collide with the floor, and I lock my legs, swaying in my attempt to stay upright.

I don't want to cry anymore, but his regret runs

deep, intensifying my own. Watching him come apart is a stake in the chest. I can't even feel my heart. It's just a gaping hole that won't stop bleeding.

Trace volunteered to remain upstairs, despite the reluctance burning in his eyes. Regardless, I don't think his presence would've stopped me from moving toward Cole. The need to console him crashes through me, trembling my chin and coursing tears down my cheeks. By the time I reach him and slide my hands over his back, he's shaking as violently as I am.

He twists at the waist and hooks an arm around my back, pulling me onto his lap. His embrace is fierce, squeezing me tighter, closer, until all I feel is his heart thundering against mine.

With my arms around him, I prefer to straddle him in this position, but we no longer have that level of intimacy. So I keep my knees together and pressed against his ribs as we hold each other in an iron grip.

He hasn't released the dress. As the tulle skirt rustles around us, I wonder what he thinks about it. I don't ask, because it doesn't matter. He'll never see me wear it.

"I buried your ashes on our wedding day." My voice breaks, thick with tears.

"I know." His breaths thrash hotly against my neck, his lips like fire as they brush my skin. "I didn't get out of bed that day. I just…I dreamed of you in this dress and drank myself into unconsciousness."

Knowing he was hurting along with me doesn't bring me comfort. "I haven't been back to your grave site since the day of the funeral. The ashes—" My eyebrows crumple together. "Were they—?"

"Just ashes. No one was cremated on my behalf."

Unsure how to respond to that, I continue with my train of thought. "Since you didn't have instructions on your burial or any family to speak of, you just have a cement marker in the middle of a cemetery." My eyes burn with damp regret. "I hated the whole arrangement and didn't want to remember that day or the image of your name engraved on that stupid block of concrete. So I never went back. I put its very existence out of my mind. Which was easy since I drowned myself in a drunken stupor for months after you died."

"I'm so sorry." He makes a pained noise and rocks us back and forth, as if it hurts too much to sit still.

I rest my head on his shoulder, tighten my arms around him, and savor the warm scent of his skin.

Feeling him against me is a balm for my heart. The scratch of his whiskers against my cheek, the deep sound of his breathing, and the bunching of his muscles—all of it creates a dipping sensation in my chest and thins out my tears.

My brain questions how well I actually know him, but my body recognizes the perfect way he fits against me, the tempo of his heartbeat, and compelling aura of his presence. My body knows exactly who he is, and it vibrates to reclaim him in every way.

"I agonized over the timing of my death." He sets the dress aside and strokes a hand through my hair. "When I severed communication with you and disappeared, I didn't trust anyone, didn't know who my enemies were. If they learned my true identity…"

"They would've found me."

"Yes. Cole Hartman had to die for reasons I can't tell you. It should've happened immediately, and every day I delayed put you at risk. But I couldn't…" He cups the back of my head, holding my cheek against his chest as he draws a shredded breath. "I put it off for months, trying to find another way. As our wedding day approached, I knew I was out of time. I couldn't let you wait for me at the altar. I couldn't destroy you like that."

"So you sent your handler to my house and destroyed me with the news of your death."

"The alternative was *your* death." He leans back and frames my face in his hands. "I know I'm asking you to blindly trust me after putting you through years of hell. But Danni, I need you to believe me when I say that everything I did, every second I spent away from you, was the only way to keep you from harm."

"There haven't been any attacks on my life." I shrug jerkily. "So there's that."

His gaze delves into mine, and he slides a hand through my hair, tucking the strands behind my ear. "You're as beautiful as I remember. Your soft little mouth, huge gray eyes, and the way you express yourself so vividly…here…" He trails a finger around the corner of my lips. "Memories of you haunted me in the best way possible. You gave me a reason to live. You kept me alive."

"Can you tell me about it?" I touch his cheekbone, tracing the sharp angle. "About the years you were hiding?"

He shakes his head, his brow heavy with sadness.

"Not even little things," I ask. "Like where you slept or who you were with?"

"It was a dingy hole in a nowhere town. I didn't speak the language there and kept to myself."

I scrunch my nose. "Do you know other

languages?"

"*Unë flas shtatë gjuhë.*" His accent changes, softens, as he says, "*Volim te više nego što misliš.*"

"Was that…?" I gasp. "That was two different languages, wasn't it?"

He sighs and kisses my forehead.

"Which languages?" I should be stunned speechless, but hearing foreign words uttered from his lips completely enraptures me. "The second one sounded like Italian."

"*No, questo è italiano.*"

"Okay, that was Italian. How many more do you know?"

"Tell me about your dance company."

"No, I want to talk about *you*."

"Danni." His voice dips, low and firm.

My knees bounce with frustration, but I'm fighting a losing battle. "I still have my company. I don't teach anymore, though. My schedule at the casino keeps me busy, and the pay is more than I'll ever need."

He folds his hand around mine, brushing his thumb across my fingers.

Electricity tingles up my arm, quivering a sigh through my voice. "I have every penny that was transferred into my account when you died."

Cole's savings and death benefits exceeded a hundred thousand dollars, and I never touched it. I couldn't bring myself to even think about it.

"The money's yours," he says tightly. "I wanted you to have it."

"No—"

"I'm going to find another job. A *safe* job that

doesn't require travel." The muscles in his neck go drumhead tight. "I'll never make as much as Trace, but I'll provide for you and—"

"What's that supposed to mean?" My chest fills with sand. "You think that's why I'm with him?"

"He's loaded. It makes things easier, doesn't it?"

Easier? He thinks any of this has been easy?

"Don't put your insecurities on me." I shove off his lap and stand over him, my voice shrilling through the basement. "You know me, Cole. You know I don't give a flying rat's ass about money."

"I'm not insecure—"

"Why bring it up then? Why even mention his money?"

"What are you doing with him, Danni? He treated you like shit. You deserve better."

"Oh, I do? I deserve you, is that it?" The vein in my forehead throbs. "You think I deserve someone who leaves me and makes me believe for years that he's dead?"

"Dammit." He leaps to his feet, his dark hair falling over his brow as he jerks his head toward me. "Listen to me—"

"No, you listen to me. That man upstairs, the man you trusted with my life, deserves every ounce of my love. Yeah, he can be a real asshole, but he's ferociously protective and generous and…and he's *here*. Always here. That's why you asked him to look after me, right? Because you knew he wouldn't abandon me. Think about it, Cole. He agreed to babysit a woman he never met for an entire year. A year that turned into four and a half years. He didn't have to do that. He didn't know me. He did it for *you*. And he never left. He stayed here." My voice tumbles into a whisper. "He never left me."

Cole flinches and flattens a hand against his chest, his expression devastated. But I'm not finished.

"Even when I deliberately hurt him, when I hooked up with that guy at a bar, he didn't leave me." My breath rushes out, taking my anger with it and leaving me depleted, dizzy. "He slept in my driveway, because he couldn't leave me."

"I didn't want to leave you." With a hand still pressed to his chest, he holds his fist in front of him, punching it down as he spits each word. "Walking away from you that morning, getting into that cab and leaving you standing there, alone…" He licks his lips, his voice fractured and hoarse. "It was the hardest thing I've ever done, and believe me, Danni, I've done some really hard things in my life."

He stares at me for a lifetime, his hands coming together against his sternum, as if holding himself away from me. *Or holding in his heartache.*

I think he's waiting for me to say something, perhaps something that'll take his pain away. But I don't have answers. I'm shivering so badly I can't even muster my voice.

His chest rises and falls, and his beautiful face contorts into a picture of tragedy as he looks away.

My trembling grows frenetic in the quiet that follows. I want to scream at the injustice of it. I want to throw myself on the floor and curse the cruelty of love. I want to throat-punch anyone who says the heart knows things the mind can't explain, because my heart is a loser. It's wired to wreak me. Not just once, but over and over. And I'm scared. So fucking afraid of how this will end.

"Goddammit," he whispers achingly, clasping his fingers on his head as he paces. "I'm not giving up on us. I won't."

"Look at us, Cole." My shoulders slump. "We're miserable."

"So what?" He whirls toward me. "Yeah, it's going to suck. Big deal. We'll work through it. We'll fight and shout and say hurtful things, because that's what people do when they care, and I care more than you'll ever know."

His hands fall to his hips, and his gaze drifts over my shoulder, hardening into a murderous glare.

I turn and find Trace standing at the bottom of the stairs. Fingers resting in the pockets of his jeans and chin angled down, he watches us from beneath a scowling brow.

"How long have you been here?" How did I not hear him?

"You said *asshole,* and I figured you were talking about me." His scowl twitches, giving me a trace of a smile.

I face him fully and don't smile back. "If you knew there was a chance Cole would return, why did you propose to me? No more bullshit, Trace. I want a straight answer."

"I didn't know he planned to retire."

My mouth opens, closes, and I glance back at Cole. "Is that true?"

"I guess I never mentioned it." He crosses his arms over his chest. "It's none of his business."

"You told him about my pussy ring. I'm pretty sure *that* was none of his business. But quitting a job you shared with him, retiring from something you were *born to do?* That very much qualifies as something you would tell your best friend."

Cole stares at me, complexion ashen. Dragging a hand across his mouth, he paces to the futon and perches on the edge. Bending over his lap with his hands laced together, he bounces a leg and scatters nervous energy through the room.

"When you asked me to watch over her…" Trace stands still, his tone accusing. "You said it could be an ongoing thing."

I whip my head toward Cole. "You lied to me?" My heart beats against my chest so violently I have to cough a few times to get it back under control. "You said—"

"I know what I said." His brown eyes thrash with unwavering adamancy. "It wasn't an easy decision. The job was a part of me. I know you understand that. It would be like asking you to give up dancing."

The air evacuates my lungs. "I couldn't."

"Exactly. But the night I told you I was leaving for a year, I knew it would be my last mission. My job endangered you. It separated me from you." He drops his gaze to the floor and lowers his voice. "With all those miles and years between us, it became very clear just how easy it would be to give it up. And I did. I quit the moment I returned to the States."

He lets me chew on that, watching me with yearning and desperation.

The only sounds in the basement are our heavy breaths and the tick of the analog clock on the wall. It's only eight in the morning, and the constant strain of the past two hours is starting to wear on me. I should be in bed, with Trace, dreaming of wedding plans.

I press my thumb against the silver band on my finger. Trace knew there was a chance Cole would come back, but he thought Cole would just leave me again. And again and again. That realization spider-webs through my mind, weaving all of Trace's actions, desires, and impulses into a sticky net of protectiveness.

"You didn't want me to be alone anymore." I peer up at Trace, hating the worry pulling at his scowl.

"I fell in love with you, Danni, and with that comes a responsibility. Your happiness and safety trumped my loyalty to Cole." Sadness darkens his expression. "You're all that I am, and the moment I accepted that, protecting you was no longer a favor or a job. It became a prerogative."

"So you bound me to you."

"No, I bound *myself* to *you*." His eyes flash to Cole and return to me. "I'm sick over the position that puts you in. But I will never regret the way I feel about you."

Cole jumps to his feet. "How about instead of proposing to her, you waited until I came home? Who she spends her life with is *her* choice, her decision to make *after* she has all the facts."

"I gave her the choice." Trace snaps his spine straight, voice booming. "She chose me."

"Because she thought I was dead!" Cole bellows, making me wince. "I will never forgive you, you selfish son of a bitch. You took the choice away from her and—"

"We all have choices. Right here. Right now." I step between them, heart racing. "Cole, you can go back to your job. If it means that much to you, you should. It'll hurt like hell, but if I can survive your death, I'll pull through if you walk away."

"I'm not going anywhere. Never again." He plants his feet, hands on his hips, staring at me with equal measures of madness and determination.

Relief whispers through me. I can talk a big talk, but I just got him back. Losing him again would gut me.

I turn to Trace. "You knew he might show back up. What was your plan for that?"

"I didn't have a plan." Trace holds his hands behind him, shoulders back, a stalwart tower of formality and calm grace.

I appreciate his reserve now more than ever. Two hotheads in one room would've ended in bloodshed. But every man fights differently, and I won't underestimate Trace. Whenever he strikes, I don't see it coming.

Cole paces around me, blustering noisy breaths and stirring up the dust. "If you thought I would back down and let you—"

"I knew if you returned," Trace says, "it wouldn't be easy. Lines will be drawn. Rivalry will ensue. Because I'm not going anywhere, either." He looks at me with that confident tilt of his head I adore so much. "I'm not leaving your side, Danni, until—" His voice loses strength, and he swallows. "Until there comes a point when I'm not the one you want. And even then, I'll convince you to see the error in your decision."

Mounting dread closes my throat. I feel so heavy, so weighed down with panic and helplessness. The ache behind my eyes returns, stabbing like a thousand needles. I suck my bottom lip between my teeth, biting down and shaking my head rapidly, but I can't loosen the grip of my emotions.

"I need…" *Time. Space. A solution that doesn't exist.*

"I need to think."

I swivel toward the stairs with thoughts of escape, in my bed, where I can cry myself to sleep.

But what if they leave? They said they wouldn't, but the thought stops me on the bottom step.

"Are you going to work?" I ask Trace.

Thankfully, today's my day off. I might find solace in dancing, but not at the casino, where I'd have to smile and entertain a room full of strangers.

"I just called in and rearranged my schedule." Trace searches my face, frowning deeply at whatever he sees in my eyes. "I'll be here."

I shift my focus to Cole. "Where are you staying?"

He goes still, his voice stunned into a whisper. "This is my home." His hand presses against his sternum. "*You* are my home."

I turn my head toward the top of the stairs, trembling against the rise of tears. "How's that going to work? Are we all going to share a bed?"

"Fuck, no." Cole flexes his jaw. "I'm not sharing you."

Trace shakes his head, expression tight.

"I guess that means we'll all be nice and cozy and *celibate* for the indefinite future." I swipe at the spill of tears on my cheek and meet Cole's eyes. "All of your things are down here. You can sleep on the futon." I motion toward it. "I spent the night there a couple months ago. It's comfortable."

Trace regards me with his lips pinned together and questions firing in his eyes.

"If you stay here," I say to him, "you can sleep on the couch in the front room."

Without waiting for his reaction, I force my heavy

feet up the stairs.

Until running footsteps pound the steps behind me.

"Danni."

The urgency in Cole's voice freezes me in place, and I glance over my shoulder.

Standing a few steps below me, he grips the railing, his eye contact strong and steady. "It's never too late to start over."

My chest constricts. I did start over, and he's standing behind Cole with enough love shining from his blue eyes to light up a whole city.

And that's the problem.

They both love me.

We're not broken.

We're just…stuck.

Despite their deceptions and missteps, their intentions were neither malevolent nor selfish. Cole faked his death for me, and Trace kept Cole's secrets to protect me.

I don't condone their lies, but what they did is forgivable. Understandable. Which means there's nothing to fix.

Maybe Cole's right. Beginning again might be the only solution.

I just wish I knew what that meant.

five

The next five days pass in tedious stagnancy. As the shock of Cole's reappearance wears off, I'm left in a fog of brooding, heart-searching, blame-storming rumination. I wish I could say I'm a meditating genius and discovered the path to enlightenment. But the truth is, I'm a fucking mess.

Cole and Trace are giving me space. By space, I mean they're not breathing down my neck. They're in my house, though, circling each other like mortal enemies and watching me with long hard looks.

And here I am, lying in bed and hiding like a damn coward. It's after ten in the morning. I need to get up, go out there, and tell them what I want.

But what I want is the forest I can't see for the trees. There's too many *what-the-fucks* between what they've told me and what they've sworn to keep secret. I'm nowhere closer to figuring things out than I was the morning Cole emerged from the mist.

Trace goes to the casino when I do. I drive separately, and he keeps his disagreement about that zipped behind his scowl. Outside of work, his ass is planted on my couch. He took over the front room, running his million-dollar empire from his laptop.

Cole moved his motorcycle out of my dining room. When he's not outside messing with it or looking for a job, he stays in the basement.

Neither of them have tried to corner me or get me alone. They haven't made any moves on me whatsoever. But when our paths cross in the house, I read their thoughts as clearly as if spoken aloud.

They're not going to back down, give up, or go away. They're just biding time, waiting for me to tell them what comes next.

The question I keep coming back to is *why me?* I know hearts are involved, but at some point, wouldn't one of them throw in the towel? Why aren't they thinking, *She's not worth this. I love her, but she's not the be-all-and-end-all gorgeoso of my dreams. There are plenty of other women out there, women who won't make me sleep on the couch?*

They were best friends, and they tossed that away. For me. It's absolutely insane. I couldn't imagine fighting over a guy. Except when I think about it, when I really dig deep, I know I'd do all sorts of crazy, irrational shit for either one of them. Letting them both stay here already classifies me as borderline nuts. It's like pouring gasoline on a raging fire.

But I can't kick them out. I don't care if that makes

me a pushover. In my worldview, a person can't have too much compassion, and right now, they both need a little mercy. If they want to stay here, I won't fight them on it. I'm not sure I could, because I want them here. Against my better judgment, I want them so badly I can't breathe.

That said, our living situation isn't sustainable. Something has to give, and soon.

"What am I going to do?" I ask the water-stained ceiling.

I should call my sister. Or my parents. I haven't talked to anyone since my life went to hell. It won't be long before Bree shows up unannounced. My sister doesn't tolerate unanswered calls.

Cole said he has a cover story about his death. I guess I should find out what that is, because if I tell her what I know, it will only raise more questions. Questions I can't answer.

Cole and Trace worked for some government entity that doesn't exist. Talking about it is criminal. Telling me anything could put them in prison.

Then there's the whole hiding-from-and-eliminating-enemies thing. What does that even mean? My imagination runs the gamut, from terrorists and international crime organizations to North Korea and missile testing. All my assumptions are wrong, because he was *fighting wars no one will ever hear about*.

My head starts to pound, demanding caffeine, so I drag myself out of bed.

Twenty minutes later, I'm showered, dressed, and sipping coffee in my empty kitchen. I don't hear Trace puttering around in the front room. In fact, the house is deafening in its silence. Are they outside?

I move to the kitchen window to scope out my driveway that runs alongside my house. Cole's motorcycle is parked in front of my MG Midget, but that's not what grabs my attention.

Virginia stands in her backyard, leaning against the fence between our houses, completely captivated by something I can't see. Something in *my* backyard.

I swallow down the rest of my coffee, slip on a fleece jacket, and open the back door to the sound of grunting. Ice forms in the pit of my stomach as I follow the angry noises around the corner. And slam to a stop.

Two half-naked grown men are wrestling and punching and going fucking berserk on my lawn. I tremble against the cold, but it's the brawl that paralyzes me in icy shock.

Cole lands atop Trace, his arms a blur of fury. But Trace is so damn fast and nimble, very few of Cole's strikes actually hit him. In the next breath, Trace slips from beneath Cole and backhands him so hard I feel my own ears ringing.

"Stop it!" I snap out of it and charge toward them. "What the hell's wrong with you?"

They don't look at me, don't acknowledge me in any way. They're too consumed by their rage, their need to maul and hurt and make each other bleed.

Grinding my teeth, I glance at the hose near the back door. I could spray them like dogs. Or just let them kill each other.

Grass and blood cover their shirtless torsos. It's difficult to determine who's winning, but the amount of red pooling in Cole's bared teeth makes my stomach turn.

Virginia moves in my periphery, waving me over.

I inch toward her, walking backwards without taking my eyes off the fight. My stomach buckles with every strike, my entire body rigid with the need to intervene.

"They've been at it for a while." Virginia hooks her cane on the metal fence and leans over my shoulder, smelling like sweet persimmon soap.

"Do you know who that is with Trace?" I ask cautiously.

"Of course, dear." She squints cloudy eyes at the brawl. "Cole told me what happened. Someone should be fired over that horrible confusion at the explosion."

This should be interesting, since he hasn't told me shit about his cover story. Though I'm not surprised he talked to her. He's been out here every day, working on his bike. It's conceivable that he's spent more time with my nosy neighbor than he has with me.

Across the yard, Trace wraps his legs around Cole's neck, both of them grunting as they try to grind an elbow, knee, or whatever body part they can into muscle and bone.

"Did he give you any details about the explosion?" I chew on the inside of my cheek, silently begging them to stop.

"Not much. Just that his company thought they had his body. It's terrible that he was detained in an Iraqi prison and forgotten about for three years. What has the world come to?"

Hatred and rage and blood. That's what my world has come to.

Cole surges to his feet and rears back an arm. I tense as Trace's leg flies out and knocks Cole's feet out from beneath him. Cole lands on his back, and his agonized groan shoots a sharp pain through my chest.

I jerk to rush toward them, but a gnarled hand catches my wrist.

"Let them work it out." Virginia squeezes my arm with a shocking amount of strength.

"I can think of better ways to work things out."

"That's how boys express their differences. They need to get all the bad out of their blood. They'll feel better after."

I doubt they'll feel anything but bruises and broken bones, but I remain where I am, cringing at the godawful din of smacking flesh.

"Did Cole tell you why he was detained in prison?" I soften my voice to sound like I know the answer.

"Something about a foul-up at the oil terminal, and Iraq thought the U.S. contractors caused it. I don't really understand how all that political stuff works."

"Yeah, it confuses me, too."

For a cover story, I guess it's vague enough to be believable. Virginia doesn't seem to bat an eyelash at it.

"Whatever happened to him was bad," she says. "He doesn't like to talk about it." Her hand relaxes, shifting to curl around mine. "You take special care with that boy, you hear? There's something different about him. A sadness that wasn't there before. He needs your love now more than ever."

My heart pinches. "But what about Trace? I'm engaged to him, Virginia."

"Yes, well, that's why they're fighting." She lifts my hand, drawing my attention to the ring on my finger.

Rings.

Why are there *two* rings?

"Oh my God." I separate the silver bands, intimately familiar with both of them. "I didn't—"

"Cole slipped it on your finger last night while you slept." Her cataract eyes glitter in the sun. "Trace found out about it, and there you have it." She gestures at the grappling, grunting tangle of limbs in the grass.

My eyes widen. "How do you know this?"

"They were arguing about it this morning. Spitting and swearing and disturbing the peace." She lowers her voice to a conspiratorial whisper. "They've been watching you while you sleep. They argued about that, too."

Damn her sharp hearing. She'll be wagging her tongue about my drama up and down the street by lunchtime.

"They've been sneaky about it." She clutches the loose skin on her throat. "Tiptoeing into your room without the other one knowing. I guess they ran into each other early this morning."

And I slept through it. What else am I sleeping through? I pinch the bridge of my nose and peek at the scuffle.

Cole attacks Trace with flying knuckles, eyes wild and muscles flexed, like he's pumped up on faith and glory. And Trace, all graceful arms and legs, dodges the strikes and snaps his fist so fast it's inhuman.

"I should stop them." I twist the rings on my finger.

"You will do no such thing. The good Lord sent them to you for a reason. Don't get in the way."

I gape at her. "They're fighting over me. I'm

already in the way."

"Did you choose one over the other?"

My neck shrinks, pulling my ears toward my shoulders as that wretched goddamn word ricochets through my skull. *Choose. Choose. Choose.*

"I can't." I choke on a rush of tears and curl my fingers around the rings. "I'm engaged to them both, and I can't be. Two is a lie." I squeeze the silver bands so hard they dig into my skin. "Loving two men is wrong."

"A mother loves more than one child. Is that wrong?"

"It's not the same thing."

"Love is love, Danni."

"Not when it's poisoned by jealousy."

We fall quiet as the fight across the yard breaks apart. Cole and Trace lie on their backs with several feet of distance between them. Chests heaving and splattered in blood, they stare at the big blue sky, lost in their misery.

"Love them. That's all you can do." Virginia grabs her cane and shuffles back to her house, mumbling, "The rest will work itself out."

six

Love them. That's all you can do.

Virginia's words nestle into the squishy parts of my heart as I gather towels and first-aid supplies from the bathroom. When I reach the kitchen, Cole and Trace are sitting where I instructed—on the floor, side by side, backs to the cabinets, and hands to themselves.

"Look at that. You're sharing air without snarling and foaming like rabid dogs." I step over Cole's bent leg and stand between their slumped postures. "I'm tempted to pat your heads."

That earns me double frowns, and a grunt for good measure from Cole.

"I learned something interesting while you were molesting each other outside." I lower to my knees, facing them, and set the supplies between their hips.

"You're sneaking into my room at night when I'm sleeping? Both of you?"

Trace meets my gaze without flinching. Cole wipes the blood from his nose and glares at the floor.

"Watching me sleep… Wow." I rub my forehead. "That isn't creepy or anything."

"I've been watching you sleep for two months." Trace leans in and drops his voice. "I miss you, Danni. So fucking much."

Cole flares his nostrils. "You son of a—"

"That's enough," I snap at him. "This is already hard, for everyone involved. But watching you do this to yourselves, seeing you carry around all this animosity and resentment, I can't do it."

"What are you saying?" Cole searches my face with panic in his eyes.

"Chill the fuck out. That's what I'm saying."

He releases a heavy breath and rests his head back against the cabinet.

"I know this situation is a shit load of fucked, but this…" I gesture at the blood smudged across their chests. "This is an unwanted, avoidable travesty. Like a wet fart in a tight leotard." I purse my lips. "You should be ashamed of yourselves."

"A wet fart…" Cole's mouth bounces before settling into a small lopsided grin.

The appearance of his dimples unfurls a ribbon of warmth inside me. Trace regards me with amusement gleaming in his eyes, and I thaw further, melting at the beautiful sight.

A smile possesses my lips. My cheeks lift, and for the first time in five days, I feel relieved. It's a slapdash feeling, there and gone as quick as Cole's dimples. But I cherish the tender moment, appreciate the clarity it offers. We can still make each other happy.

I lift a towel and reach my other hand toward Trace's face. As my fingers slide against his sculpted jaw, my pulse spikes and my breaths quicken. For once, my reaction isn't nerves or anger. It's excitement. Affection. Cautious desire.

He always affects me, though. Even now, with his chest and arms all scratched up and caked with dirt. I could stare at him for hours—his unsmiling lips, rumpled blond hair, and eyes so blue they conjure greatness, like the vast sky on a summer day with the top down on my car. Like the first day we spent together, running errands, trading flirty arguments, and kissing outside of the pharmacy.

Was our time together just a fool's paradise? Can we get back to that place again?

With my hand on his jaw, I angle his head side to side, checking for injuries. Blood smears across the smooth angles of his face, but there are no lacerations. No swelling.

I turn my attention to Cole, his grumpy features lined with abrasions and gashes around his eyes, down the bridge of his nose, and cut through the corner of his mouth.

"If you're the one with specialized training..." I squint at Cole. "Why are you more banged up than Trace?" I look back at Trace and wipe the wet towel across his cheeks, revealing pristine skin beneath the grime. "Did you even get hit?"

"He got my mouth once, and my ribs are bruised." Trace gingerly touches his side.

"He's full of shit." Cole drapes an arm over his bent knee and flexes his fingers, his gaze never leaving mine. "He just wants your hands on him."

Trace regards me in that way he does, with his head down and eyes up. It's distractingly sexy.

I clear my throat. "You didn't answer my question."

"Trace was trained in hand-to-hand combat," Cole growls. "Ranked top of our class."

"What class? Was it military training?"

Cole's expression empties, giving me nothing.

Christ almighty. "What about your skill set?" I ask him.

"I'm more proficient in…other areas."

The boding descent in Cole's tone warns me not to inquire further. Doesn't stop my mind from jumping to images of him snapping a sniper rifle together and crawling through a jungle wearing a ghillie suit. But what the fuck do I know?

Absolutely nothing.

"Why do you fight him," I ask Cole, hooking a thumbing at Trace, "if you know you're going to lose?"

Trace huffs an annoyed breath. "He's bullheaded enough to get his ass handed to him, which is pretty fucking pathetic."

"I have the courage to get my ass handed to me." Cole licks the cut on his lip. "Which is pretty fucking poetic."

Cole's temper is definitely poetic, like a murky river—calm, easygoing, and seemingly innocuous, until something disturbs what lies beneath, and all hell breaks loose in a terrorizing rage of teeth and blood.

I return my attention to Trace, giving him another

clinical perusal. Scratches and red spots mar his torso from rolling on the ground. The skin is torn on a few of his knuckles. But nothing requires bandages.

"I can't do anything about your ribs." I climb to my feet and rinse off the towel in the sink. "Do you need a doctor?"

Cole snorts, and Trace shakes his head.

"While I clean up Cole's face," I say to Trace, wringing out the towel, "why don't you go take a shower?"

Trace's scowl tightens, his reluctance so potent it pulses through the air.

"Cole will shower after you." I brace my hands on my hips. "Then we're all going to sit down and have a chat."

Bending forward, Trace prepares to stand. And pauses. Clearly, he doesn't want to leave me alone with Cole, and if I were in his position, I wouldn't, either.

He's clinging to a delicate web. One more mistake—a hurtful word, a cruel action—could shove me into Cole's arms. Right or wrong, I'm looking for anything to sway me into a decision. Which isn't fair to either of them. Especially since I know exactly what it feels like to see someone I love with another woman.

Trace knows how I feel about Cole, and in order to be with me, he has to suffer through seeing me with Cole. Yet he stays and endures and doesn't give up.

When I caught him with Marlo, I didn't fight for him. I walked away. No, scratch that. I *ran.* Straight to another man, a stranger, just out of spite.

So watching Trace struggle with leaving me alone with Cole stirs me with deep sympathy, tempting me to back down. But I tend to sympathize *too* much. It makes me weak. Vulnerable. Easily trampled.

I silence the temptation and push back my shoulders.

Trace reads my eyes and shoves off the floor. I don't breathe until he vanishes around the corner and shuts the bathroom door. A moment later, the pipes groan through the old house.

"I got a job." Cole touches my hand.

"You did?" I kneel beside him and dab the wet towel on the cut across his cheekbone. "That was fast. What's the job?"

"Security at the stadium." He studies my expression, as if seeking my approval. "It doesn't pay much but—"

"A rent-a-cop?" A sinking feeling invades my stomach. "I know nothing about your prior job, but aren't you overqualified to stand around at concerts and baseball games? Are the security guards even armed?"

"Yes, they're armed." He scratches his jaw and drops his hand. "I have a skill set that over-qualifies me for any job in the private sector. The scope of my training applies to this much of the world." He holds his finger and thumb a hairbreadth apart. "There aren't a lot of options for guys like me."

"But you could—"

"I had a career. That's not what I want now." He shoots me a meaningful look. "I just need steady pay, something that doesn't require travel, with hours that match yours."

"Please don't do that for me. I'm not putting any demands on what you choose to do with your life."

He stiffens. "Four years ago, you didn't hesitate to

tell me, no less than a hundred times, to quit my job."

"Yeah, well, you didn't listen."

"I was a dumbfuck, and my stupidity cost me everything." His expression shatters, his voice a grief-stricken whisper. "I'm listening now. What do you want?"

"I want you to be happy," I say on a tattered breath. "Both of you."

His eyes close, and the sunlight from the window glances off the sharp lines of his cheekbones, highlighting the sunken hollows beneath. He lost too much weight, but he's still criminally handsome. The stubborn lock of his jaw, the sexy shadow of whiskers, the swell of pouty lips—it's a visage of danger and fortitude.

I always knew there was something roguish about him. Not just his temper, but something more, like a mysterious edge I couldn't put my finger on. But as he lifts his dark lashes, I see it now—the troubling secrets in his eyes. He's experienced things he won't ever be able to share with me, and I hate that. It's a wall between us, a part of his life I don't have access to.

I reach for his chin, cupping the chiseled shape as I clean away the rest of the blood. "If you can't tell anyone your work history, what did you put on the job application?"

"I didn't fill one out." A bitter smirk pulls at his lips. "Trace has connections at the stadium. He got me the job, no questions asked."

"He did?" I widen my eyes.

"He didn't do it out of the kindness of his heart. He's motivated, Danni. He wants me working and moved out and far away from you."

My chest constricts. "Don't tell me you don't want the same things from him."

"You know what I want?" Eyes bright and searching, he slowly lifts a hand toward my face. "I want to be your lover, your husband, your home. I want to be your everything."

I hold still, lost in the familiarity of his molten dark gaze. He gently touches my lips, and a teetering sensation trembles behind my breastbone, like my heart is slipping, readjusting, and settling with a contented sigh.

"I miss your smile. And the scent of your skin." His fingers shake, gliding downward to caress my neck. "When I was away, I burned Nag Champa incense, trying to recreate your fragrance, but it wasn't the same. It wasn't you."

"They say smell is strongly linked to emotion and memory." I busy my hands with the first-aid supplies. "I used to sleep with your clothes, desperate to hang onto every memory I could." Sadness creaks into my voice. "It was hard, Cole. Every fucking day was an endless crawl through hell."

"I know, baby." His face collapses, and he pulls me toward him. "I'm so fucking sorry."

"I was angry." I push against his shoulder and lock my arm, keeping space between us. "I cursed you. Blamed you. And some days, I hated you." My words tremble from the ache in my chest. "I hated you for leaving me."

"I deserve that."

"No, you don't. You had an obligation to your job, and our relationship was brand new. You did what you had to do, and I just…I didn't know how to cope. When you died…" I lower my head to my hands. "It took me so long to let go of the past, and now here it is. You're back, bringing all those painful feelings to the surface, and I don't know what to do."

"Do me a favor." He bends his neck, tugging my arms down to see my eyes. "Imagine yourself in a place you want to be. Don't think about it. Just let your heart take you there. Where are you?"

"Dancing on a stage with Beyoncé."

"Right." He shakes his head with a soft chuckle. "I knew that." Swiping a hand over his mouth, he sobers. "Who's in the audience? Who's watching you dance?"

Since this is a fantasy, there's no deliberation. I open my mouth to tell him he's there, sitting in the front row and wearing his dimpled smile. Except he's not alone. Trace reclines beside him, and they lean their heads together, sharing a private conversation before erupting in laughter. I close my eyes and try to erase one of them from the vision. But the attempt makes my chest collapse, and a sharp burn fires through my sinuses.

When I open my eyes, Cole studies me expectantly. I press my lips together and look away, blinking back tears.

"Is it him?" he asks. "Is he where you want to be?"

"You're both there."

He sucks in a breath. "That can't—"

"I know it can't happen. That's not what I want!" My outburst reverberates through the kitchen, and I lower my voice. "I don't know how to do this."

He reaches a hand toward mine, his fingers twitching, stretching, before making contact. "The half-naked girl I met on the street that morning, the one who straddled me on my bike and stole my heart… She didn't know what she was doing, either. But she was beautifully bold and shameless. She did whatever the fuck she wanted, with mischief in her eyes and laughter on her lips."

The sob in my throat hiccups into a coughing, helpless grin. "I wasn't half-naked."

"Your perfect round ass hung out of a pitiful scrap of cotton."

"They were cheeky boyshorts."

"They were torture. I had to go to work hard as a rock." He twines his fingers around mine. "I would've married you that day. I *should've* married you. I'm a fucking idiot."

My pulse kicks up, filling my chest with fuzzy warmth.

"Go back to that morning with me." He puts his face in mine, his gaze fierce. "We'll start over. Let me prove how much I love you. I can convince you—"

"You didn't have to convince me of anything the day we met, and you shouldn't have to do it now. That's not how love works, and that's never been how *you and I* work."

He gives me the look. The one I know so well. It says he'll do anything to win me back. Lying, stealing, maiming, killing—there's no limit to the depths he'll go. Knowing what I know now about his occupation, the thought makes my stomach cramp.

"If you hurt Trace, it's the same as hurting me." I untangle my hand from his and rub antibiotic ointment on the gash across his nose. "You understand that, right?"

"Yes." He regards me so intently it takes all my

energy to keep from squirming. "It's the damnedest thing…" His head cocks. "When I look at you, I see what other men see. A stunning knockout with lips that summon filthy thoughts and eyes that turn the biggest badass into a bumbling fool. But there's so much more. Your compassion and vulnerability, your ability to love so deeply, with your entire existence. You're the whole package, and anyone who meets you knows this."

A flush rises through my cheeks. "Cole—"

"It's a miracle I'm not fighting off dozens of men. At the moment, I only have one contender." He rubs his sternum, his timbre losing strength. "The problem is, you love him, and that's pretty damn hard to compete with. But lucky for me, I still have part of your heart." His eyebrows gather. "Right?"

"You already know the answer to that."

"Good." He blows out a breath. "That's good, because I'm yours. All of me. Forever. I'm not going away, Danni. Not when things are hard. Not when this"—he gestures between us—"seems impossible. Through the good and the bad and all the madness in between, I'll be wherever you are, fighting and laughing and appreciating every goddamn second you give me."

A twinge of yearning quivers in the heart of my chest. His voice…that gravelly, passionate sound of his timbre is one of the things I missed the most. More than that, I missed his words, the rawness in every sentence he strings together.

He makes me a believer.

seven

They say a girl's first love isn't the first person she kisses or the one she gives her virginity to. Her first love is the guy she'll compare all others against. He's the one she never forgets, even when she convinces herself she's over him and moved on.

As Cole rests a hand on mine and leans so close I smell the recognizable scent of his skin, I know with certainty I never got over him.

The heat radiating from him, the dark depths of his gaze drilling into mine, his very presence speaks to my soul, enchanting and ravishing and slaying. It's the sweetest torment, drugging me into a Cole-induced stupor.

If he kisses me, I won't be able to stop him. I haven't tasted his intoxicating lips in four and a half years, and I'm helpless against the magnetic pull he has over me.

I still haven't come to terms with the fact that he's here. Sitting on the floor in my kitchen. Alive and real and a kiss away from spiraling me into total bliss.

"Danni." He stares at my mouth, and his tongue slips out to wet his own. "I need you so fucking much I can't see straight."

I whimper, angling closer, until all that separates us is a finger-width of air and a head full of uncertainty. *My* uncertainty. Given the way he's looking at me, the only thing he's worried about is his ability to strip off my clothes before I change my mind.

His fingers glide around my neck and twist through the hair at the base of my skull, his breaths growing shallow, heated. He edges closer, oh-so slowly, deleting the minuscule distance between our lips.

I close my eyes. Part my mouth. Tense against a riot of nerves. And jump at the burst of noise on the kitchen counter.

Try by Pink blares from my phone, sounding an incoming call.

"Ignore it." Cole clenches his hand in my hair.

But I'm already pulling back, shaking out of my trance and scrambling for the distraction.

I was going to kiss him. With Trace within hearing range. What the hell is wrong with me?

Grabbing the phone, I groan at the caller ID.

"My sister." I hit ignore and peek at Cole.

He drops his head and clutches the back of his neck as frustration ripples through his bent posture.

"I haven't talked to her since you returned." I crouch beside him. "I need to tell her what's going on."

He slides his hands to his face, scrubbing his forehead as if struggling to dial back his temper.

That's where he and Trace differ the most. Trace is the master of self-restraint. Hell, he spent nearly every day with me for four months burying his feelings for me.

Cole would never do that. I don't think he can. He has zero control over his emotions. When he wants me, he takes me, and the claiming is a powder keg of hunger and ferocity. At least, that's how it used to be.

Nothing is different between us, the chemistry and passion just as wild and uncontainable as the day we met. Yet everything has changed. When he died, part of me died with him, leaving behind a ghost of the woman he fell in love with. I can't connect with him when it comes to his career, and he'll never be part of my relationship with Trace. We didn't have those separations before, and in some ways, it makes us strangers.

That doesn't mean he isn't the one for me, but it's a scary revelation. I might have gotten him back, but that doesn't mean our relationship is recoverable.

"You better call Bree," he says, "before she shows up and pisses herself when she sees me."

"You need to walk me through the cover story."

Ten minutes later, I'm alone in my bedroom, listening to Bree's heavy gasps through the phone.

"Holy shit cakes, Danni." She makes a strangled noise. "All that time in an Iraqi prison? Is he okay? Mentally, I mean. Surely, they're providing therapy for him."

"He's doing okay." I hate lying to her. It goes against every instinct I have. But I don't know the truth, and that's probably a good thing, because I'd be tempted to confide in her.

In the next room, the shower turns on, the pipes groaning through the walls. That means Cole's in there. Removing his pants. Revealing inch after inch of his mouth-watering physique.

Does he still go commando? I haven't seen him without jeans on since he returned. Is there a black snake still tattooed around his thigh or did he have that one removed, too? What does he look like now without clothes on? Thinner? Harder? Any new scars?

I have so many photos of him, pictures I stared at for days on end after he left. But none are of him naked. He doesn't have a body one could easily forget—broad chest, narrow cut of hips, and a well-endowed package between powerful legs. Nevertheless, I ache to see him in the buff again.

The door to my bedroom opens, interrupting my thoughts as Trace steps in, wearing only a towel.

Bree continues to blabber in my ear about what-ifs and what-nows, but my attention fixates on Trace, on the definition of muscle along either side of his spine as he stands in my closet, selecting something to wear.

I feel like a hussy, imagining one naked man and two seconds later, ogling another. My ability to switch so easily from Cole to Trace and back again is upsetting. It shouldn't be that way, but I don't know how to shut off my feelings.

"Are you shitting the bed right now?" Concern spikes through Bree's voice. "Oh my God, does that mean you're engaged to both of them?"

"I don't know what it means."

"Oh, Danni. I can't imagine what you're going through. You love them both so much." Her whisper rasps through the phone. "There's no way you can choose between them."

Cole suggested I keep his connection to Trace a secret. It opens too many questions that would raise suspicion. Since Bree thinks he and Trace just met, she has no idea how deep the heartache goes. Whoever I don't choose doesn't just lose his fiancé. He loses his best friend, too.

Trace releases the towel at his waist and drops it to the floor. My nostrils widen with a sharp breath, my gaze sliding over the hard flanks of his backside. He's ridiculously, beautifully sculpted, with layers of lean muscle, a high tight ass, and long legs, all enwrapped in taut flawless skin.

He glances over his shoulder at me, and whatever he sees on my face makes him smirk. Without looking away, he slowly, methodically, pulls on a pair of black boxer briefs, followed by charcoal slacks, letting both hang low on his butt without zipping up.

"Tease," I mouth.

His smirk transforms into a full-fledged grin that cartwheels across the space between us and hits me square in the chest. His smiles are so rare that when he gifts me one, I hold it tight to my heart.

"Do you want me to come over?" Bree asks. "Angel has a soccer game in a couple hours, but I'm free until then."

"No, they're both here, and I need to hash things out with them."

Trace loses his grin and turns back to the rack of clothes.

"This is crazy." Bree exhales. "Do you have a

plan?"

"Do I ever?"

"No, but surely you have some idea of what you're going to do."

Trace emerges from the closet, tucking a white button-up into the open fly of his slacks. I have a fascination with watching him put himself together. His meticulous movements, attention to detail, the way his hands move confidently over his body—it's as if every action is intended to seduce. He's too damn sexy for his own good.

He finishes dressing and approaches the bed, with a curious glint in his eyes. His blond hair brushes his brow, not yet tamed for the day. Stubble dusts his jaw, waiting to be shaved. Yet he looks like he's ready to take on the world, prowling toward me in that effortless way he moves, his suit molding to every delicious inch of his frame.

"Hang on a minute," I say to Bree and mute the phone.

He places a knee on the mattress and leans over me to graze his lips against my cheek. "I love you."

"I love you, too." My veins flood with warmth as I recall something he said the day Cole returned.

You're all that I am, and the moment I accepted that, protecting you was no longer a favor or a job. It became a prerogative.

"When did you know you loved me?" I run a hand through the corn-silk strands of his hair.

He slants into my touch and sighs. "The first time I saw you at Bissara—"

"When you went there to check up on me."

"To watch over you and keep you safe." He turns

his head and kisses my wrist. "I walked in and saw you dancing. I haven't caught my breath since."

My heart skips, knocking the wind from my lungs.

"When did you know you loved me?" His blue eyes bore into mine.

"When you gave me the concert ticket for Beyoncé." I grin.

His expression falls, and he nods stiffly. "That's the night you saw me with that woman on my lap." A tic bounces in his jaw. "It was all for show. You know that, right?"

"Yeah."

"I'm so sorry. Despite what I said that morning in your basement, I *never* wanted to hurt you. I made so many foolish attempts—"

"I understand why you did it." I trail my fingers along the honed lines of his face and shift back, glancing at my phone. "I need to finish this call with Bree. I'll be out in a minute, okay?"

Dense lashes fringe pale blue eyes that roam over my features, as if absorbing every detail to memory.

"Take all the time you need." He rises from the bed, straightens his collar, and leaves the room, shutting the door behind him.

With a heavy exhale, I un-mute the phone. "I'm back."

"You need to date both of them," Bree bursts out, loud and rushed, as if the words were burning her lips for weeks rather than the thirty seconds I had her on hold. "Two men. Lots of sex. That's an order."

"I'm not doing that." I press the heel of my hand against my chest and whisper, "It's selfish."

"You know what? Fuck that. For once in your life, you're going to put yourself first. Jesus, Danni, you give and give until you have nothing left. You love with all your heart, and you never ask anything from anyone. You don't even know the meaning of selfish."

The shower shuts off in the next room, reminding me how thin the walls are.

"I'm going to turn on some background noise." I slide off the bed and grab my tablet from the dresser.

A moment later, *Issues* by Julia Michaels strums through the bedroom.

"You know them, Bree." I move to the full-length mirror on the wall beside the closet door and flatten a hand against the glass. "We're not talking about your everyday, passive men here. They're overbearing, jealous, growly cave-grunters who don't share their toys."

"You're not a toy," she says harshly.

Cole used to call me his dirty little fuck doll, and it turned me on like nothing else. But I'll keep that tidbit to myself.

"Figure of speech. You know what I mean." The crisp plucky notes of the song snap through me, gripping my hips and hooking me into the rhythm. "I'm not going to string them along."

"You didn't put yourself in this position." She blows out a breath. "Cole did this."

Trace played a part as well, but she doesn't know that. It's something I'll have to keep in consideration if she starts rallying for Trace, which is likely since she was never a Cole fan.

Examining my form in the mirror, I ripple my core, sending vibrating waves of motion to my ribcage and pelvis. As the melody races up and down the scale, I hold my hand against the glass and twitch my hips to the contrasting beats, as if dancing with my reflection.

"You need time," she says. "Am I right?"

"That's *exactly* what I need. I feel so blindsided by this I've been walking in a fog for the past week." I sway my head through the song's haunting chorus. "This is a for-the-rest-of-my-life kind of decision, you know? But how long can I drag it out before it becomes a pathetic excuse for procrastination?"

"For however long it takes. They love you. They wouldn't be there if they didn't. So they'll wait for you. They'll wait indefinitely, while you figure out which one deserves you the most. Meanwhile, you need to spend time with them. Get to know them on every level under the sun and…under the covers—"

"Bree—"

"Enjoy yourself. Enjoy *them*. Let it evolve naturally, organically. As you spend time with each of them, you'll gravitate toward one more than the other."

"What if I don't?" I splay my fingers over the reflection of my face as the song slows.

"What if you do? Think of it like one of those online dating sites. Except you don't have an algorithm narrowing down the choices. You already know your top two picks. You don't have to weed through hundreds of overinflated profiles or go on dozens of painful dates. You've vetted two candidates, and you know you're matched in every way."

"I guess that's one way of looking at it." I prowl backward, away from the mirror, exaggerating the flex of my legs with the low bass drop and breathy vocals.

"Whatever you do, make sure you're doing it for *you*." Bree hardens her tone. "I'll be severely disappointed if you're not one-hundred-percent selfish about this."

"Wow. Aren't you full of well-meaning advice?"

"It's my job as the smarter, prettier sister. Your job is to listen to me."

I roll my eyes. Her grade-school-teacher-ness is shining through. It makes her forget she's eighteen months younger than me.

"I'm hanging up now." A smile teases through my voice.

"I love you."

"Love you, too."

I end the call and turn my attention to the intermittent rhythm of *Issues*, moving with the beat, starting and stopping. It's a flow and a snap, a ripple and a crash. I stretch up, up, up, and let my limbs tumble down, as if I'm tied to puppet strings that are tightening and slackening.

The lyrics are so angsty I feel every word, from the curl of my fingers to the flick of my head. My skinny jeans restrict the energy that vibrates to let loose, but as the music melts through me, I'm possessed by it, swaying and jerking to the tempo that circulates through my blood and dominates my muscles.

My hands rove over my body, caressing each joint and encouraging every deep bend. By the time the song ends, I'm breathing lighter. My insides feel softer, and there's a warmth in my core that wasn't there before. A peace that connects me to life. And love.

Five minutes later, I stand in the living room with my arms at my sides and a steady flow of confidence in my veins.

Trace and Cole settle into opposite corners of the couch, both fully dressed. Trace, with his face now shaved and hair slicked back and textured. Cole, in a white t-shirt and jeans, with whiskers darkening his cheeks and raw intensity in his eyes.

"Before I get into this, I need you to answer something." I hold up my left hand and meet Cole's gaze. "You put this ring on my finger. Twice. Is it safe to assume you still want to marry me?"

"Yes." He leans forward, expression aglow with eagerness. "You're my heart, Danni. I can't live without you."

I swallow and look at Trace. "I'm still wearing your ring. Do you—?"

"I'll marry you today. Right now." Trace licks his lips, his eyes wide and unblinking. "My path has never been this clear, my future never so beautiful."

"Thank you." My stomach flutters. "I'm just going to talk through this, because I really don't know what I'm going to say." I flex and relax my hands. "Just…let me speak without interrupting me, okay?"

They're both perched on the edge of their cushions. Cole shifts first, seemingly forcing himself to recline and loosen up. A heartbeat later, Trace follows suit.

"The way I see it, I have three options." I stare down at my hand. "Option one. I return one of these rings and end that relationship. Then I plan a wedding with the one I keep."

A wave of tension ripples through the room, and my pulse goes erratic. I breathe through it and continue.

"Option two. I return both rings and start over.

Without you." I glance between them, meeting their hardening gazes. "We go our separate ways, or at least, I do. I like to think you two could resolve your differences in that scenario."

Cole works his jaw, and Trace's mouth forms a flat line. I can tell they're chomping at the bit to speak up, but they respect my wishes and remain silent.

"Option three." I twist the bands on my finger, my throat scratchy. "I return both rings and start over. *With you.* Both of you."

Cole adjusts his position, leaning forward then back while rubbing a hand over his mouth. Trace is still—calmly, eerily frozen.

I don't want their reactions to influence me, because Bree's right. Whatever choice I make should reflect who *I* am, not who they are.

"Part of me wants to put these options up for a vote." I draw in a steeling breath and strengthen my backbone. "But I'm not going to do that. I'm going to put on my big girl pants and tell you how it's going to be. Can you live with that?"

Their nods are stiff, but what shines from their eyes threatens to knock my feet out from under me. Pride, respect, loyalty—it's all there in bright sheens of love. There's a chance I'm about to destroy one or both of their worlds, and they still have it in them to look at me with admiration.

I grip the engagement rings, eyes on my trembling fingers as I rotate the bands around and around, aching to keep them right where they are.

Love has been good to me. It's also been vicious and cruel. I don't know what it plans to do to my heart next, but there's a blessed kind of comfort in knowing it isn't finished with me. I have to give up one of the men I love, but I don't have to give up on love altogether.

I remove the first ring from my finger and hold it out to Cole. He sucks in a breath, and another, refusing to take it. His face turns stark white, and a horrified look seeps into his eyes.

I set it on the coffee table before him and slide off the second ring, offering it to Trace.

Trace's throat bobs, and a tremor races through his fingers as he reaches for the band.

"I choose option three." Nervousness crops up in my voice. "I want to start over. I want to date both of you."

Tension visibly loosens from Cole's shoulders, and he exhales softly.

Trace is harder to read. He closes his hand around the ring, and an indiscernible quietness falls over him. If he's upset, I don't blame him. He went from blissfully happy and engaged to this frightening place of uncertainty. In a way, it feels like I'm breaking up with him, and it makes my stomach erupt with dread.

"What's the living arrangement?" Trace asks, low and hushed. "If you're dating both of us."

In my mind, dating two men requires separation. I need to be with them individually, not crammed together under the same roof.

"You're moving back to the penthouse." I lift my chin, bracing for an argument.

"And him?" Trace scowls at Cole and turns his glare back to me.

"Cole can get his own place or stay in the basement—"

"He's not staying here!" Trace leaps to his feet, hands on his hips. "You're not going to shack up with him while I—"

"Sit down and let me finish." My shoulders tense as I wait for him to lower onto the couch. "I spend half of my waking hours at the casino, where *you* live. We've been going back and forth between here and your penthouse for months. I'm okay with continuing doing that for a while. But…" I narrow my eyes at both of them. "I'm not sleeping with you. Dating two men is complicated. Adding sex to this would be a disaster."

As my words sink in, silence creeps through the living room, heavy with apprehension and maybe a little bit of relief. I'm doing this to give myself time, but it gives them time, too.

"For how long?" Cole lifts his head and meets my eyes. "How long will you *date* us?"

"Until I know."

eight

My chest feels like a lead balloon as I stand on the front porch, watching Trace put the last of his belongings in the trunk of the sedan.

I keep telling myself this isn't the end. It's the beginning of a new chapter. But if that's true, why does it hurt so much?

Cole made himself scarce while Trace and his driver cleared his clothes out of my closet. I think it's the first time any of Trace's employees have been inside my house. It's weird. Hell, this entire situation is dicked in the head. We love each other, and I'm kicking him out of my house, like we're going backward.

Not backward. We're starting over.

I clutch my throat, swallowing around a painful lump.

Trace shuts the trunk and opens the rear passenger door. I told him he had to leave, that he needed to go work and I would see him when I return to the restaurant tomorrow.

Today's my day off, and I want to visit the homeless shelter. I haven't been there since Cole came back.

Across the front yard, Trace lingers beside the open door of the sedan. The dark suit makes his blond hair look paler than normal, and his eyes are so light they shimmer in the sunlight.

I can't see the emotion there, but I don't have to. Every inch of his rigid posture vibrates with devastation. It's killing him to leave me. *To leave me here with Cole.*

But I made these rules. Now I have to own them.

He flattens a hand over his necktie, as if to keep it from lifting in the chilly breeze. Then he turns and lowers into the backseat, making that hand on his chest look more like he's holding a breaking heart.

My own heart gives a painful thump, and it pounds harder as he closes the door and disappears behind tinted glass.

He didn't say goodbye, and now the car is rolling into motion, carrying him away from me.

Even though I made this happen, I can't handle it. The sight of him leaving without giving me something to cling to—a whisper of hope, a tender touch—rises panic through me.

What if he's in a car accident? What if he dies and I never see him again?

I fly off the porch, my bare feet racing through the cold grass and onto the quiet street. But I'm too late. He's already a block away.

I keep running, chasing, aching for the confident strength of his arms around me.

The brake lights illuminate, and the sedan slows to a stop. My breath rushes out, my legs burning with exertion as I close the distance.

Then the sedan reverses, shrinking the gap, until the rear door opens. Trace's long leg slides out before the car stops moving. But I'm already there, tumbling into the backseat and onto his lap.

"Danni." His timbre is breathy and deep, fanning across my face.

I shut the door and straddle his thighs, panting, with my arms enfolding his neck and my forehead resting against his.

He combs his fingers through my hair, runs his hands up and down my back, and lifts them to frame my face.

I get a glimpse of sad blue eyes a millisecond before his mouth covers mine. My pulse skitters at the warm, soft, delicious feel of his lips.

This is what I needed, and my insides purr with contentment.

His fingers drift into my hair and tighten as his tongue traces the seam of my mouth. I open for him, inviting him with hungry licks and whimpers.

He takes over, angling my head and plunging deeper, faster, his urgency apparent in the clench of his hands and the flexing muscle beneath his suit.

And just like that, I'm wildly aroused, like he injected lighter fluid in my veins. One touch below my neck and I'll catch fire. It's all I can do to keep from wriggling on his thickening cock.

He delves inside my mouth, sweeping with expert strokes, controlling the pace and depth, and demanding I meet the frantic rub of his tongue. A groan reverberates from his lips, and I devour it, unable to catch my breath or control the beat of my heart.

My chest swells with peace and happiness, but it's also filled with fear. I don't know what will become of us. I only know that what we have doesn't come around very often, and by some miracle, I managed to capture this rare, wonderful thing with two men. I can't let go.

"I didn't mean to get you worked up." I trail a path of kisses over his smooth cheek. "I just wanted…I needed to make sure you know I love you."

"I know, Danni." He nibbles on my ear lobe. "But I never tire of hearing it." His embrace constricts, pressing me impossibly tighter against his chest. "All I can think about is you kissing him like that."

"Think of it this way. We just shared the last kiss of our first relationship. Cole got one of those four years ago." I push back until his arms loosen. "We're starting over. Right now." I slide off his lap and kneel on the seat beside him. "This is ground zero."

The muscles in his face tense.

"I'm going to go slow." I touch his jaw. "With both of you. It's a new beginning and…" A smile pulls at my lips. "I have a feeling this beginning will be a thousand times better than our last one."

He closes his eyes, but I don't miss the shadow of guilt in the depths.

"I love you, Trace Savoy." I open the door and back out of the car. "I'll see you tomorrow."

"Not nearly as much as I love you." He reaches out and grazes a knuckle beneath my chin. "And I'm counting down the minutes."

With a nod, I close the door.

This time, when the car motors away, I don't feel as panicky. The sensation is still present, gnawing inside my stomach, but he knows I love him. He knows this isn't over.

I hurry back to the front yard, my toes turning purple in the nippy air. But instead of heading toward the front door, I veer down the driveway alongside my house, expecting to find Cole outside.

Sure enough, he crouches beside his motorcycle, surrounded by a clutter of tools.

He looks up at my approach, his face lined with unbridled interest as he scans me from feet to tits, making a slow study of my skinny jeans and off-the-shoulder sweatshirt. When he finally lifts his eyes to mine, I'm standing a few feet away with my eyebrows arched.

"When do you start your new job?" I ask.

"In a couple days." He rises to his full height and wipes his hands on a rag.

He's not as tall as Trace, but he's still almost a head taller than me.

I angle my neck to hold his warm gaze. "Got any plans today?"

The shake of his head is slow and somewhat absent, like he's not really paying attention to my words. It's the flirty smile that makes me suspicious. Whatever he's thinking is private in nature and probably dirty as hell.

I'm reminded that he hasn't had sex in over four years. Without Trace here, it's going to be a harrowing test of will to keep all that pent-up hunger out of my bed.

A sigh ripples past my lips. "There's somewhere I need to be. Do you want to see what I've been up to while you've been gone?"

"I'd love to." His smile explodes in shards of light, popping his dimples and vanishing the shadows between us. "Where are we going?"

"Anticipation—"

"Heightens the pleasure." He winks, making me melt. "We'll take the bike."

"I hoped you'd say that."

"Let me clean up, and I'll be ready to go."

Fifteen minutes later, I wait for him in the driveway, huddling against the chill in the faux-leather jacket, gloves, and boots he gave me shortly after we met. Black leggings, made to look like leather, complete my outfit.

I'm not a biker chick, but I always felt kind of badass when I rode behind him dressed like this. I'm giddy with excitement to experience that nostalgic rumble between my legs. God, it's been so long.

He steps out, carrying our helmets, and covered neck to toe in faded denim and leather. With an animal of prey in his movements and a glowing fire in his eyes, this is the man I met on the street all those years ago. I'm as lost in his potency now as I was then, shivering against a frenzy of surreal emotions. I never thought I'd see him again, let alone ride on the back of his bike.

Setting his half-helmet on the seat, he lifts mine and adjusts it on my head. He takes care to gather my hair down my back, his fingers tenderly gliding across my face and along my neck, prickling my skin with goosebumps.

The gentle touches are so chaste for Cole, a sign

that he's capable of behaving himself. But for how long? He's never had to restrain himself with me, and I wonder if this celibacy rule will eventually break him.

"Did you encounter beautiful women while you were away from me?" I chew on the corner of my lip.

His hands still on the straps that dangle beside my face, his expression perplexed.

"Yes," he says cautiously. "Why do you ask?"

My mouth has no filter. That's why. "I'm not trying to be accusatory. I'm just curious about the time you spent away from me."

He has an insatiable sex drive. How has he gone so damn long without? Surely, he was tempted.

"I already told you, Danni. There's been no one else." His tone resonates with all the nuances of *we're done talking about this*.

"I'm sure there was someone—"

"No." He buckles the strap under my chin, yanking harder than necessary. "I love *you*. I want you and only you. The idea of touching another woman makes me sick."

Yet I did more than touch someone else. I fell terribly in love with another man.

My chest aches, but I remind myself that our situations were different. I thought he was dead.

"You're stunning." He steps back and looks me over. "This was one of the fantasies I jacked off to."

I glance down the length of my body, taking in my curvy shape in skin-tight black pleather. "This?"

"Yes, *this*. You bring a man to his knees." He steps into my space, hands curling around my hips and his nose sliding along mine. "Do you still have your piercing?"

"That question might be too personal for a first date."

"Is that what this is?" His fingers press hard against my butt. "A date?"

"If you want it to be." I blink up at him.

"So submissive." His voice is smoke and whiskey, his breath a mint-scented drug. "Fucking love that about you."

He releases me, leaving me swaying in the wake of his rumbling timbre, as he puts on his half-helmet and swings a leg over the bike.

"Hop on, baby." He angles his neck to watch me over the sloping ledge of his shoulder.

I place a hand on that thick muscle and slide up behind him, squeezing my thighs around his narrow hips.

I'm not an advocate for the leather industry—it's unnecessary and inhumane—but I don't mind smelling that wild distinct scent on him. It brings back so many wonderful memories of my nose buried in his jacket and my arms hugging his waist as he opens the throttle and arrows us through the wind.

He slides his hands back, molding his fingers around my thighs and yanking me closer to his back. "Where are we going?"

"You need to eat." I grip his legs, squeezing the lean muscle.

I'm worried about his weight loss. He's still defined and hard as stone, but nowhere near as bulky as he was when I met him.

"I'd like to eat *you.*" He glances over his shoulder, brown eyes full of naughty intentions. "Is that on the menu?"

With a groan, I snuggle against his back and rest my helmet on his shoulder. "You're not making this easy."

"Loving you is easy. Everything else… Well, if it gets too hard…" He turns over the engine and raises his voice. "I'll just love you harder."

nine

The cold wind whips through my hair and stings my cheeks as Cole zooms out of the neighborhood. He takes a corner, and I lean with him, plastered to his back and relishing the feel of gravity pressing the motorcycle toward the ground. There's nothing in the world like the feeling of being wrapped up in Cole and putting my life in his very capable hands.

I've never been nervous or frightened riding on his bike. He's proven his ability to maneuver through the physics of friction. And my God, he looks so damn sexy with all that raw power between his legs.

The way his strong fingers make quick twists of the throttle, the constriction of his muscles as he leans heavily into turns, and the heat of his body snug against mine on a cold day—it reminds me what it felt like to ride *him*.

As he shifts gears, the purr of the engine revs my excitement and fuels my senses. From the vivid green landscaping and the blinding blue sky to the architecture of old homes and the oily asphalt, the view from the bike gives me a renewed appreciation of the world around me.

It also puts me more in tune with him. I feel every twitch in his body, the tempo of his breaths, and play of his sculpted abs against my palms. I probably shouldn't have slipped my hands beneath his jacket. But it feels so natural, so right, being with him in his element, on a bike, taking risks.

The smell of fresh bread tickles my nose as we approach Miller's bakery. Can there be anything better? Only perhaps the scent of Cole's skin after he's made love to me for hours. But for now, I'm content with the bakery, and he seems to agree as he pulls into the parking lot.

We're in a quiet area on the edge of downtown. Lots of old brick buildings and cobble sidewalks. I love this part of St. Louis, with its thriving population of family-owned businesses and diverse cultures.

He parks the bike and shuts off the engine, twisting at the waist to meet my eyes. "Sandwiches sound good?"

"Perfect. I haven't eaten here since…"

"Since I brought you that day?"

I nod, smiling. "It was pouring down rain."

"You were trembling and soaked and so fucking beautiful."

I slide off the seat, ducking my head as a flush heats my cheeks.

He stores our helmets and laces his fingers through mine, leading me toward the entrance. Until something catches my attention at the far end of the parking lot.

"Wait." I dig my boots in.

A young couple huddles around a small child, holding a cardboard sign. I can't read the scrawled words from here, but I know the look—the defeated postures, dirty hair and clothes, overall desperation radiating from them.

I let go of Cole's hand and jog toward them, with the sound of his footfalls trailing behind me.

When I reach the family, my heart sinks. The child—a girl around Angel's age of four—holds a scroungy little dog against her chest. The sign in the man's hand is the usual *Will work for food,* and the woman's blank stare and deep frown suggests she's given up on life.

"Hi there." I hold out a hand to the woman. "I'm Danni, and this is Cole."

Cole offers them a smile and a chin lift.

"Oh, um… I'm Holly." She shakes my hand and tries to smile back, but it strains her face. "This is my husband, Frank, and our daughter, Aubrey."

"That's an adorable dog, Aubrey." I crouch before her. "Do you like sandwiches?"

She nods, her gaze wary, skittish.

"We're headed into the bakery." Cole hooks a thumb over his shoulder. "You want to join us? My treat."

They accept with enthusiastic nods, and I give Cole my biggest, most grateful grin.

Later, after our bellies are full, the little girl steps outside the bakery to untie the dog and walk along a grassy area.

I lean across the table and eye her parents. "Will you tell me what's going on?"

Frank explains their circumstances, a story I've heard countless times. He and his wife lost their jobs in California. Then they lost their house and everything they own. They came to the Midwest for the lower cost-of-living and had to sell their car along the way to feed themselves and put a roof over their heads. They've been staying in a motel and were forced to check out this morning. They're out of money with no hope in sight.

"There's a homeless shelter about ten minutes from here." I soften my tone. "I can—"

"We appreciate your help. We really do." Holly's chin trembles as she gazes out the window at her daughter and the tiny mutt. "But that dog is all she has left. Homeless shelters don't take pets—"

"This one does." I grip her hand on the table between us. "It has private rooms for families, healthy food, and fantastic programs to help you find jobs and get on your feet again. I'm actually on my way there now."

Cole arches a brow at me, his eyes asking, *This is what you've been up to?*

"It's called Gateway Shelter," I say to her and nod my head at Cole. "Cole's never seen it, and I'm taking him there to show it off, because it's such a great place."

"Are you sure about the dog?" Her voice scratches with disbelief. "I've never heard of shelters allowing pets."

It's true. Most don't because of the hassle and cost. As a result, many people—women specifically—tolerate abuse just so their cats or dogs will have a home. I come across homeless families all the time, just like this one, who refuse to seek shelter because their companion animals aren't welcome.

A while back, I put a bug in Father Rick's ear—the manager at Gateway—about modifying the *no pet* rule. Unsurprisingly, during the latest round of renovations, he made changes that would accommodate dogs and cats.

"I promise." I squeeze her hand. "Your dog is welcome."

Holly and Frank share a look, and their eyes take on a bright shiny glimmer.

"We'd love to check it out," Frank says. "It's ten minutes away?"

"A ten-minute drive." I glance out the window, squinting at the motorcycle. I'll have to call a cab.

"Give me a minute." Cole steps outside and puts his phone to his ear.

"He's really handsome." Holly blushes, tucking a strand of short auburn hair behind her ear.

"Yeah," I sigh. "He really is."

Frank, who isn't hard on the eyes either, shakes his head.

When Cole strides back into the bakery, he pockets his phone and meets my eyes. "Trace is sending his driver. The car will be here in a few minutes."

He called Trace? That's so…expected. My chest feels like it's filled with sunshine and dimples, and I have the sudden urge to dance. Like jump up on the table and shake everything I have. But I refrain myself, settling on a smile.

"Thank you." I reach out and grip his hand.

Twenty minutes later, we arrive at the shelter.

Father Rick welcomes the family with open arms and gives them a tour. Cole and I tag along, so he can see the scope of the renovations that have been ongoing for the last six months.

"Danni and her fiancé funded all of the expansion." Rick beams as he guides us through one of the new shower rooms.

He shifts his eyes to Cole, and his smile slips. Cole stands behind me, his jealousy blatant in the glower lining his face. I elbow him in the ribs, and he grunts. Then he wipes a hand over his mouth and grins down at me.

Rick regards us suspiciously. What must he be thinking? He attended my engagement party with Trace, and now I'm here without a ring, flirting with another man. I need to clear things up before we leave.

Continuing the walk-through, Rick shows off the remodeled kitchen, massive pantry, private rooms for families, and finally the dining area, where everyone congregates.

No one hangs out during the day, since they're expected to be out and about looking for jobs.

"The doors will open in…" Rick glances at his watch. "About thirty minutes, and it'll be a mad rush to feed everyone and get them settled in for the night." He turns to me. "Are you sticking around for a while?"

"Yep." I walk toward the little girl and her dog and bend down. "Do you like to dance?"

A smile struggles on her lips and flickers in her green eyes. "Yes."

"Wonderful." Rick claps his hands together and motions at her parents. "Come on. I'll introduce you to Susie. She's our job consultant. Then we'll get you set up in one of the private rooms."

They exit the dining hall, leaving Cole and I alone, grinning at each other.

"Did Trace give you hell when you asked for his car?"

"Nope. He was absolutely relieved to hear the sound of my voice."

My eyes bulge. "Really?"

"No." He grimaces.

"I hate that you two had a falling out because of me."

"You're worth it. He and I at least agree on that." He looks around the large room. "When did you start volunteering here?"

"When you died." My tone sounds more acidic than I intended.

I play it off and move to the table at the far wall where I had a stereo system set up.

"Danni." He touches my lower back, his expression broken.

"It's okay, Cole." I power on the speakers and brace my hands on the table. "I was depressed and didn't know what to do with all that negative energy. This place gave me purpose. I started volunteering in the kitchen. Then I got a wild hair up my ass to shake things up."

"You dance here." He takes in the small dance floor and music equipment.

"Line dancing." I lift a shoulder. "I like giving sad people a reason to smile."

"You're pretty fucking amazing, you know that?" He brings my hand to his lips, kissing my fingers. "Whenever I'm with you, I feel like I'm flying. But you also scare the crap out of me."

"What? Why?"

"You're the best of everything. Your soul is so pure I don't want to darken it."

"Cole—"

"Beauty and love and freedom… That's you, all wrapped up in a tiny seductive package. Christ, I want to indulge in every inch, inside and out." He turns my hand over and presses his mouth against the inside of my wrist. "You taste like life."

I step into him, hugging his waist and resting my cheek on his chest. "I missed you, Cole. So much."

"I feel you, baby." He embraces me tightly, pressing his lips to the top of my head.

A throat clears near the entrance of the dining hall.

Rick crosses his arms and cocks his bald head, probably wondering why I'm all up against a man who isn't Trace.

"I never told him about you," I whisper. "It was just too…hard. But I should—"

"I'll talk to him." Cole untangles from me and strides toward Rick.

I don't mean to stare, but that predatory swagger, those low-rise jeans, the hard flex of his backside… Sweet sassy molassy, I can't peel my eyes away. My legs twitch to chase him. My fingers itch to do things to him. Naughty things that shouldn't be done in public, with a priest watching, or anywhere at all. Because we're just dating. Without sex.

A groan sticks in my throat, but my gaze remains stuck to Cole's ass. It doesn't hurt to imagine him naked, to fantasize about the hard swollen length of him springing free as I unzip those jeans. I ache to feel him between my legs again, pounding, stretching, throbbing—

My eyes collide with Father Rick's narrowed stare, and I turn away.

God help me, my mind is a slut. A fuckhappy, back-door Betty on the horizontal. Easy like Sunday morning.

But I want to be easy with Cole.

And Trace.

It's the worst idea ever. I've banged more than one guy within the span of a few days, but they were just flings. Sleeping with two men who hold my heart is a whole other level of free love. I'm not sure I have the emotional dexterity for it, so I need to just get it out of my sluttenous head.

I distract myself with the stereo system, setting up the line dance song I'll play on repeat for the next couple hours. Then I wait.

Cole returns just as the doors open, and the hall clamors with the shuffle of disheveled, hungry bodies. The shelter sleeps two-hundred homeless now, and it still fills to max occupancy every night.

It takes an hour to get everyone checked in and guided through the food line. Cole and I assist where needed, but the volunteers have a well-oiled system in place.

"How did your conversation go with Rick?" I lean against the wall beside Cole in a vacant corner of the dining hall.

"I told him the truth about us. How we met. Our engagement. My deployment and disappearance."

"Then you gave him the cover story?"

He nods. "It has to be this way, Danni."

"I know." I release a breath. "It's fine."

"For a priest, he sure is smitten with you." He forehead wrinkles. "And Trace."

"Rick is *not* smitten with Trace." I laugh.

"He admitted it took a while, but he eventually warmed up to Trace. He said your *other fiancé* spends a lot of time and money here." His mood sours. "The Trace I knew wouldn't be caught dead in a place like this."

I think back to Trace's conniption fit when I gave Rick that first ten-thousand-dollar check. "People change."

His lips flatten.

"Don't read anything into that, Cole." I rest a hand against the zipper on his leather jacket. "I love you just the way you are."

His mouth bends into something beautiful and gentle, and I know my words bring him relief because I feel his happiness deep in my bones.

"Are you ready?" I walk backward toward the speakers, swaying my hips to a soundless tune. "'Cause it's about to go down."

"Last time you said that, you straddled my lap on the bike and molested me."

"Poor baby." Grinning mischievously, I press play on the stereo and flick my wrist above my head to the mellow, catchy beat of *Uptown Funk.*

I choreographed an easy-to-learn line dance to this song, using a variation of the electric slide, with fun booty shakes and sexy hip twists. The dance sequence is the tits, if I do say so myself, and Cole's going to be my first victim.

I move into the taped-out section on the floor in the

dining hall and raise my voice to the crowd of two hundred. "Hi, I'm Danni. When you're finished eating, come on over. I'll teach you the steps."

Then I turn to Cole and crook my finger.

He shakes his head, less in defiance and more because he thinks I'm crazy. Maybe I am. But he's already on his way over here to be crazy with me.

Shrugging off his jacket, he tosses it next to mine and rolls his neck. Someone catcalls from the crowd, and I laugh because that was definitely a man's whistle.

"I think you have an admirer." I wink at Cole.

"We already exchanged numbers." He prowls around me, wearing a straight expression. "He promised me a special evening tonight."

"Good for you, but first, you're gonna groove with me."

"Nuh uh." He taps my lips. "First, you're gonna say the magic word."

I put my hands on my hips and inject some attitude into my voice. "Please?"

He closes his eyes and inhales deeply. "I'm imagining you doing something completely and wildly inappropriate while panting that word."

I smack his rock-solid abs, making his eyes blink open and his mouth bow in an adorable dimpled grin.

"I'm going to show you the steps." I move into position. "Focus on my feet. Then I'll help you move your hips."

At his nod, I travel through the routine, sliding right then left, easing into an oscillating descent toward the floor while shaking my backside. Another hop, a twist, with a hip tilt and lift. Add in some arm movements, and bam! This is my jam.

As I repeat the steps, I glance over my shoulder and narrow my eyes.

The pervert isn't watching my feet. His hooded gaze is fixated on my rear.

"Cole." I snap my fingers until he lifts his head. "Do you have it?

"No." He rubs the back of this neck. "But I want it. The way those pants stretch across your ass..."

Oh for the love. I slip in front of him, pressing in with my butt brushing his groin. "Do what I do, okay?"

His hands instantly fall to my hips. *Perfect.* I wait for the song to restart, give it a few counts, then we're moving.

It's clumsy at first. His boots are too bulky. His legs are too long, and he seems nervous and uncomfortable. But after a few iterations, he starts to get the hang of it. He might not be a dancer, but he has rhythm, and he's never afraid to let loose with me, no matter who's watching or where we are.

Once he has the steps memorized, I swing around and move in behind him. With my hands on *his* hips, it's my turn to study his backside.

I nuzzled and licked every inch of him during those ten months we spent together. But I'm an ass girl, and that round firm part of Cole's body is mac-a-licious, like a honey bun. I want to nibble, munch, and sink in my teeth, passively or carnally. Any manner of biting would do. Because I'm hungry.

Focus, you hussy.

I shimmy up against his back, guiding his hips with the grind of mine. I try to keep it PG-rated, but Cole has other ideas. Ideas that involve his hands roaming along my faux-leather leggings and reaching back to cup my butt.

Spinning away, I dance around him, sharing his smile and savoring the ripple of his muscles as he adds extra gyrations to the routine.

If I ever decide to become a full-time line dancer, I'm totally going to hire him. His charisma and energy is contagious. People are already congregating along the edge of the dance floor, nodding their heads to the beat.

I wave them closer and spot Aubrey, the little girl from the bakery, hovering in the crowd.

Holding my arms over my head, I boogie toward her.

"You want to try it?" I hold out a hand. "I'll teach you."

She glances back at her dad, who sits at a nearby table, holding the little dog. Returning to me, she bobs her head and smiles.

That smile… Despite everything this little girl has been through and the hard road she faces ahead, she manages a smile that's pure and genuine, and *that* is why I come here.

She curls her tiny fingers around mine, and for the next hour, she stays at my side, laughing with me, dancing with me. It's a moment of mindless joy, one I hope she hangs onto when life feels impossible.

When she starts to yawn, I lead her back to her parents and bend down to whisper in her ear. "Whenever you feel sad, do a little dance. Shake it out."

She purses her lips, looking skeptical.

"That's what I do." I shrug. "It always makes me feel better."

"Okay." She climbs onto her mom's lap and snuggles in.

"Thank you." Holly runs a hand over Aubrey's head. "For all of this. I can't express how much—"

"You're welcome." I give her a watery grin and turn away to find Rick watching me from the other side of the room. So I head that way.

Cole seems to have everything under control on the dance floor, guiding thirty-some women effortlessly through the dance. Their ages range from late teens to grannies, and they all follow him with googly, heart-shaped eyes.

I share their fascination. Over six-feet of rough-and-ready brawn clad in a white t-shirt and frayed jeans, he exudes coarse intimidation. But that warm light in his eyes softens his gruff bearing, makes him approachable, magnetic, and oh-so handsome. So insanely handsome, in fact, it's impossible to look away.

"I like him," Rick says as I approach.

"He has that effect on people." I smile as Cole reaches out to steady the middle-aged woman shuffling beside him.

"What are you going to do, Danni?" Rick crosses his arms and lifts a hand to smooth his gray mustache.

"That's the million-dollar question." I sigh. "Got any priestly advice?"

"You love them both?"

"Is that wrong?"

"No, not wrong. But God's plan for marriage is one man for one woman. Otherwise, He would've created more Adams for Eve." He gives me a sympathetic smile. "You'll have to choose one and set the other one free to find his own wife."

I won't correct him on his religious views of marriage, but if I believed in a god, that god would accept all variations of genders and sexual orientations in a relationship. I do, however, agree with him on one thing.

"I know I need to choose." I hug my waist and lift a hand to clutch my dry throat.

"Take some time and truly assess your feelings for both of them. You'll find that you really love and have more of a connection with one of them."

"That's the plan."

"Until then, prepare yourself for double the highs, double the lows. A relationship with one person is a lot of work. But with two?" He pats my back and stares at me like a father would a daughter. "I don't envy you, young lady."

"Yeah." I chuckle, and it sounds more like a groan. "Thanks."

"Anytime you need to talk, you know where to find me."

"I appreciate that."

I return to the dance floor, giving Cole a reprieve to sit and watch. And watch he does, reclined in a chair, legs spread, and eyes like liquid fire as he devours every move of my body.

His face is hard, cut in a lethal way that conjures seedy hotel rooms, guns in his hands, and a cigarette perched between his lips. I don't know what his job looks like, but as I watch him watch me, I realize he's probably a very dangerous man. Not dangerous to me. But I have a gut feeling he's killed people, and I don't know how to process that.

So I do what I always do and let the music eclipse my thoughts. I shake and twirl and move in sync with dozens of smiling people who have very little to smile about.

Later that night, I ride home on the back of Cole's motorcycle, both invigorated and tired, but also a little worried.

He's going to put the moves on me when we get home. I just know it. I saw it in the melty way his eyelids fell at half-mast while he watched me dance. He waited for me for over four years, and he's not the kind of man who goes without sex.

With a hand on the gas and the other on the clutch, he's the epitome of power and seduction. That sounds so silly and girly, but I've always had this reaction to him. Like I'm sixteen all over again, crushing on a boy to the point of foolish obsession.

But that's not all this is. Our love runs deep, enduring miles and years and even death.

I hug his broad back, relishing the proximity of his strength, *his life*. I love this man, and I want to show him with every inch of my body. But I can't. Because Trace…

I stop myself at that thought and make a personal vow. When I'm with one of them, I won't think about the other one, until which point I can't help myself. Then I'll know. If I'm longing for the one I'm not with, I'll know which one I want more.

As we motor out of downtown, a light drizzle forms in the chilly air, hovering like a spook-white mist against the black sky, lifeless, motherless. I nuzzle into Cole's warmth and remain there long after he shuts off the engine in my driveway.

"Danni?" His gravelly voice rumbles through me.

I snuggle closer. "You're so warm."

"I'll make you warmer inside."

"So will a hot shower." I reluctantly peel myself off his body and head indoors.

We take turns in the bathroom, and I'm surprised he doesn't suggest we shower together. Maybe this won't be as hard as I thought.

I lie in bed, finger combing my wet hair and listening to the rattle of the pipes as he finishes in the bathroom. When the shower shuts off, I sit up and stare at the closed door to my bedroom.

We didn't say goodnight, and it's only nine o'clock. Will he go to the basement or try to seduce his way into my bed?

Nervous energy has me reaching for the drawstrings on my pajama pants. I double-knot them, as if that'll keep him out.

Then I grab my phone, looking for a distraction. There's a few missed texts, probably from Trace. I ignore those and pull up my playlist, selecting a mellow song on low volume.

As *Lust For Life* by Lana Del Rey trickles in the background, I close my eyes and sway to the melody.

I don't know what I expected from spending the day with Cole. It's too early to make a decision, but I feel more lost than ever.

No, not lost. I'm more certain about my feelings for him than I was this morning. Spending my life with rugged, sexy Cole Hartman would be as epic and passionate as I always imagined. No woman in her right mind would walk away from him.

I press my face in my hands and try to keep my

emotions under control. I need time, and that's okay. As long as he and Trace aren't miserable, I can forgive myself for being indecisive.

A knock sounds on the bedroom door, and I whip my head up.

I'm going to open that door, and he's going to weaken me with the look. The one I can't refuse. And he's going to smell clean and yummy with his hair all wet and tousled.

Shitty, shit, shit. I draw in a deep breath just as Lana launches into the chorus about taking off clothes. That won't give him the wrong idea or anything.

I slide off the bed and crack the door wide enough to slip out. Then I shut it behind me and lean against the heavy wood before lifting my eyes to his.

Damn. The hallway is dark, but his gaze is darker. Shadowy black, like a mysterious cave, luring me in with its promise of dangerous thrills and reckless adventure.

Beads of water trickle along the grooves of his chiseled chest. I want to follow those glistening trails with my tongue, around his hard nipples, down the corrugated steel of his abs, and lower, below the low-slung waistband of his workout shorts. The material is so thin I can see the long hard shape of him jerking to be released.

"Are you going to bed?" He rests a hand on the doorframe above my head and angles toward me.

"Mm hmm." My pulse kicks up.

"I want to taste you."

My knees wobble. "Not on our first date."

"Remember our last first date?" He bends closer, sliding his whiskered cheek along mine and whispering into the space beside my ear. "I was inside you the entire night. We didn't make it to the bedroom until we christened every square foot of this house."

My thighs quiver in memory. "It has to be different this time."

"I know." He eases back, just enough to look at me. Or rather, my mouth. "I'll settle on tasting your lips."

A kiss. That's perfectly acceptable for a first date.

Except Cole kisses like he fucks—deeply, intensely, with the most fulfilling, raunchiest, kinkiest techniques known to man, and he does it with his soul engaged while stealing every hollowed-out corner of mine.

I might die if he puts his mouth on me. I'll surely die if he doesn't.

"Close your eyes." He runs his nose alongside mine, his breaths warm and minty clean.

I let my lashes flutter downward, my fingers digging against the door at my back.

The first brush of his lips stops my heart. The second caress shocks my system into a vibrating funnel of blood and desire.

He tilts his head, pressing harder, deeper, parting my mouth and sinking his tongue. I tremble and pant, wrapping my arms around his neck and meeting every tantalizing rub and lick.

His mouth is made for this, designed and sculpted to bring a woman the kind of slow-burning pleasure that melts beneath the skin and lingers like a fantasy.

Bowing into and around me, he crowds so close I have nowhere to go. But I'm exactly where I want to be as he holds me on the cusp of madness in the cradle of his body.

We kiss for an hour and a minute, tangled in the

fabric of eternity. My hands slide through his hair, over his shoulders, down his biceps, palming and scratching his pecs.

He's hard everywhere, and the hardest part of him feels like an iron bar, jabbing against my stomach. He doesn't grind. He's just so big and close I feel every thick inch, like an urgent plea for entry.

Then he goes wild, feverish, sucking, nibbling, and making up for lost years. The door rattles in the jamb with the press of our bodies. A picture frame falls off the wall. Friction, skin burns, bite marks… Holy lordy, what a kiss.

Eventually he edges back and lets me catch my breath. Ghosting his lips along my jaw, he pauses at my neck.

"We'll take it from there on our next date," he breathes against my skin. "Sweet dreams, baby."

Then off he goes, prowling toward the basement door and vanishing behind it.

I must be every shade of aroused, staring after him. God knows, I'm a hot wet mess between my legs.

Because that kiss was perfect. The kind of kiss I can't live without.

My heart drums a battle of emotion as I worry about how long I can draw this out.

In my bedroom, I turn off the music on my phone and open the text messages.

Trace: I'm lost without you.

Trace: You are my smile.

Trace: I never thought love was worth fighting for.

Until I met you. I'm ready for war.

Trace: I miss you.

The texts came over the span of the day, letting me know I haven't been far from his mind. I feel an overwhelming need to soothe him, so I send a quick message.

Me: I'm tucked in for the night, alone and missing you, too.

Then I turn off the light and count my blessings. I've been alone. Agonizingly, helplessly stuck in the isolation of mourning and depression. I'm not in that place anymore.

As impossible as my love life feels right now, it could be so much worse.

ten

The next morning, I'm up early, showered and dressed in yoga pants and a tank top before nine o'clock. I guess going to bed before midnight has its advantages. Or disadvantages, depending on how I look at it. Celibacy and curfews aren't things I aspire for in life.

As I roll into the kitchen, the floorboards vibrate to the tune of something rude and destructive blaring from the basement. *Cole and his punk rock racket.* If there's one thing I didn't miss about him, it would be his taste in music. I mean, I can't dance to it, so can it even be called *music*?

I inch along the kitchen counter, squinting at numerous plastic containers of whey protein, keratin, L-Citrulline-whatever, and other bulk supplements. Looks like someone went shopping this morning at the steroid-man store.

Coffee's already brewed—*God love his sweet ass*—and there's even an empty mug waiting for me. I fix a creamy cup and follow the noise pollution into the basement.

I find him standing amid a pile of dumbbells with his back to me, curling some serious weight. His biceps bulge with each pump, his spine deeply cut beneath shredded muscle. If the music wasn't so loud I bet I'd hear him hissing through each lift.

I used to watch him work out all the time. It turned him on when I did that, and he always fucked me after, slick with sweat and hard all over, right there on that weight bench.

With a sigh, I set the coffee on the bottom step and creep toward his futon. His bedding, all twisted and tangled, looks way too inviting. I snuggle in and press my nose to his pillow.

My eyes flutter closed as the scent of him—musky and manly—mixed with the spicy aroma of his shampoo saturates my senses.

The music shuts off, and I lift my gaze, colliding with his.

He braces his hands on his hips, cocking his head and panting with exertion. "Are you smelling my pillow?"

"What's the point of pillows if you can't stop and smell them every now and then?"

"You mean roses."

"Roses die, but pillows are forever." I steal another sniff and roll to my back. "I'll take a bouquet of yours, accented with your breath. Not baby's-breath, because that would be weird."

"Or we could just share a pillow." He prowls toward me. "And a bed. And body fluid."

"You lost me at body fluid." I feign a grimace. "You look sticky."

"You used to love getting sticky with me." He leans over my sprawled position and slides a palm from his sternum to the thin trail of hair low on his torso. Then lower, lower…

Ohmygina, his fingers are going in, dipping beneath his waistband and giving me a glimpse of how well he's keeping up with the manscaping.

"Cole." I groan. "You need to stop."

"Your breathy voice says otherwise." He places a knee between my legs and straddles one of my thighs.

Half of his hand is still visible above the waistband, so he's not touching himself. But the heated look on his face tells me he wants to. Or more accurately, he wants *me* to.

"Do you still have the snake tattoo around your thigh?" I stare up at him, falling fast and hard into his dark chocolate eyes.

"Yes. Want to see it?" He lowers his hand another inch.

"Better not." I swallow. "Are you finished with your workout?"

"I have push-ups left." His dimples make an appearance, like double divots of mischief. "Do you want to get sweaty?"

"Oh, no. Don't you dare—"

He grabs my waist and falls on top of me, rubbing his slick skin all over mine and using my body like a damn towel. I shriek and laugh, shoving at his pumped-up chest, but it's a wasted effort. He out maneuvers, overpowers, and wrestles me into a sweaty, worn-out tangle of limbs.

"You win." I sag beneath his heavy weight and run a hand down the curve of his back.

"I won the day I met you." He nuzzles my neck and circles his hips lightly against mine.

He's hard. So beautifully, deliciously long and swollen and ready. Four years ago, I would've reached my hand into those shorts and stroked him to climax. But I need to do the right thing and keep the disasters in my life to a minimum.

"How about those push-ups?" I comb my fingers through his hair.

"As hard as I am…" He lifts his head and grins at me. "Maybe I can pull off a cock push-up."

"Oh God. That doesn't sound remotely sexy." I trace a finger beneath the ridge of his pecs. "Are you up for doing ninety-pound push-ups?"

Me, sitting on his back, is the only way he used to do them.

"Hmm. Ninety-pounds?" He rises on his knees and makes a show of examining my body. "I think you've added a few pounds. Or twenty."

He knows damn well I haven't gained an ounce since he met me. If anything, I've gotten leaner—a side effect of depression.

"Sounds to me like you're afraid to try." I arch a brow.

"Fuck that." He jumps to his feet.

I follow him to the mat near his workout machines, savoring the effortless way his body moves.

He lowers into the push-up position, elbows bent,

face down. "Climb on, baby."

I sit on his spine and cross my legs, facing his feet. As a dancer, I have superior balance, so my job is easy. He, on the other hand, has his work cut out for him.

He used to be able to do twenty of these, but he's lost a lot of muscle mass. I count silently, watching his ass flex through each dip and rise. And damn, his sexy grunting noise. Those always got to me, like the rigorous, full-throttle sounds of sex.

His back begins to shake on the tenth lift, and I know he only has one or two left in him. But he powers on, pressing out three more before he collapses beneath me.

"Thirteen." He grunts, breathing heavily. "Fuck."

I slide off his back and stretch out alongside him. "You'll get there."

"Yeah." He inches toward me and brushes the hair from my face. "I will."

We goof around the house for the rest of the day, doing mundane things, like laundry and housecleaning. He changes the oil on my car, trims back the old oak tree in my yard, and fixes the leaky faucet in the bathroom.

Between him and Trace, Cole is definitely handier around the house, and I'm so grateful for that. But I wouldn't choose him just because he keeps things in working order. A non-leaky faucet doesn't top the list of things that are important to me.

Dancing is important to me, and Cole seems to appreciate my need to constantly move my hips, whenever, wherever. Like today, when I crank up my Beyoncé playlist and dance around him while he prepares a late lunch. He doesn't get annoyed or tell me to grow up. He shakes his head and laughs and tells me I'm beautiful.

Then it's time for me to go to work.

He walks me to my car, lingering beside the open door as I buckle my seatbelt. Hands on his hips, he stares at the pavement, looking for all the world like he's seconds from dragging me back into the house.

The cords in his neck go taut. His expression hardens, and it takes him long uncomfortable seconds to meet my eyes. I know the question is coming before he asks it.

"Will you come home tonight?"

I ache to siphon all the pain from his posture, but I won't lie to him. "I don't know." Stretching toward him, I touch his stubborn jaw and guide his gaze to mine. "I won't have sex with him."

His nostrils flare, and he grips the back of his neck.

"Is this too much?" Worry tinges my voice. "Are you miserable? Because I can't bear—"

"As long as you're not fucking him, I can handle this. I'm just… I'm being a selfish prick."

My breath stutters. "I'm the one who's selfish. I'm dating two—"

"No, Danni." He crouches beside me and leans into the car to hug my waist. "I did this to you. I put you in this position because of decisions *I* made. I'm fully prepared to pay for that."

"Cole—"

"Make no mistake. This is the most important fight of my life, and I'm going to give it all I got." His timbre scratches, gruff with emotion. "I might not have trained for this, but I was trained to win. And winners never quit."

eleven

Cole is decidedly some kind of soldier. Retired or not, the snake is his spirit animal and venomous aggression burns hotly in his blood. So I'm not at all surprised when he shows up at Trace's restaurant later that night.

When he ambles in, I'm on the circular platform at the center of the dining room, four hours into my belly dance routine. He doesn't look at me, his attention on the young hostess as he leans down and says something to her. Then he points at the only empty table near the stage.

Trace's table. Trace isn't here now, but he's been in and out all night, sitting in that very spot. He probably reserved it for the evening.

The hostess shakes her head and leads Cole to a different table. But instead of following her, he veers through the dining room toward me.

He got his hair cut. Faded up the sides and spiked on top, it's similar to the high-and-tight style he wore when we met, only more rebellious. And way sexier.

Dressed in dark jeans and a black collared shirt, he sits at Trace's table a few feet away and lifts his gaze to mine. I don't let the clean-shaved face, nice clothes, and new hair cut fool me. He's up to no good.

The hostess rushes over, and he crooks a finger at her. When she bends down, his lips form one word. *Menu.*

More head shaking, her mouth moving as she points across the dining room. When he waves her away, she huffs and storms off, probably to call Trace. This should be fun.

Cole returns his attention to me. He's seen me belly dance, but not on a stage in a packed room. I found the job at Bissara shortly after he left as a way to keep myself busy in his absence and earn some extra cash for the wedding.

Tonight, I'm wearing a black balconette bra with a scalloped trim and a strappy halter accent that divides my minimal cleavage. The black wide-leg pants flow like a skirt and sit so low on my hips it's impossible to miss a single ripple or twitch in my abs.

Cole's eyes rake me from head to toe as I undulate my core to the erotic beats of *Beautiful Liar* by Beyoncé and Shakira. The choreography to this song focuses on synchronized hand rotations, head tosses, and dramatic hip kicks to punctuate the hard beats.

With his unadulterated attention on me, I rev it into high gear, writhing my curves with enthusiasm while holding his gaze with a flirtatious smile.

He sucks in a breath that lifts his chest and parts his lips.

I toss him a wink and spin away. Then I perch my rear in the air, flatten my palms against an imaginary wall, and watch him over my shoulder as my lower half twists and shakes to the sensual music.

His hand flies to the back of his head. I'm not good at reading lips, but I think he curses a prayer to Jesus. Then he twists in the chair, likely scanning the audience in a surge of possessive jealousy.

The restaurant patrons are enraptured. This is an adult-only venue, and the people who dine here aren't prudes. Most are frequent guests who come just to watch the show.

There are as many women in the audience as men, and this seems to appease Cole as he swivels back to me, his shoulders more relaxed.

I'm halfway through the next song, when Trace's tall silhouette appears in the entrance. I tense through a pelvic shimmy as he strides directly toward Cole.

Black suit and tie, crisp white shirt, and all glowering business, he stops beside Cole and folds his hands behind him.

Cole reclines back and casts Trace a devil-may-care expression, but there's mischief in those dimples. Surely, he didn't come here to pick a fight?

I try to focus on the dance routine, but I'm glued to the interaction before me.

Trace towers over Cole, staring him down for a tense moment before taking a seat beside him. They launch into a stiff conversation, which quickly elevates to fists curling on the table, heated whispers, and red faces.

For fuck's sake. This song can't be over soon enough. The moment it ends, I do the customary bow and hop off the stage to the sound of applause.

The next song in my set list streams through the speakers as I stroll over to the table and lower into the chair across from them.

They stopped arguing when they saw me approach, and now they're staring at me as if bracing for a fight.

Rather than give them one, I prop my chin on my fist and smile at Cole. "I like your haircut."

The displeasure radiating from Trace heats my face, but I keep my focus on Cole.

"Thanks, baby." Cole grins back.

"Do you like Moroccan food?" I ask.

"Yes."

I catch a passing server and ask for a menu. Then I turn to Trace. "Are you finished working for the night?"

He gives a starched nod, his neck looking strangled in that tightly buttoned shirt.

"Why don't you loosen the tie?" I gesture at my own throat. "Relax a little?"

"Take the rest of the night off." He bends closer, with the small table separating us. "Spend the evening with me."

"I'm going to finish out my shift." I tilt my head, eying Cole. "Did you come here for the food, the show, or to ruffle Trace's feathers?"

Trace leans back, scowling at Cole, though it looks more like a pout.

"The food and the show." Cole smirks. "Trace can ruffle his own feathers."

"You're not welcome here," Trace says curtly.

"Is this your first time at the casino?" I study Cole's sobering expression. When he shakes his head, I ask, "Did you come here after you met me? To visit Trace?"

"Yes." He frowns.

He used to go to the casino *while living with me*, to hang out with a best friend I didn't know about. It's a bitter sore spot for me, a deception I struggle to forgive, even though I understand why he kept their friendship a secret.

Had I met Trace through Cole, if I'd been introduced to him as the friend of my fiancé, would I have still fallen in love with him after Cole died? Or would I have kept him in the friend zone? It's hard to say and doesn't really matter at this point, but I wonder how different things could've turned out.

"I know you haven't been to this restaurant." I accept the menu as the server approaches and hand it to Cole. "It's only been open for six months."

"I thought I'd check it out, see where you worked." Cole glances around. "It's a nice place."

A sneaker slides against my barefoot beneath the table and hooks beneath my calf. I narrow my eyes at Cole but don't move my feet.

"The entertainment here is exquisite." He opens the menu and stretches his other leg toward me, capturing my ankles in the cradle of his. "I'm jealous of that light you dance on."

"Jealous?" I laugh. "Why?"

"It has the best view in the house."

Oh my God. I rub my forehead, grinning.

"Ridiculous," Trace mutters.

"I bet she makes you a shit ton of money." Cole

glares at Trace.

"My money will be her money." Trace bores his steady gaze into mine. "The moment she takes my last name."

His quiet intensity is nerve-wracking, making me shiver all over.

"Danni doesn't give a fuck about money." Cole inconspicuously tightens his legs around mine and scans the menu.

"You're wrong." Trace's eyes don't stray from mine. "A large bank account means endless donations to whatever charities she's passionate about." He shifts his glare to Cole, his tone eerily calm. "Keep your fucking feet to yourself or I'll have you removed from the property."

I widen my eyes, surprised Trace knew what was going on under the table.

Cole doesn't move. "You'll have your paid servants remove me, because you're not man enough—"

"Stop it." I pull back, tucking my legs beneath my chair and sitting straighter. "Instead of taking pot shots at each other, how about you have a pleasant dinner together?" I look at Cole. "The cuisine is amazing. I recommend the *Kefta Mkaouara* with the tasty bread to soak up the sauce." I turn to Trace. "When you're done, you can show him around the restaurant. Meanwhile, I have to finish my set."

Without waiting for their reactions, I return to the stage. The room erupts in cheers and whistles as I find my footing mid-song and roll into the choreographed routine.

Trace and Cole order dinner and eat quietly without turning the steak knives into weapons. They mostly ignore each other and focus on me. But there are a few conversations through the next two hours. Conversations I so badly wish I could hear. Their mannerisms and expressions are serious, stormless even, as they talk.

When they finally stand from the table, Trace heads toward the exit.

Instead of following him out, Cole steps up to the stage. I dance toward him, encased in the beam of light that shines from beneath the acrylic platform. He studies it for a moment and reaches out to test the motion sensor, trying to make it follow his hand.

The spotlight stays under my feet, chasing me from side to side as I move through the footwork. Maybe it's attracted to sweaty women, because sweet mercy, I'm burning up. Thankfully, the light doesn't put off heat. Trace had it designed specifically for me, as well as the renovations for this restaurant, the addition of the stage, and my own private dressing room. All of it—as I recently learned—was constructed for my employment before I even met the scowly casino owner.

Cole lingers at my feet, staring up at me as if he can't bear the thought of leaving. I hate it. No matter the *hows* or *whys* that put us here, I seem to be the one pulling the strings now, and what I'm doing is cruel.

I twist mindlessly through belly dance movements while playing out an agonizing resolution in my head. I could end things with Cole right now. Tell him I moved on, that I love Trace more—*a lie*—and demand he pack up his shit and go. Cut ties. Change my locks. Block his number. Force him to find new love and deeper happiness with someone else.

It would be excruciating for me, but it's the compassionate thing to do. In the long run, his life would be better for it. Nothing good can come from being with a woman who loves two men.

A pang stabs my chest, and my face crumples. I spin away, pretending the twirl is part of the routine. With measured breaths, I focus on rippling my mid-section and composing my expression. Then I turn back.

He grips the edge of the stage, bulldozing me with a look that says *I* am his only mission now, and a soldier doesn't back down from a fight.

It also tells me the scenario I just imagined is total bullshit. Our love won't end with changed locks and blocked numbers. It's stubborn and unshakable and *fated*.

I lift my gaze to the man standing near the entrance of the dining room. Fingers in the pockets of his tailored slacks, Trace rests a shoulder against the far wall, watching me with single-minded focus.

Maybe he's the one I need to let go. But we haven't had any one-on-one time since Cole returned. Perhaps I'll stay with him tonight and talk to him openly about this.

Cole removes his hands from the stage and straightens, as if preparing to leave. I can read his demeanor—the tense shoulders, the pinched lips, the *stalling*. He might not admit it, but this is hurting him.

I glide toward him and press my lips to my fingers. Then I bend down and touch those fingers to his mouth, letting my caress feather along his jaw and float away from the indention in his chin.

"Love you," he mouths.

I nod and soften my eyes with all the things I want to say but can't on a stage in a crowded dining room.

He strides toward the exit and joins Trace.

Together, they vanish beyond the door, taking all the air with them.

Love is a deep breath with wings. It flutters in the chest, swooping and dancing to the beat of the heart. Without it, I feel strangled and lifeless.

Without them, I might never breathe again.

twelve

I slip off the stage at midnight, physically exhausted but emotionally energized. Dancing clears my head and breathes life into my soul. I feel blissfully empowered and eager to talk things out with Trace.

I haven't seen him or Cole since they left Bissara. I assume Cole went home. Trace could be anywhere on the property.

Rather than heading to my dressing room, I swerve toward the main floor of The Regal Arch Casino and Hotel. Past the clanking, flashing slot machines and around the crowded gaming tables, I veer down a quiet corridor and punch in my access code to call Trace's private elevator.

Inside the lift, I press *31*. After a short ride, the doors open, and I step out.

The penthouse is quiet, seemingly vacant. Dim lights illuminate the open kitchen on the left. Straight ahead, the living room is dark, drawing my attention to the glittering St. Louis cityscape beyond the windows.

"Trace?" I make my way down the hallway, stopping at the first doorway and poking my head into the workout room and indoor pool area. "Are you home?"

Silence.

Dang it. He must be in one of the bars downstairs, hobnobbing with clients.

The humidity and aroma of chlorine swaddles me in a vapor of tranquility, and I suddenly feel like swimming.

I follow the exposed brick walls to his bedroom and find it as tidy and vacant as the rest of the penthouse. An industrial warehouse theme dominates the top floor of the hotel, but the soft red and charcoal textures in this room give it a welcoming, cozy feel without losing the masculine ambiance.

His maid service comes three times a week. Today is an off day, yet his king-sized bed is made, accented with coordinating pillows. I smile at the image of him straightening and fluffing. He's such a damn clean freak.

I take a quick shower, washing off make-up, glitter, and eight hours of sweat. When I finish, he still isn't back.

In his ginormous closet, I dig through drawers in search of my favorite pink bikini. It's no secret I'm a little disorganized and a lot messy—the complete opposite of Trace. His suits and shirts hang in color-coded rows while my shit rarely makes it onto a hanger.

He cleans up after me constantly and never complains. For a man who tolerates very little, he puts up with my quirky, annoying habits like a champ.

Now where did he put my bikini?

I find it in a drawer labeled *swimsuits – imagine that*—along with a few others I've never seen before. He doesn't have a personal shopper. He's too controlling for that. Picturing him standing in a clothing store and picking out these skimpy things makes my heart smile.

I pull on one of the new suits, a strappy silver monokini, which is essentially a few tiny pieces of fabric webbed together with dozens of spaghetti strings.

Making my way down the hall, I cross the workout room and enter the glass enclosure on the roof of the casino hotel. In the warmer months, the windowed panels slide back, bringing the outdoors inside. But October in St. Louis is chilly. With the pool area sealed up for the winter, it feels like a sauna in here.

I stop at the digital panel beside the pool entrance. I love how the smart home system plays music in any room in the penthouse. It also does security stuff and other things, *more important things* – Trace's words—but I only access it for the sound system.

With my playlist already loaded, I select *Don't Let Me Down* by The Chainsmokers and crank up the volume.

Gathering my damp blonde hair, I knot the waist-length strands on top of my head and bounce my legs. I can't help it. I'm a slave to the music, and within seconds, I'm dancing beside the rectangular pool.

The catchy lyrics spur me to sing along and wriggle my hips. By the time the chorus hits, I'm straight-up grooving, belting the words like the singer I'm not, and completely caught off guard when an arm snakes around my waist and spins me around.

Devious blue eyes illuminate my horizon right before strong lips swallow my gasp.

Trace grabs the backs of my thighs and lifts me up his body, kissing me so passionately the world tilts and infinity stands still.

I hook my legs around his hips and melt against him, matching the sinful strokes of his tongue. He tastes like warmth and love and feels like sex. His hunger vibrates beneath the crisp suit, and his fingers dig unapologetically against my backside. Impatient. Greedy. Carnal.

I brace my arms on his shoulders and twine my hands in his hair, holding on as he licks inside my mouth, chasing my tongue and groaning his pleasure.

With a tight grip around my waist, he loosens the knot on my head and caresses my hair down my back. It's diabolical the way he gently separates the tangles, his fingers absently moving while his tongue annihilates my senses.

He's divinely beautiful and devilishly tempting, like a warrior angel fallen from grace. But he's always graceful, every action calculated, his movements precise and controlled and erotically appealing.

The song fades, silencing all sound but the heavy panting of our breaths.

He breaks the kiss and stares at me with a stern frown in his brows and an even deeper frown on his lips. It's such a natural expression for him—severe, imposing, seemingly displeased. His scowl used to annoy me. But now that I understand the man behind it, I find it oh-so tasty and lickable.

"Hi, sexy." I lower my tiptoes to the tiles.

He's so much taller than me I have to tilt my head way back to smile at him.

"Hi, gorgeous." His expression softens, and he trails a knuckle along my jaw. "Thank you for the text last night. I won't say I slept well, but your message made it easier. I missed you."

"I missed you, too." I glide my hands down the crisp lapels of his suit jacket.

"Stay with me tonight."

"Okay." I rest my cheek against his chest and close my eyes as I breathe in the seductive scent of his aftershave. "Swim with me?"

He holds me for a peaceful moment before stepping back to prowl a circle around me.

"If I get in the water with you while you're wearing this…" He pinches the crisscrossed straps on my waist. "This abstinence bullshit ends." Stopping behind me, he trails his fingers from my thighs to my ribs, his arms slipping under mine to flick the strings beneath my breasts. "Take this off."

Tendrils of heat curl through my body, hardening my nipples and prickling my flesh. Taking off the swimsuit is a no-go. I'm tempted to grab his tie and tip him—suit and all—straight into the water with me. But he'd have to remove his ruined clothes. Then he'd be all wet and naked and irresistible.

Damn my no sex rule.

I twirl out of his grip, take a running leap toward the pool, and cannonball into the deep end. The water temperature is perfect as it rushes over my head and saturates my skin.

Skimming along the bottom, I swim toward the

shallow end and come up for air near the stairs.

Trace lowers onto the edge of a lounger a few feet away. In his shiny shoes, starched black slacks, and tie, he should look out of place. But it's the other way around, like the lapping sound of water and chlorine-dense atmosphere shouldn't be here. The clothes and the surroundings don't make the man. *He* sets the ambiance and commands the space, no matter what he's wearing or where he is, as if his aura defines the very air that touches him.

Perched on the end of the lounger, he bends his knees, supporting his elbows and the lean of his upper body. His bearing exudes lazy nonchalance, but the glare in his arctic blue eyes reminds me he's not at ease, not tonight. There are too many uncertainties about us and the future.

I wade over to him and fold my arms on the decking. "What did you and Cole talk about?"

"I will not spend my time with you discussing Cole."

"So you're going to pretend he doesn't exist?"

"For now…yes."

"We need to talk, Trace. Sooner rather than later. Like tonight."

He stares at me, motionless, expressionless, without a glint of capitulation on his beautiful face.

I release a frustrated breath. "I'd like to swim for a few minutes. What are you going to do?"

"Watch you."

He's already watching me. Intensely. Compulsively. I look away, chewing the inside of my cheek. Sweet Jesus, this man…this buttoned-up, rigidly-layered, wickedly good-looking man with a gooey center is so deeply under my skin I can't swallow the thought of separating myself from him. The agony of pushing him away would be unbearable.

Shaking off those thoughts, I propel my body into motion and slice through the water. Back and forth, I dive and float, without direction or purpose. But each time I come up for air, my gaze falls unerringly to his.

Still as a statue, his posture is that of a powerful man, as if to say, *I'm the biggest and meanest in all the land and you better pay attention.*

What's remarkable is that he's a leader without being aggressive or loud. He captures my attention with sophisticated subtleness—the cool tone of his voice and the calm calculation in his body language, like the know-it-all mannerism he always slips into with his hands clasped behind his back. He's comfortable in his position no matter where he is or who he's with. Including sitting in a humid pool room wearing a heavy suit.

I finish my swim and use the stairs to exit the water, studying him out of the corner of my eye, waiting for his gaze to stray. It doesn't.

He's told me time and time again he enjoys looking at me, but that isn't the only reason he watches me. It's his nature to be in charge of everything, to be aware of everything going on around him. And around *me.* If he had it his way, he'd control the air I breathe, the water on my skin, and the beat of my heart.

I love that about him, and I suppose it means I'm submissive. But I also like making him work for it. To keep things challenging and interesting.

When he gets his way—he usually does—I don't mind. Because his intent is genuine. He doesn't try to oppress or harm or degrade me. He wants to protect me from all of life's dangers, like drowning in a pool, getting robbed in my unlocked house, and spending years mourning a dead man.

My chest clenches. I might whine about him being an overprotective controller, but he knows as well as I do his overbearing ways please me to no end.

As I dry off, he stands and follows me to his bedroom and into his closet. I drop the towel and reach for the straps on my shoulder, eying his hovering frame in the doorway.

"A little privacy?" I give him wide, innocent eyes.

He knows I'm not modest about nudity. He also understands my need for inhibition during this confusing point in our relationship. Yet he makes no move to leave.

Instead, he stands taller, hands on his hips with his chest open. Like a fluffed rooster with a make-me-if-you-dare attitude.

The simplest way to battle stubborn Trace Savoy is to simply not submit, which I think he actually gets off on.

First step is to out-stare him, and I'm not above cheating. The trick is to look at the bridge of his nose because seriously, his eyes are bone-melting lasers, and no one can compete with that.

His nose is perfect like the rest of him. It fits his face, proportional and aristocratic with sleek sidewalls that support a blocky masculine shape and a natural degree of flatness sloping down the bridge tip.

Okay, it's just a damn nose. I really want to fall into the luster of his cerulean eyes, but I also want to win.

"I can do this all night." I feel myself caving by the second.

"Or you could just remove the swimsuit." He adopts a wider stance, legs apart, shoulders back, with those pools of ice blue never looking away.

Time for the second step. Touch him, *before* he touches me. Because if I make the first move, I get the upper-hand, right?

I reach out and glide my fingers along his jaw, dipping into that sexy hollow behind his necktie. "Turn around. I'll just be a second."

He slowly releases a breath and scowls his nonconsent.

My gaze slips, as if pulled and grabbed by his tractor-beam eyes. It's a trap. I'm not holding his unflinching eye contact. He's holding *me.* With just a look, I'm caught and shackled.

Damn. This is no longer about removing my swimsuit. It's become a battle of wills, and I don't know why, but I want to beat him.

The third step in a stand-off with a man like Trace is to appear friendly and demure while ignoring his finespun signals. Like the way his fingers slide into his pants pockets with thumbs angling toward his cock, as if to remind me who has the biggest tool.

Seeing how I don't have a tool and the whole point of this charade is to *not* draw his attention to the assets I do have, I'm at a loss. But I can negotiate. Somehow I managed to haggle a helluva counteroffer when he hired me to dance at Bissara.

"Where are you sleeping tonight?" I give him my back and search the drawers for pajamas.

I won't find any, because I've only ever slept naked with Trace.

"I'm sleeping in the bed." His deep timbre shivers up my spine. "With you."

"On two conditions."

"It's nonnegotiable."

I won't let Cole share my bed, and I should apply the same rule with Trace. But I'll make an exception, because I unequivocally trust Trace's self-control. Cole? Not so much.

But I'm only doing this if Trace meets my conditions.

"The first condition," I say. "I sleep in clothes, and they remain on all night."

His hand moves in my periphery, yanking a white button-up from one of his hangers and holding it in front of me.

The shirt is thin, almost see-through, but I accept it and remove a pair of white panties from a drawer.

"The second condition." I peer at the hovering scowl behind me. "Step out while I dress."

"This is bullshit, and you know it." He drifts closer, his chest brushing my back, as he caresses his hands over my shoulders, slipping the straps down my arms. "I've kissed every inch of your body. I know each curve, dip, and delicate freckle. You have nothing to hide—"

"I'm not hiding." With a hand on my hip, I lift my chin over my shoulder. "Respect my wishes, Trace."

His jaw hardens, and he storms around me, walking in fast, angry strides deeper into the closet. With his back to me, he kicks off his loafers, and they land in the vicinity of his orderly shoe rack. His breaths heave furiously as he yanks off his suit jacket and whips it toward the hamper.

He's beyond pissed, and I know I'm not going to

win this. So I turn around and quickly change into the shirt and panties.

That done, I shift back and find him slipping on a pair of navy boxer briefs over his hips, the long length of his spine taut with frustration.

He pivots to face me, and our eyes lock. Uncertainty trickles over my skin, and I wrap my arms around my waist.

Whatever he sees in my expression causes his posture to go from self-assured to anxious. He rubs the back of his neck and shifts from one foot to the other.

Then he drops his arms, holding them out to his sides. "Come here."

thirteen

At some point over the past six months, scowly Trace Savoy, with his knotted necktie and starched personality, negotiated his way into my heart. He's given me a whole new perspective on *asshole* – a perspective that makes me appreciate the rare glimpses of his vulnerability. Like when he stands before me with his arms out, wearing nothing but boxer briefs and naked tenderness.

Like now.

I step into his waiting arms and hug his firm waist, breathing in the masculine scent of his bare chest.

He inhales slowly, deeply, as if it's the first gulp of air he's taken in months.

"Are you hungry?" He strokes my hair, twining his fingers affectionately through the strands.

"I ate during my break a couple hours ago."

Without warning, he lifts me, holding me in the cradle of his arms as he carries me out of the closet and tumbles us onto his bed. He lands atop me with his hips wedged between my legs and his heart thundering against mine.

Together, we toss the decorative pillows to the floor and wriggle until the bedding is kicked out of the way. Then it's just him and me and the kiss that's been brewing beneath every word we exchanged in the closet.

His lips move sensually against my mouth, his tongue rubbing and teasing and coaxing mine to dance. I cling to his biceps, loving his weight on me, the feel of his tall, muscled frame pressing down and pinning us in the moment.

Our legs entwine instinctively, and his hands return to my hair, rougher now than before, yanking at the roots as he controls the pace of the kiss. Deeper, harder, he eats at my mouth with fervor, angling our heads and fitting us perfectly together.

The thick, heavy length of him grinds against the crotch of my panties, but he doesn't thrust or try to remove the barriers between us. Thank God, because my willpower is plummeting quick.

He seems to sense that and eases back, positioning us on our sides, chest to chest. His large pupils, hooded eyes, and labored breaths all signal his desire. If I looked down, I'd find his underwear tented.

I'm torturing him, and the thought clenches my chest.

There's nothing wrong with a little abstinence, but I feel guilty about it. I feel like a damn tease.

"I don't like this…this distance between us." I run my fingers over the sculpted lines of his face, relishing the scratch of his five o'clock shadow.

"It's temporary." He tucks my hair behind my ear.

"How temporary? It's already been a week. I need to—"

He touches a finger against my lips. "Don't force it. You're not in a race, and I'm not going anywhere."

I grip his hand and lace our fingers together between us. "You're okay with this? Starting over and dating and stuff?"

"Stuff?" He casts me a smoldering look. "I'm interested in hearing more about that."

"I mean it, Trace. Where's your head at on all of this?"

"The situation is less than ideal, but it's a hell of a lot better than you starting over without me." His mouth twitches, and he nudges his thigh between mine, inching us closer. "I can handle the competition."

I wish his confidence would rub off on me, because I'm feeling pretty sucky about my indecisiveness. "Who were you with before you came home tonight?"

His eyes darken. "Cole."

All that time? And they didn't kill each other? My curiosity is wildly piqued as I try to picture them hanging out together. "Where were you guys? For *hours*?"

"In my office."

"Doing what?"

"Talking."

"No more curt answers, dammit. What did you talk about?"

"Things." His eyes glimmer.

I groan. "You're infuriating."

"You're stunning." He kisses my bottom lip and

slowly draws it into his mouth.

"Stop flirting." I pull back, fighting my grin. "I'm being serious."

"So am I." He clutches my thigh beneath the oversized shirt and tightens our hips together. "You're seriously breathtaking."

"Thank you." Basking in his compliment, I snuggle closer against his hard body and try to remember what we were discussing. Oh, right. "I know you don't want to talk about this, but the two most important people in my life worked together, used to be best friends, and I just…I want to understand more about your relationship. It's important to me."

He plays with my hair absently, and his eyes lose focus for a few seconds before clearing and latching onto mine. "Before I was his handler, I was an operative, like him."

I perk up, lifting on an elbow. "An operative? I don't know what that is."

"It'll stay that way. Don't go searching on the Internet. You won't find answers, but someone will know you're digging."

"Someone?" A chill sweeps across my scalp. "The government? Are they watching me?"

"The *government* watches everyone. Especially those who are linked to people like Cole and me." He rests a hand on my cheek and strokes his thumb across my lips, back and forth. "We were in the field together, inseparable for a few years on several missions. When you're with someone like that, doing what we did, you get to know them on a level I can't explain. You trust him with your weaknesses, your fears, your…*life*. You become brothers."

His throat bounces, and his entire expression hardens. I wrap my hand around his and bring it to my mouth, kissing his knuckles, one by one.

As his ruminating silence lingers, everything inside me goes still, silently urging him to continue. But I force myself to be patient.

He doesn't make me wait long. "I was offered a promotion to be his handler."

"Like his boss?"

"Yes, I was his boss, but it's different than what you think. It's a relationship built on trust. I guided him through every operation, and he trusted me not to get him killed."

"Guide him how?" I strain toward him, tense with the need for answers. "I know you can't give away trade secrets, but I keep imagining him killing people, like an assassin. Surely, you can tell me if I'm on the right track."

Grooves form across his brow, as if he's considering his response. "It isn't a secret that gathering information plays a significant role in national security."

"Like secret intelligence? Cole was an intel guy?"

His lips quirk in a smile that says, *Aren't you cute?* "Sometimes the only goal in a mission is to retrieve a piece of information. Sometimes it takes years."

"Information from who? An enemy?"

"An enemy, informant, defector, or from our own internal agencies. I'm generalizing here, but there are those who make the laws, and those who enforce the laws on the law-makers."

"Jesus. That sounds sneaky. And dangerous." My heart speeds up as I search his flinty eyes. "But you can't steal information by donning a ski mask and breaking and entering. It takes finesse, right? If you're spending years on a single mission…"

…had to change my appearance, assume another alias, and stay far, far away from you…

My eyes go wide with realization. "It's undercover work, isn't it?"

"Processes and style of operation are off-limit topics. I haven't given you classified information, but some of the terms I used might raise flags if you repeat them."

"I won't."

"Not to Bree or your parents—"

"I promise, Trace." I lower to the pillow and lean my face to his. "Thank you for sharing that with me."

It's far more than Cole gave me, and now I have a clearer understanding of the job they did. I lean back, studying Trace's relaxed expression.

Suspicion creeps in. Why is he telling me this now?

He and Cole are at war. I don't put it past either one of them to leverage every angle they have to one-up each other. And Trace just gifted me something Cole wouldn't. *Candidness.* Is it just a play in his game? I hate thinking that way, and maybe I'm wrong. I hope I am.

I run my fingers through his hair. "What did you and Cole discuss tonight?"

His nostrils flare. "You already know the answer to that."

Me, probably. "I don't want to assume. Will you tell me?"

"He spouted threats. I returned some of my own. Now we're on the same page."

"What kind of threats?"

"Danni—"

"Please?"

"Death threats." He blows out a breath. "I'll admit his were more creative than mine. But the one about my mother…"

I narrow my eyes. "What did he say?"

"If I put my dick in you again, he'll skin me alive, dry my hide in the sun, and use it as a condom to fuck my mother's corpse."

My body goes cold, my voice a horrified whisper. "He did not say that."

"He was pretty fired up when that one slipped out."

"Oh my God." I roll to my back and glare at the ceiling. "And you made threats on his life, too?"

"Yes." A steadfast response, shameless in its delivery. "If he has sex with you—"

I whirl toward him, mouth gaping. "You can't kill each other.

"Sure, we can. But we won't." He frames my face in his hands. "We won't do that to you." His eyes flicker. "I'll just pound the ever-loving hell out of him."

"No, you will not."

He laughs without smiling. "I can't tell you how many times we've beaten each other to near death over the years."

"When? Before you met me?"

"Yeah." His lips twist with a sinister delight. "He's a stubborn son of a bitch. Sometimes the only way to set him straight is to break his ugly face."

"You did that when you were friends?"

He shrugs.

My stomach cramps. "That's fucked up."

"Ready to change the subject?"

"Definitely."

If I never hear about his relationship with Cole again, it'll be too soon. Except that whole exchange doesn't sit right with me.

I squint at him. "You just manipulated that conversation, didn't you? So we'd stop talking about him?"

Something flashes across his expression, an almost smile, before he drags me across his chest and holds my face inches from his. "So goddamned smart and beautiful. I'm fucking doomed."

"Doomed?" I shake my head, grinning. "Now you're just being dramatic."

"Am I?" He brushes my hair from my cheek, watching the movement of his fingers as they slide around my ear.

"I need to ask you an important question."

His eyes flit back to mine.

"If you and I go our separate ways—" I reposition myself on his suddenly rigid chest and hold his unwavering gaze. "Can you just try to imagine that scenario for a second? See yourself far into the future? You could find love again, right?"

"I'm not doing this." He pushes me off his body and perches on the edge of the bed with his back to me.

"Why not?" I crawl toward him. "I'm just trying to get a feel for—"

"You're trying to determine who will be less heartbroken." He sneers at me over his shoulder. "Do you really want to base a decision on that?"

My breath catches at the scorn in his tone, and I lean back, putting several feet between us. "I'm trying to reduce the amount of devastation."

"Alright, let's play out *that* scenario." He twists at the waist, glaring blue flames in my direction. "You decide who's more likely to find happiness without you, and you let him go. That leaves you with a sensitive, temperamental douchebag who can't find his dick without your hands leading the way. We both know who that is."

"Don't be an asshole."

"It's a fucking cop out."

"You're being an asshole." I shove off the bed and pace through the room as helplessness quakes through my limbs.

"I *am* an asshole, Danni. I'm not going to alter my personality to sway your vote for first place."

"This isn't a competition." I ball my hands at my sides and take a wide stance before him.

"You're turning it into one."

"That's not fair," I whisper and stumble back, my heart banging against my ribcage. How am *I* turning this into a competition? "I didn't ask for this. I just want to do the right thing."

My throat closes, and tears sneak up. I turn away and pace to the wall of windows, resting my palms against the cool glass.

"Cole and I agreed on one thing tonight." His reflection in the window rises from the bed, approaching my back. "Neither of us will pressure you into making a decision."

"What do you mean?" I watch his mirrored silhouette prowl closer.

"We're not putting you on a timetable. You don't

need to *do* anything." He pauses inches behind me. "Just let it happen on its own."

"Let the decision happen?" I roll the words around in my mouth, tasting the idea. "Like fate?"

"Yes." He touches his brow to the back of my head. "It's the way you approach everything else in your life. All heart and no plan."

"I don't think either one of you wants to wait around for fate. I won't string you along."

"I can assure you that you're not stringing me along." He slides his hands over my shoulder, caressing one down my arm while the other curls around my throat and tightens. "I'm in control. Always."

"But I'm making the rules." I clutch the fingers around my neck as an avalanche of desire crashes through me.

His growing hardness against my backside hitches my breath and trembles my legs. He's power and temptation concentrated in one strong hand, securing me in place and demanding my attention.

Oh, how I want him. I want his dominance, his hunger, and his stamina. I press back against him, sagging against his hard chest while warring with the need to pull away.

He shifts closer against my back, adding upward pressure against my neck—a silent command to lift on my tiptoes. When I do, he slides the swollen head of his erection down my buttcrack and nudges it against my pussy. He's so damn hard I'm surprised he hasn't torn a hole through his boxer briefs.

"I want inside your tight little body." Squeezing my throat, he splays his other hand over my stomach and dips lower, lower, sinking between my legs to rub the crotch of my panties. "If I feel like forcing the issue, I can have you begging for it within seconds. Do I make myself clear?"

I nod in the shackle of his hand. He's in charge, and I have no complaints. It's the way we both like it. He takes the weight of worry and decision off my shoulders, and I trust him to honor my limits.

Except my stupid rules mean I have a lot of limits at the moment.

He releases my throat and straightens the collar of the borrowed shirt around my neck. Then he braces a hand on the window above my head and points behind him. "Get on the bed and tuck yourself in."

The harshness in his tone makes me jump to follow his command. Not because I'm afraid of him, but because I hear his restraint unraveling in the strain of his words. He's painfully aroused, and toying with him would be unnecessary and cruel.

I slip under the covers and watch as he reaches toward his groin, head down, breathing heavily. His back is to me, but I can guess what he's doing. I've seen him hold off his release by squeezing the base of his cock. He's doing that now, not that he's on the brink of coming, but maybe it helps him stifle his impulses.

He remains in that position for several minutes before his breaths taper off and his shoulders relax. When he turns toward the bed, his cock is still engorged, but soft enough to bend downward in his briefs.

He crosses the room, flicks off the light, and slides in beside me. I roll into him as his arms come around me and his leg rests over mine, effectively caging me in. I love being swaddled in his embrace and burrow closer, taking shelter in his strength.

Dark silence crawls in around us, grasping at my breaths and pillaging the air for answers. His quiet stillness suggests he said everything he wanted to say. But the discussion feels incomplete.

He wants me to let the decision happen on its own and claims there's no hurry. That sounds ideal—all things considered—but I don't know how to sit back and rest on this. I need a resolution.

This thing between the three of us is a delicate balancing act. Even now, I'm sleeping with one man after I refused the other from my bed last night. I have my reasons, but it still niggles, begging to be examined.

"Trace?"

"Hmm?" His deep voice penetrates my chest.

"I want to tell you something, but I don't want you to use it against Cole."

He stiffens against me. "I hate that you're thinking about him while lying in my arms."

"I'm thinking about the situation and everything that comes with dating both of you."

"I told you to let it go."

"You told me to let the choice happen on its own." I flatten a palm on his chest, chasing the tempo of his heart with my fingertips. "But there are other decisions I have to make every time I'm with one of you."

"Go on."

"I'm sleeping in your bed. *With you.* I'm not doing that with Cole."

"I'm afraid to ask why." He runs his fingers through my hair, petting me.

"You already know why."

"Because he has no control over his dick." His

hand pauses. "Do you know how many women he's fucked?"

My molars crash together. "You don't need to be hateful. I know all about his women. I also know it's been years since he's had sex. So cut him some slack."

"Is that what you're going to do the next time you see him? Give him some leeway because he traded the love of his life for a job?"

"You know what? Forget it." I push against his chest. "You really are an asshole."

His arms tighten, refusing to let go. After a moment of struggling, I slump, too tired to wage a physical fight against a man twice my size.

He tucks me against him and releases a heavy breath. "I'm sorry. I was out of line."

I pin my lips together, still sore over his rude reaction.

"Tell me what you wanted to tell me." He nuzzles my neck. "I promise not to show my ass."

"No." I wriggle away from him.

"Danni," he says, all surly and grumbly.

"Instead of growling at me, maybe you should try to convince me nicely?"

"Roll over."

That's barely an octave away from a growl. I shouldn't give into it, but curiosity wins. When I shift to lie on my chest, he climbs over me in the dark and straddles my hips.

I lift my head to see what he's up to then immediately face-plant, because sweet mother of God, his fingers…along my spine…working my muscles…*heaven.*

Moaning into the pillow, I liquefy into butter

beneath his strong, magical, amazing-as-fuck hands. "Don't stop."

"I've heard you say that before, while eating a pillow for a different reason."

"This might be better than sex."

He yanks the shirt up, exposing my back, and his fingers dig in around my shoulder blade.

"Oh God." My eyes roll back in my head. "Right there."

"I've heard that—"

"Shut it."

"You're really tight."

I half-snort, half-grunt. "Hilarious."

"No, your muscles here…" He rubs a knot in my shoulder while shoving the shirt out of the way. "I'll put you on a regular schedule with the hotel's in-house masseuse. I don't know why I didn't think of it before with the constant beating you put on your body."

"Don't do that. It'll take away from our time together. Besides, I prefer your hands." I sigh at the pleasure. "Jesus, that's good."

He continues to work my back, breathing through the movements like a pro. I drift into a blissful coma, sinking peacefully into almost-sleep when I remember what prompted him to do this.

"What I was going to tell you earlier," I say, "is that I don't have any misgivings about sharing a bed with you. Because I trust you."

His hands fall still, his voice cautious. "You trust me and not Cole?"

"I trust your self-control." I squirm beneath him, forcing him to slide off me as I flip to my back.

We settle into our favorite position, lying on our

sides, limbs entangled, face to face.

"I don't want to take advantage of your restraint." I trail my fingers along his jaw and down the strong column of his neck. "I'm afraid I'm going to touch you, tease you, and push too hard because I know you won't cross the line and break my rules. You'll keep your needs bottled up, and I'll keep pushing and push—"

"Danni." He grips my wrist and holds my hand against his chest, his eyes pitch-black in the darkness. "Do those things with me. Touch me. Use me. Push me all you want. Take whatever makes you happy."

"No, I can't." My heart stammers. "It's wrong."

"You can't take advantage of what I'm freely offering, and I'm offering everything—time, support, respect, love, protection… The list goes on. Just know that you have *me*. I'll be what you need for as long as you let me."

fourteen

In the spirit of letting decisions happen on their own, I coast through the next couple days without forethought, itinerary, or course of action. The only schedule I'm committed to is working at Bissara three to midnight, five nights a week.

The morning after I stayed with Trace, we slept in, lazy and contented. Later that day, with his hand in mine, I called my parents and my closest friend, Nikolai, to tell them about Cole. They took the news about as well as Bree did, offering their condolences and support while I figured things out.

After I ended the calls, Trace and I didn't discuss it, focusing instead on each other until I went to work.

There's something to be said about spending time with an incredible man without sex in the equation. We talked and cuddled, kissed and flirted, whispered and laughed more that day than we have in the six months I've known him. I enjoyed it so much I stayed with him two nights in a row.

The third night is now upon me, and as I hop off the stage and end my shift, Trace meets me at the entrance of the restaurant.

Pressing a hand against my lower back, he turns to guide me toward the elevator that will take me to his penthouse.

I didn't have a plan for tonight, but the need to see Cole digs my feet in.

"I'm going home." I pivot to face him.

A black look shrouds his expression. "Bored with me already?"

He assured me he could handle the oscillation of this dating thing for as long as it takes. I also know he's prepared himself for the inevitable nights I spend with Cole.

"I wasn't sure how to tell you…" I peer up at him, feigning a grimace. "I've been bored with you for months."

He chuckles, a gloriously dark and gravelly sound. Then he grabs my waist and lifts me to capture my mouth in a plundering kiss.

I fold my legs around his hips and feed him my moans, my desire, and my love. Our lips remain locked as he carries me down the empty corridor. We continue licking and nibbling as he blindly taps in the access code on the panel for my private dressing room.

The door opens, and I break the kiss, dropping my feet to the floor. Restless and dreading what comes next, I smooth my hands over the crisp lines of his suit.

"I had an amazing last couple of days with you. *Because of you.*" I straighten his yellow tie and step back. "Turns out, you were right. Assholes make my pulse race."

"And your panties wet." He pins me with a knowing look, the smug ass.

"I'll see you here tomorrow."

Two more days of work. Then I get a two-day break. I don't know what I'll do on my days off or who I'll be doing it with, and I kind of like not knowing. There's no expectations. Nothing to fret about.

I slip into the dressing room and close the door partway, leaving a foot-wide crack filled with stony blue eyes and a gorgeous scowl that I want to kiss right off his face.

Leaning in with his hands on the doorframe, he regards me for a weighted moment, licks his lips, and whispers, "I love you."

"Love you more."

"Impossible." He straightens his spine then his suit jacket. His hands slip into his pockets, and he turns on his heel, vanishing around the corner.

I close the door and sag beneath the force of my feelings. The desperate urge to run after him and hug him with all my might is a powerful pull. But it would only make it harder to say goodbye.

It's time to go home. I haven't seen or spoken to Cole in two days. He started his new job tonight, and I want to hear about it.

And I miss him.

As much as I already miss Trace.

Fuck me, my life is a mess.

They gave me their hearts, willfully, recklessly. If I choose one, I break the other. What the fuck am I supposed to do?

I want to keep them both. But even if we were the last three people on Earth, that wouldn't happen. Not with two men as possessive as Cole and Trace.

I take a shower and pull on jeans and an oversized sweater and coat. It's after one in the morning when I drive home and park the Midget in my empty driveway. No motorcycle. Cole's still at work?

Bracing against the cold, I race inside, through the back door, the dance room, the kitchen, and pause. *I didn't lock up.*

Since Cole has his own keys, I retrace my steps to the back of the house. As I pass through the dance studio, the mirror on the far wall catches my eye. I swivel toward it, squinting at the pristine new glass, and press a hand against my tightening chest.

I broke that mirror three years ago in a drunken rage of grief. Then I left it, splintered and sad, as a reminder of what I look like when I give up.

And Cole replaced it.

Anger lances through me, spiking my pulse. But I shake it off. He didn't know. He was just trying to be helpful.

Do I even need the reminder anymore? The night I dragged myself out of that dark place, I hoped I would look back someday and appreciate the distance I covered.

I started dancing again. And smiling. And living. And I fell in love. That's a pretty good distance. A happy distance.

The near future won't be easy, but I like to think I'm past the hardest obstacle of my life. Cole's alive and breathing and able to share those dimples with those lucky enough to know him.

As if on cue, the purr of his motorcycle vibrates along the side of the house. It shuts off, and I rush toward the door, yanking it open and shivering against the chilly air.

Cast in shadows, his dark silhouette swings off the bike and approaches in long, unhurried strides. I step back, making room as he enters.

"You just get home?" Glancing at my coat and gloves, he sets his helmet on the chair by the door.

"A few minutes ago." I lock up and pull off my outerwear. "Thank you for fixing the mirror."

"You're welcome." He shrugs out of his leather jacket, takes my coat, and hangs everything on the hooks behind the door. "How did the glass break?"

"It got in a fight with a bottle of whiskey."

His bog-brown eyes scan my face. Not prying. Just looking. Taking in my features like the first day we met.

It's always the visual connection that sparks first between us. The silent greeting of eye contact. The instant physical attraction. It creates a crackling glow that wraps around us until the rest of the world fades into the void it was without him. We float in a luminous bubble, staring and gravitating closer together and smiling foolishly.

The helmet left his brown hair in spikes of sexy defiance. Dimples dent his cheeks, and a black t-shirt stretches across his wide shoulders. Black slacks and a gun holster on his hip complete the security uniform. It's uninspiring as far as uniforms go, but my God, he knows how to work it. I bet he turned every female head in the stadium tonight.

"Do you know how to use that?" I point at the gun on his hip, assuming his prior job required expertise in all manner of firearms.

He arches a brow and huffs. "We'll go to the shooting range, and I'll show *you* how to use it."

"Sure." I shrug. My interest is solely in watching him handle a gun. "How do you like the new job?"

"It's just a job."

I circle his wide stance, taking in the delicious fit of his clothes. Sitting low on his trim waist, the cargo pants highlight the powerful muscles in his legs and the firm shape of his ass. He's covered head-to-toe in black, like a formidable shadow, except for the white lettering on his back that reads *Security.*

He went from a high-speed operative with a top-secret clearance to the sheriff of Nothingham with an iron-on decal on his back.

"You hate it, don't you?" I return to his front and study his dark gaze.

"I hate being in this house without you here."

My shoulders slump. "I know this is hard—"

"Hey." He lifts my chin with a knuckle and glides his hand beneath my hair to hold the back of my neck. "I didn't say that to make you feel bad. The job gives me something to do while you're working. That's all it is to me."

"And a paycheck."

"I don't need much beyond what's standing right here." He folds his arms around me and holds me tight to his chest. "This… This is everything to me."

I clutch his waist, balling his shirt in my hands and sinking into his molten eyes. His beautiful lips are right there, a breath away. The need to kiss him is so deep-rooted and intrinsic I've never had to think about it before.

But I don't want to turn this into a passionate make-out session that ends in frustration. And it will, because we never go halfway on anything. When we met, we fell instantly. When we kiss, we go wild. A feral, uncontrollable kind of wild that always leads to sex.

I shift back, putting a sliver of space between us. "Are you tired?"

He shakes his head, eyes warm and hooded.

"Want to have a picnic on your futon and watch movies?" I ask.

"You mean, watch one movie? The *only* movie?"

"You remember." I grin.

"Are you kidding? I watched *Dirty Dancing* countless times over the past four years, just so I could come home and recite it with you."

"You know the words?"

"All of them."

I bounce on my toes, unable to contain my excitement. "I'll get the snacks."

"I'll take a quick shower and meet you downstairs."

Later, with my belly stuffed with cheese, crackers, and beer, I lie face-down on the futon, with his pillow scrunched beneath my chin. He mirrors my position beside me, wearing lounge pants and a white t-shirt. With our legs angled toward the top of the bed and our heads at the foot, we're glued to the TV on the wall a few feet away.

There's only a couple scenes left in the movie, and he's proven that he does, in fact, know all the words.

Midway through, we fell into our own speaking parts, with him reciting Johnny Castle's lines while I perform Baby's. It's turned *Dirty Dancing* into a whole new viewing experience, and I can't stop laughing.

He shifts to his side, facing me, as he reels off his next line. His eyes glitter, and his mouth sensually forms each word, delivering the dialog with passion and drama.

I squint at his intense facial expressions. "Are you making fun of this movie, Cole Hartman?"

"Never." He inches closer and trails a hand down the back of my t-shirt.

While he showered, I slipped into pajamas, opting for the most coverage. The shirt is tight but longer than most, gathering around my hips. And the flannel pants have a double-knotted drawstring at the waist.

He turns his attention back to the TV and continues his speaking parts. But that hand is still moving, roving lower on my back, rubbing, and exploring. I soften beneath the affection, mesmerized by his presence. So much so the movie fades into the background.

Under the guise of massaging my tailbone, he works open a gap between my shirt and waistband. When his fingertips find my skin, goosebumps skitter up my spine.

He rests his cheek on the pillow, watching me intently. His deep brown eyes are magnetic, beguiling in their focus, baiting me to tip closer, peer deeper, and fall in.

Closing the distance, he presses his hips against mine and seizes my mouth with warm, soft lips.

His fingers stretch beneath my shirt and splay across my back as his other hand cups my head. With his arms around me, he pulls me flush against his body, chest to chest, mouths fastened, and tongues plunging.

Our legs twine together, rubbing, sliding, my fingers tangling in his hair and my nails scratching his scalp. Holding my head, he adjusts the angle and deepens the kiss. Groaning, breaths quickening, he dips his other hand beneath the waistband of my pants and palms the curve of my butt.

I tense, knowing we're headed toward a landslide that won't quiet. Not until we're both moaning with release.

"Don't get stiff on me. I just want to feel you," he breathes against my lips. "This ass…" He squeezes a handful of flesh. "Fuck, I missed this goddamn ass. The round, toned shape, this tight little hole…"

He sinks his fingers between my clenching cheeks and strokes the rim of my back opening.

I whimper. "Cole—"

"Let me touch you, baby. I won't push for more. I just…need…" His brow rests heavily against my temple as his entire body vibrates and rocks closer. "Christ, Danni, it's been so fucking long."

So long since he's touched me. Since he's been with a woman. Since we've let ourselves come together in the spontaneous, unrestricted, explosive way we both want.

If I let him fuck me, I'll have to tell Trace, and it'll shatter him. Or I don't tell him, and the guilt will eat away my insides until I'm sick with it.

Or I do the smart thing and resist Cole's advances.

"No." I clutch his wrist and try to remove his hand from my pants. "We can't."

He fights me for a moment, his fingers tightening

against my backside. Then he snaps his hand away and rolls to his back.

"Goddammit." His guttural whisper breaks something inside me.

"I'm sor—"

"Go upstairs, Danni." He closes his eyes and rests his forearm across his brow, shutting me out.

My shoulders curl forward, and an ache swells in the back of my throat. I feel bruised, rejected, which is stupid since I'm the one who rejected him.

He continues to lie there, with his cock standing like a flagpole in his lounge pants. He holds that arm over his eyes and fists his other hand in the bedding, waiting for me to leave.

Because he wants me out of his sight.

He can't even look at me.

My chin quivers as I climb off the futon. My bones feel heavy and wounded, and I can't stop the hurt from rising up my throat and choking past my lips.

I make it halfway to the stairs before the futon creaks beneath his weight.

"Are you crying?" Concern roughens his timbre.

I'm always crying, because I'm not strong enough for this. Hell knows what he sees in me. A wise man wouldn't waste his time with me. I'm fucking pathetic.

The tears slip free and course down my face. I keep walking, taking the steps two at a time as his footfalls give chase. He catches me at the top and swings me around in the doorway.

"Fuck." He swipes his thumbs across my damp cheeks and drops his hands to my waist, pulling me against him. "I'm a prick."

Thick shadows encase the stairway, snagging and

snaring every crevice and crack without mercy. He stands one stair beneath mine, putting us at eye-level, his gaze somber and inklike in the phantom darkness.

I sense his unease, his creeping sadness. I recognize it, because it's coming from me, too.

The last four years changed us, and now everything hangs in the balance. Our hopes and dreams are on pause, and I'm terrified to press play. I don't want to know the ending.

As my tears continue to fall, he kisses them away, whispering between the brushes of his lips. "I sent you upstairs because I don't trust myself. I don't want to fuck this up, and when I'm with you… Dammit, Danni, I want all of you, in every possible way."

"I'm making it worse." I grasp his tense neck, holding our foreheads together. "I'm not good at saying *no*, especially when I'm dying to say *yes*. I'm failing—"

"No, baby. The person failing here is me. I'm impatient and selfish and demanding. I make mistakes and lose my temper."

"You're passionate and impulsive and yeah, sometimes you get out of control. But if I can't handle your worst moments, I don't deserve your best ones."

"Jesus. I must've done something right to have been given a chance with you." His voice rasps, deep and throaty. "You have such a beautiful mind. You're incredibly understanding and gracious. And those qualities are shaped into a stunning flesh-and-bone work of art. I only have to look at you to know I have something special and rare." He releases a breath. "Sometimes you feel like an unattainable dream."

"I'm just a girl, Cole. And I'm right here."

"You're everything, and I want more." He palms my backside, fitting our hips tightly together as he speaks against my lips. "I want you to belong to me. I want my ring on your finger, my babies growing inside you, and your future welded to mine. I want to watch you teach our kids how to dance and see you swing on that pole when you're ninety years old—"

"Gross."

"Never. You'll always be beautiful." He kisses the corner of my mouth. "I had my grave marker removed from the cemetery yesterday."

"You did?"

"I'm going to buy a larger plot. When you die, I want you buried beside me."

The air whooshes from my lungs. "That's kind of morbid…in a really romantic way. Now I feel all glowy and mushy." I grin a soggy, hot mess of a grin. "Is that weird?"

"No." He trails kisses over my face, tingling an electric thrill through my body. "Not at all."

"I've felt this before, right outside, when a sexy hunk of a man rolled up on his motorcycle."

"I was right there with you, baby." He touches his smile against mine. "But now I feel it more."

He's right. There's a powerful charge in the air, like the stirring of energized matter, seeking and fusing into a cocoon of untamed chemistry that only Cole and I can create. It's an unexplainable connection between us, one that bridges the gap between lust and love. I can't see it or hear it, but I feel it, feeding light into a flickering moment, making it shine brighter than all the hours that haunted me in the dark.

In the sheath of glowing heat that envelops us, I

anticipate a hard fall into a feral kiss. His hands bite into my backside, and his hungry breaths spin around mine. But he doesn't attack my mouth, seemingly fighting an internal war. A war that eventually ends with him backing me out of the stairwell and leading me to my bedroom.

My pulse kicks up, and my legs wobble. Is he going to fuck me against the wall? Bend me over the bed? Take me on top of the dresser?

He does none of those things as he tucks me beneath the covers. He digs for the sheet beneath the blanket, which has been kicked to the foot of the bed. I help him, but it gives me pause. The bedspread is so tangled up… This isn't how I left it two days ago.

"You slept in my bed." I stare at the sheets, glad they've been washed since last time Trace slept here.

"It used to be *our* bed."

"But I wasn't here."

"Your scent is." He pats the pillow and pulls the bedding over me. "It's one of the countless layers that will always be a part of you. When we're wrinkled and toothless and fucking like arthritic animals, you'll still smell like you."

I burst into laughter and sink onto the mattress, clinging to the thread that connects us. "I never stopped missing you."

"I'll never stop loving you." Switching off the light, he leans down and gives me a lingering kiss. "Sleep well, my beautiful girl."

When he slips out of my room, I'm not sure I'll sleep at all. It hurts to watch him walk away, and he's only going downstairs.

There's no way I could watch him walk away forever.

fifteen

The next morning, I wake with the sunlight from the window warming my face. My muscles feel rejuvenated, and my mind is clear. By some miracle, I conked out quickly last night and slept straight through.

I climb out of bed and head to the bathroom, cringing at the raucous noise thumping from the basement. Cole's already hard at work, lifting weights and blaring his punk rock music. A grin lifts my cheeks as I picture him lip syncing and banging his head with belligerent intensity.

After emptying my bladder and brushing my teeth, I find freshly-brewed coffee waiting for me in the kitchen. I prepare a cup, sipping and sighing and feeling sweetly spoiled.

To return the favor, I blend up a protein shake for

him and carry the chocolaty, foamy concoction to the basement. The loud, insistent music leads the way, contaminating my ears with violent lyrics.

My blood heats in anticipation of watching his ripped physique flex through his workout. With the music drowning out my footsteps, maybe I can spy on him for a while, observe him in all his unguarded, sweat-dripping, muscle-shredding glory.

I step off the last step, round the corner, and stumble to a gasping stop.

On the far side of the basement, he grips the edge of his workbench, an arm braced on the edge to support the weight of his upper body. His other hand isn't pumping iron. The dumbbells lie at his feet, forgotten, as he pumps the hard, swollen jut of his erection instead.

My hand flies to my mouth, muffling my squeak, and the protein shake starts to slip from my fingers. I tighten my grip, saving it from crashing to the floor.

I should go. Turn around and sneak upstairs before he sees me. But the erotic sight paralyzes me in place, tingling my skin and accelerating my breaths.

The thrashing music swallows his noises, but I know he's grunting. His mouth is open, and the ridges in his glistening torso contract and bunch with the rapid pace of his stroking hand. The upper curve of his ass flexes above the workout shorts, which hang precariously around his thighs.

And his cock… Holy hell, it looks longer, thicker than I remember, jerking in the fist of his hand. My mouth waters with the need to wrap my lips around him, to lap at the salty glans, and devour him whole.

He hasn't noticed me, his head turned slightly away, as he focuses on the framed photo on the workbench.

I unlock my legs and take a few steps closer, squinting at the object of his attention.

It's a picture of me in the dance studio, stretching during one of my warm-ups. He's jacking off to that?

My chest clamps and swells as conflicting emotions barrel through me. Guilt pinches the hardest. He's thinking only of me while my heart is torn in two. But I also feel relief and gratefulness and…arousal.

There isn't a warm-blooded woman on the planet who wouldn't be turned on by this. He's so damn virile and beautifully built, from the right-angled outline of his mitered shoulders to the *V*-cut contour of his abs and hips. His physique is a chiseled masterpiece of sexuality and manhood.

Desire throbs between my legs, dampening my flesh. I wet my lips and inch forward another step.

"Danni." The profile of his mouth forms the word, his voice inaudible beneath the roaring music.

I freeze, suddenly nervous and a little ashamed for spying on him. He doesn't look at me, but he knows I'm here, ogling him like a pervert.

The hand on his cock slows, stopping to cup the tight sac beneath. Then he slowly moves his head and meets my eyes.

He doesn't speak, but he doesn't have to. It's all there in the taut muscles of his face—longing, frustration, and a hunger so potent it turns his jawline to stone.

I should head out and leave him to it, but everything inside me rages against that idea. I want to give him a hand, maybe two, and bring him over the edge, panting, shaking, and blissfully replete.

His eyes harden, and he lifts his chin toward the stereo that sits against the wall. I move toward it and power it off, blanketing the basement in silence.

When I pivot back to him, his shorts are pulled into place, his palms flat against the surface of the workbench as he leans into his arms.

"I didn't mean to…" I shift my weight, tongue-tied and flushed. "I brought you a protein shake." I set it beside the stereo.

He nods and closes his eyes, breathing heavily through his nose.

The damp basement air thrashes with awkwardness. This isn't us. We fight, yell, bitch, and call each other out on our fuck-ups. But we're never awkward together.

My attention falls to the bottle of lube on the workbench beside his hand. My no sex rule exists for a reason, but that doesn't mean I can't give a little. Without over-analyzing it, I stride toward him, snatch the lube, and climb onto the futon, kneeling at the center.

"Come here," I say to his back.

"Not a good idea, baby."

"I trust you."

His shoulders heave with an unwieldy breath before he straightens, turns to face me, and narrows his eyes at the lube in my hand. "What are you—?"

"Take off your shorts." I lean to the side and glance at his feet. "And your shoes and socks. Then lie down on your back." I pat the mattress.

With a hand on his hip, he grips the back of his neck and stares at his tented shorts, at his sneakers, at the floor, all while hissing through his clenched teeth.

"Please?" I blink doe eyes at him.

"Fucking killing me here." He drags both hands down his face, groaning. Then he toes off the shoes and kicks them out of the way as he prowls toward me. "You're playing with fire, you crazy woman."

"I can handle you."

"I don't know about that." His posture is so stiff he looks uncomfortable as he lowers onto the edge of the mattress.

He removes his socks, grips the waistband of his shorts, and stares at his lap. Hesitating. I pop the cap on the lube, and the noise seems to pull him out of his head. In one fluid motion, he shoves off the shorts and rolls to stretch over six feet of golden naked brawn beside me on his back.

My attention instantly falls on the black snake inked in terrifyingly beautiful detail around his powerful thigh. The rest of his tattoos were removed in a single surgery. I don't know how or where or anything else about it, since he refuses to disclose the specifics.

"The things I want to do to you…" He clasps his hands behind his head and stares up at me with hooded eyes. "I want to violate every tight little hole in your body until you forget he ever—"

"Enough of that." I cover his mouth with my hand until his face slackens. Then I run my fingers through his hair. "Relax. Can you do that for me?"

"Maybe." His eyes lower to my chest, zeroing in on the taut nipples threatening to poke through the cotton. "If you take off your shirt, I'll do whatever you want."

"Liar." I crawl between his legs, lifting and adjusting his heavy muscles around me.

When I have us in the position I want, he's lying on

his back in the spread of my thighs, with his ass snug against my crotch. His legs drape over mine and stretch out behind me while my legs rest along either side of his torso.

He grips my calves and rocks his hips, clenching his abs with the bob of his cock. His gaze burns into mine, and I can practically feel the testosterone thundering through his veins.

I squirt a dollop of lube on my palm and rub my hands together. "This might hurt a little."

His eyes widen.

"I'm kidding." I grin and look down at the swollen hardness pointing up at me.

He's enticingly thick and well-endowed, with a plump head, lickable veins along the shaft, and a heavy sac that he keeps smoothly shaved. The dusting of hair above his cock is dark brown like his whiskers and leads to an inviting happy trail on that flat brick of muscle low on his abs.

With a deep breath, I grip the base of his erection and slide my oiled hands, one on top of the other, up the length, teasing inch by inch. Sweet mercy, he's hard as steel. When I reach the tip, I glide a palm over it in a firm massaging motion that bows his spine off the mattress.

"Goddamn." His eyes squeeze shut, and his chin snaps up, elongating the cords in his neck. "Fuck, that's incredible."

Power hums through me, and I repeat the technique, going faster and gripping tighter with each pass. It doesn't take long before he's panting, shaking, and thrusting his hips in urgent need.

I float into languid caresses, sliding my lubed hands all over his balls, his cock, and back again to tease the skin behind his sac. I'm not stroking him as much as I'm simply feeling him, running the width of my hands over every inch of his well-hung package. But I maintain a rhythm, adding just the right amount of pressure while pacing him steadily, maddeningly toward orgasm.

Tremors skitter across his thighs, and I know he's close. I hear it in the sporadic sound of his breaths, feel it in the pulsing swell of his cock, and see it in the dark lust dilating his eyes as he watches me.

"I'm gonna come," he chokes, bucking vigorously into my fist. "Fuckfuckfuck. Ahhh, God. Danni…Danni…"

He grunts and jerks in my grip, his entire body contracting as jets of ejaculate spurt over my hands and splatter his thighs and abs. I continue to rub him, moving slower, softer, until the aftershocks of his pleasure ebb into silence.

His fingers uncurl from the bedding and lift to cup the back of my neck. He pulls, I give, and our breaths collide in a chaotic enchantment of love.

"Thank you." He licks my lips.

"You're welcome." I nibble back, rolling his taste around on my tongue.

"You pulled one over on me."

"How's that?"

"I'm nude, and you're fully clothed. That's not how this works." In a blink, he flips us, sending me to my back with his weight on top of me. "Your turn to come."

He clutches the hem of my shirt and pulls it upward. With his naked body between my legs and his handsome face staring down at me, I quiver on the cusp of saying *fuck it all.* The pounding, clamping heartbeat between my legs demands to be stroked and stretched by his huge, hungry, still-hard cock.

But there's another man across town, alone with his uncertainty and no doubt missing me at this very moment. Trace's feelings are so deeply woven through my heart I tense at the thought of hurting him.

Guilt seeps in, twisting me up. Am I betraying him? I don't know. I'm dating both of them.

"Danni?"

I hide my confusion behind a wide smile. "We're all covered in come. I call dibs on the shower." Pushing him off me, I race out of the basement, shouting, "You can wash up when I'm finished. I'll be quick."

I fly up the stairs and sprint into the bathroom, stripping off my clothes as the door slams behind me. My stomach hurts, and my heart curses me for running headlong into lust-induced spontaneity without thinking it through.

Fighting back my tears, I move mechanically beneath the spray of water. Shampoo, rinse, I don't let myself dwell on what happened as I reach for the conditioner.

The bathroom door opens.

Footsteps pace back and forth in the small space, and I turn to face the wall, shoulders hunching. He must know I'm upset or he wouldn't have barged in here. I hug my waist, waiting for him to either yank open the shower curtain or say something.

He does both, sending the metal hooks squealing along the tension rod. "Don't you dare shut me out."

"I'm naked."

"I see that." His feet squeak on the bottom of the tub as he steps in, and the heat of his body smothers my back.

"Cole—"

"Danni." He touches the shampoo bottle, seemingly making an effort not to brush any part of himself against me in the small space. "Do you still need to wash your hair?"

I shake my head. "You shouldn't be in here."

He moves his hand to the conditioner and waits.

I nod.

For the next few minutes, he focuses on massaging the cream rinse through my waist-length strands. He doesn't rub up against me or ask me why I'm all wooden and sullen. He's giving me time to open up on my own before he starts growling and pushing. It's like he knows I need a breath—or a hundred breaths—before speaking because I'm on the verge of crying.

When he shifts away to wash his own hair and soap his body, I drag in gulping drafts of air.

Am I'm putting too much thought and worry into this arrangement? Maybe all the helplessness and confusion I feel is just part of my path? Instead of running from my feelings, I should try to figure out what they're telling me. The answer's inside me. It has to be. I just need to breathe and remember I'm not alone. I can talk to them. They might not like what I'm thinking, but they'll always listen.

"Am I being a pain in the ass?" I glance over my shoulder, just as he runs suds over his erection. My breath hitches, and I look away. "Am I making this more complicated than it is?"

"I can't read your mind." He sets the soap on the ledge and faces me with a hand on the wall. "But I can guess this has to do with *him*."

"I feel like I'm cheating." I pivot toward him and lean my back against the tiles with my arms at my sides. "Right now, being naked with you feels like betrayal. And when I'm with him, I feel the same. Like I'm cheating on you."

His eyes taper, and his brows pull in and release. Instead of telling me to just choose him, he gives me the response I need the most. "I understand."

He slides a knuckle under my chin, dipping lower to follow the line of my neck, then lower still, down my chest and pausing to graze my nipple. My breasts feel fuller, tighter, and my pulse picks up.

He hasn't seen me naked in over four years, so I forgive his sudden detour from the conversation and hold still while he looks.

Opening his hand, he molds his fingers around my breast, testing the weight, kneading the flesh. His nostrils go wide, his voice barely a whisper. "You're as perfect as I remember."

"So are you." I trace the outline of his bicep and touch his pouty lips, smiling softly.

As his gaze begins to descend below my waist, he sucks in a breath and snaps his head up, fastening his eyes on mine. "You're not cheating."

"So if I shower with Trace, you won't consider it a betrayal?"

His chin lowers to his chest, but I glimpse the sudden tension in his face.

"It would be his betrayal, not yours." He steps closer, placing his hands on the wall on either side of my head, hemming me in.

"He told me about your death threats."

"Is that right?" He peers at me from beneath a furrowed brow.

"One specifically about his dead mother."

His eyes close briefly. "The discussion escalated. I was pissed and said shit I shouldn't have said. I would never—"

"I know." I rest my hands on his waist, savoring the heat of his skin.

"You're not being a pain in the ass or making this complicated. Neither of us will ever blame you for the situation we put you in. And we won't resent you for the actions and decisions you make. Any anger that arises will never be directed at you. This is between him and me."

"Did he say that?"

"Yes. We discussed it."

"I don't want that negativity between the two of you." My face falls. "I've ruined your friendship."

"*You* didn't do anything, and I'm done talking about him." He nuzzles my neck. "I owe you an orgasm."

My thighs clench together, and I sink my nails into his hips. "I don't think—"

"This is happening, baby. My ego won't have it any other way."

"Fuck that—"

"Oh, we're going to fuck, but right now, I just want to concentrate on you."

Those are words every girl wants to hear. Add to that the determined look in his eyes, and I'm defenseless, debilitated, and too damn weak in the knees to stop him.

His hands glide down my body, and I whimper. He kicks my feet apart, and my heart skips. Then he sinks his fingers between my legs and devours my moan in a kiss.

"You're still wearing one of my rings." He flicks the piercing and growls against my mouth. "I bet it pissed him off every time he saw it."

I'm tempted to tell him Trace sucked on my pussy ring every chance he got, but I won't stoop to that level. "I thought we weren't talking about him."

"You're right." He grips the hair on the back of my head and plunders my mouth.

His minty, masculine taste sweeps over my tongue, and his hand delves through my folds. The roots of my hair spark with delicious pain as he pulls, angling my head and deepening the kiss.

The hard lines of his body pin me against the wall, our skin wet and slipping together, creating a diabolical friction that heats me up and revs my pulse.

His fingers tease my thrumming center, but it's his primal kiss that gets my juices flowing. His tongue moves with expert strokes, licking the seam of my lips and curling deeper, flicking and rubbing and claiming.

I can come from just his kiss. The spinning, whirling, all-consuming sensation he creates with the movement of his mouth should be illegal. It makes me mindless, starving, horny as fuck, and my inner muscles clench to the point of pain.

"Cole, I need…I need you inside."

"So impatient." He bites my lips. "That's the girl I remember."

He bends his knees and ducks his head to latch onto a nipple. Then he plunges his fingers into my pussy. Two, three…I don't know how many fingers, but holy fuck, they spark greedy flames straight to my core.

My hips start to move, and my hands rake through his hair as I hold on and ride his fingers. Pleasure surges through me, and I know I won't last long. Hell, I was ready to come the instant he took my mouth.

"This is going to be fast." I drop my head back against the wall, my legs shaking against the onslaught of stimulation.

His teeth sink into my breast. His fingers curl inside me, and his thumb circles my clit. I'm a goner. The orgasm detonates, knocking the air from my lungs and the strength from my legs.

He holds me up, banging me hard and fast with those strong fingers as he laves my nipples and stares up at me with so much love and devotion.

I melt against him, boneless and satiated, hugging his neck and peppering breathy kisses across his face. "I needed that. Thank you."

It's a sappy whisper of honesty, but the possessive glint in his eyes suggests my words have a greater meaning to him. I just admitted that I haven't come in a while, that I didn't orgasm during the two nights I spent with Trace.

He finishes washing me, lavishing extra attention on the parts that'll soon be covered up. Then he dries us off and leads me into my bedroom.

I enter the closet and change into a soft pair of blue velour pants and a matching hoodie. When I step out, I find him sitting on the corner of my bed, with his elbows on his thighs and a towel around his waist.

His jaw works, and he rubs it, lifting his gaze to mine. "His penthouse only has one bedroom."

I don't know how he knows that, but I can guess

where he's going with it, and my stomach caves in.

We won't resent you for the actions and decisions you make.

His words sink in, giving me strength as I lower to the bed beside him.

"You slept in his bed." His hand clenches between his knees. "With him."

It isn't a question, so I remain silent, waiting for him to continue.

"I'll be sleeping in here from now on." He stands and strides toward the door.

"Please don't take this the wrong way, but I don't trust your self-restraint."

"And I don't trust his."

We engage in a silent glaring stand-off before I sigh and lower my head. Arguing is futile. All I can do is give and love and listen, with the hope that I won't lose my voice or be used in the process.

sixteen

That night, I climb off the stage, stiff and sore and more exhausted than usual. My joints protest every little movement, and I dread the short walk to my car. It's been a grueling night of dancing, and I need sleep in the worst way.

Trace meets me at the front of the restaurant, looking as chipper and sexy as always in his tailored suit. I stop beside him, shoulders sagging as he studies me with questions burning in his blue eyes. *Are you staying with me tonight? Going home? Did you fuck him? Did you choose him?*

"I'm staying." For no other reason than my legs ache and my eyelids feel like sandpaper. "I'm really tired."

Smiling an almost-smile, he takes my hand and

leads me to the elevator.

I lean against him as we ascend to the 31st floor. "I don't know why my ass is dragging like this."

"Late night last night?" His tone is light-hearted, but jealousy clips the edges.

"We watched a movie." I toss him a glare. "Nothing to get snippy about."

"I'm not the one being snippy." The elevator opens, and he lifts me off my feet, cradling my lolling body against his chest. "What's wrong with you?"

"I don't know." I lean my head against his shoulder and take savoring breaths of his aftershave. "There's nothing going on in my head, if that's what you're thinking. I'm just drained."

He carries me into the penthouse, down the hall, and through his bedroom. When he reaches the bathroom, he sets me on the vanity and starts the shower.

"I'll get you something to sleep in." He ambles toward the door, hands clasped behind him, like a policeman patrolling his territory. "Do you need anything else?"

"You and your arms. That's what I want to sleep in."

Steam from the shower curls around his tall frame as he pauses with his back to me and lowers his head. His shoulders rise and fall. Then he pivots and retraces his steps.

He has that look, the predatory flicker in his eyes. Like he wants to eat me. If I weren't so damn drowsy, I'd give him a playful reaction. But all I can muster is a faint smile.

When he reaches me, he leans his brow against mine and strokes my hair. "Do you need help in the shower?"

There isn't a hint of insinuation in his voice, but two showers with two different men on the same day… That's a big *no*. I turn down his offer with a shake of my head.

I should contact Cole and let him know I won't be home tonight. Except my phone is in the dressing room downstairs. "Shit."

"What's wrong?"

"I need a favor." Other than the practical reason for asking this, I have a strong need to right some of the wrongs between the two people I love most in the world. "Will you let Cole know I'm not feeling well and that I'll be staying here tonight?"

His hand stills in my hair. Then he releases me and steps back. "Of course."

"Thank you."

A phone call won't make them besties again, but maybe it'll open a line of cordial communication.

After he leaves the bathroom, I take my time in the shower, letting the heat seep into my overworked muscles. When I finally step out, I find one of his button-ups folded and waiting for me on the vanity.

I hold it to my nose, breathing in his scent, before dressing, cleaning my teeth, and running a brush through my hair. He didn't bring me a pair of panties, but the shirt hangs to my knees and frankly, I'm too wiped out to care.

He's already in bed when I emerge from the bathroom. The soft glow of the table lamp illuminates the gold in his hair and the alertness in his eyes as he watches me approach.

"I'm worried about you." He opens his arms, offering exactly what I need.

I crawl into his embrace and snuggle in with a breathy sigh. "Just…tired."

"I'm cutting back your hours at Bissara." He reaches toward the nightstand and shuts off the light.

"No, you're not." I yawn. "Tell me about your day."

"We'll talk tomorrow." He caresses my hair. "Close your eyes."

"'kay." I rest my head on the strong beat of his heart, and in the span of a few breaths, all my aches slip softly asleep in his arms.

And I sleep through most of the next day.

I wake sporadically to use the restroom, pick at the food Trace brings me, and ogle his carved physique in his workout shorts. I'm not ill or feverish or congested. Just achy and bone-tired. But as the sun arcs over the skyline beyond the floor-to-ceiling windows, I grow restless with the need to get up and dress for work.

I throw back the covers and slide my feet to the floor.

"I already contacted the restaurant staff." Trace's deep voice rumbles from the doorway behind me. "You're not going in."

"Trace." I groan and fall back on the bed. "I feel fine."

His stubborn footsteps sound his approach, and he leans over me, placing a palm on my forehead. "You don't have a fever. Are you nauseous? Any pain?"

"No. I'm just run-down."

At some point, he changed from workout shorts to a suit, and now that crisp black jacket is sliding to the floor. He removes his shoes next, then his shirt and pants, and slips into bed with me, wearing only his boxers.

Leaning toward the side table, he taps something into the digital remote for the smart home system. A second later, the seductive electronic beats of *Pillowtalk* by Zayn tiptoe through the bedroom.

"If you feel fine…" He rolls on top of me and settles between my legs, his gaze dipping to my mouth. "You won't mind if I have my way with you."

My pulse hiccups, and a thrill tickles up my spine. With a hand on his nape, I touch the pad of my thumb to the seam of his parted lips, holding it there.

"I don't know why my body refused to get up today." I drift into his eyes. "But my soul didn't want to leave your bed without a kiss."

His cock jerks against my inner thigh, swelling and lengthening. His expression remains soft, his eyes unblinking and hooded as we lean closer, little by little, breaths mingling and fraying in mutual desire.

Our noses touch, and I slide my thumb to the corner of his mouth, caressing my fingers across his cheek. His hand meanders up my thigh and rests on my waist beneath the shirt as the other tangles in my hair.

When our mouths finally meet, we exhale as one and surrender to the powerful pull, reaching and holding and sinking into each other.

He encircles his arms tightly around me, and his tongue chases mine, catching and releasing. Then he angles deeper, licking and sucking with abandonment, as if trying to drive away my doubts and taste the desire I keep tucked beneath my awareness.

His weight grows heavier, his muscles tightening

and pressing against me. I glory in the heave of his hunger and give beneath him. My skin heats and prickles, responding to the sliding friction of our bodies. My jaw slackens, submitting to the demands of his mouth. And my legs fall open, yielding to the savage drive of his need.

Every inch of him vibrates and coils with the urgency to thrust, to fuck, to chase his release. But he doesn't remove his boxers, doesn't shove a hand between my legs to test my wetness. Instead, he flips to his back, taking me with him.

Our mouths remain fastened as I straddle his hips and roam my hands along his sculpted biceps and shoulders. He palms my bare ass and kisses me with so much passion I feel the strength of his love beneath my bones, reminding me how much I have to lose.

I lean back, anchored by his sexy sleepy eyes, as the vocals in the background croon about fucking and fighting, paradise and war.

"We can skip the war and..." His lips crook into a rare smile.

"Make love?"

His erection pulses beneath me, hindered only by the thin material of his boxers and...my consent.

My thoughts flit to Cole sleeping alone in my bed, and a pang stabs my chest.

I want this—the frenzy, the burning heat, the passionate sex—with Trace, but I can't bear the guilt that comes with it.

The song changes, and a soft feminine voice streams through the hidden speakers, singing the tremulous lyrics of *I Hate U I Love U* by Gnash. I sway to the gentle beat, loving that he chose my playlist.

"How do you feel?" He runs his palms up my thighs.

I'm too tired to dance for eight hours on a stage, but… "I feel like grooving, slow and easy, on your lap. I love this song."

"Do it." He groans, clutching my waist and flexing his hips beneath me. "Grind on me."

The melody spirals through my core, gathering a sensual energy deep inside me that builds and spreads outward, lifting my ribcage and rolling my pelvis.

His fingers dig against my skin, and his breaths fall out of rhythm. I hold his gaze, communicating with my eyes how much I adore him, how I love when he watches me, and how I'm going to come, just like this, grinding on his hard-as-steel cock.

I keep my movements small and unhurried, letting the pulse of the song carry me over his shaking body. I hold my hair on top of my head, my arms framing my face as I let go and ride the tempo. Gravity does the rest, driving me against him and pushing my clit along his erection.

"Fuck, you're beautiful." The intensity of his eyes bores into mine, and his hands skim upward, beneath the shirt, cupping and kneading my breasts. "So soft and strong at the same time. A fantasy and a reality. You're a hell of a woman."

His gravelly words shove me to the edge, and I hover there, rocking and panting and reaching…

His arm snaps up, and he grips my throat, pulling my mouth to his. I choke against the collar of his hand, mouth gaping as he licks my lips, thrusts against my clit, and propels me into a writhing, trembling, gasping orgasm.

Pleasure crashes through me for endless, strangling breaths before he releases my throat and hugs me to his chest.

"Watching you come is such a fucking turn-on." He kisses my neck, my cheek, then moves to devour my mouth.

I pull back, twitching with the remnant sparks of bliss. The sexy song serenades me as I slide down his chest, eyes locked on his and lips curling with naughty intent. I grip his waistband, taking the boxers with me as I move down his legs.

He lifts his hips, easing the removal of that last scrap of clothing. The fact that he hasn't spoken or tried to stop me is a testament to how badly he wants this. The moment he's naked, I don't make him wait.

Kneeling between his legs, I lower my head and take him fully into my mouth. He hits the back of my throat, and a low, needy grown vibrates in his chest.

Then I suck him, relaxing my throat, working my fist on his shaft, and massaging his balls.

His hands fly to my hair, controlling the pace and depth as he whispers commands in his deep, eloquent voice. "Faster…tighten your fingers… Fuck. That's it…roll your tongue…so fucking good… Goddamn, Danni. I'm almost there…"

I keep my gaze on his, lost in the pleasure glowing on his expression. His thighs shake beneath my hand, and the sinews in his neck stretch with the bow of his spine.

"Fuck!" He slams against the back of my throat and stiffens with a long guttural grunt.

The force of his climax fills my mouth, and I

swallow, licking his glans and sucking softly as he comes down from his groaning high.

"Incredible." His chest heaves, and the fingers in my hair loosen.

I climb up his chest and spread kisses across his lips. "What's incredible is how you can whisper *Suck me harder* and make it sound like a love song."

He chuckles into my mouth, and the kiss that follows flows through my blood like a drug. I'm addicted to this man, an addiction that transcends lust and orgasms and physical attraction. Not only do I need his love, I need his patience and dominance, the kind only he can give me. It's a soul-deep craving, one I will always come back for, again and again.

The kiss lasts forever and ends too soon. He sits up, pulling me with him as he straightens the oversized shirt around my shoulders.

"You're staying here tonight." He pulls on his boxers and reaches toward the nightstand to silence the music. "I already sent a message to Cole."

This is so weird. I'm thrilled they're communicating, but it feels as if they're discussing my schedule like parents with joint-custody.

"I decide where I stay."

I don't know why I bother saying anything. One, he's more stubborn than I am. And two, the little workout I just performed on his lap didn't help the lethargic fog that's taken up residence in my body. I don't want to go anywhere tonight.

I decide to pick a different battle, one I'm far more interested in. "I want to see your texts."

"Which texts?" He grabs the TV remote and

reclines back against the pillows.

He knows which texts, and his phone is probably in the pocket of his pants on the floor. I eye the crumpled pile, wait a beat, and dive for it.

The moment I find it, I turn back toward him, expecting him to snatch it away. But he hasn't moved, doesn't even look at me as he scrolls through the channels on the TV.

I realize why when I try to access his messages. "What's your password?"

"It's top-secret."

"Bullshit. Cough it up, Savoy."

"No." He thumbs the buttons on the remote, eyes fixed on the TV.

"No more lap dances for you, then." I toss the phone on the bed and walk toward the door.

If he wants to hide shit from me, he can sleep by himself.

"Where are you going?" His tone is casual, unconcerned.

I flip him off over my shoulder and keep walking. Childish, I know, but I'm determined to win. The last time I gave him the middle finger, he sneaked up behind me and—

An arm hooks around my waist, and he lifts me off the floor. Before a yelp leaves my lips, he slams a stinging hand against my butt, shooting fiery pain across my skin. I cry out, shocked and squirming in his hold as he hauls me across the room and drops me on the bed.

"Brat." He tosses the phone on my lap and rattles off a series of numbers.

I shoot him a glare, betrayed by my triumphant grin as I unlock the screen and open the text window.

He returns to his reclined position, eyes fixed on the TV. He isn't fooling me. The ridiculous Ancient Aliens episode about Nazi UFOs that's playing isn't holding his attention.

I find his messages to Cole and scroll to the first one, timestamped around the time I took a shower last night.

Trace: She's staying with me tonight.

Cole: Why isn't she answering her phone?

Trace: She left it in the dressing room. She doesn't feel well.

Cole: Let me talk to her.

Trace didn't respond until two hours later, long after I passed out.

Trace: She's asleep.

"You left the bed after I fell asleep last night?" I squint at him.

"Yes." He folds an arm beneath his head and watches me out of the corner of his eye.

"Why did you get up?"

"To send that text."

I guess I should be grateful, but it seems strange. "But why? I mean, I'm glad you did, but I question your motivation."

"I didn't want him showing up downstairs and raising hell."

"Oh." I blow out a breath.

Cole would totally do that. My stomach clenches as I return to the thread of messages. The next one came this morning.

Cole: I want to talk to her. Answer your fucking phone!

Trace: She's still asleep.

The messages go back and forth like that all day. The more frustrated Cole became, the more exclamation points he used. I don't blame him. Trace's texts are as warm and forthcoming as his stony personality.

I slow my scrolling when I come to the one Trace sent before he walked in here.

Trace: She's still in bed and not going to work. I'll have her call you in the morning.

Cole: Let me talk to her, you motherfucker!

Cole: I'm calling. Pick up!!

Cole: Answer the fucking phone!!!

Cole: If you don't answer the phone, I'm coming for you.

Trace: Security has been notified.

Cole: You know damn well your security can't stop me. I'll be inside that penthouse in two hours. You have my word.

My pulse races. "Is that true? Can he get past your security team? And the cameras?" My eyes widen. "And the access codes?"

"Probably." Trace lifts a shoulder.

Cole's threat came an hour and half ago. That means he'll be here in thirty minutes.

"What the fuck?" I smack Trace's shoulder. "Why didn't you tell me about this? I would've talked to him."

"I've been a little distracted." His blue eyes burn into mine. "With your mouth on my cock."

"Don't give me that shit. You're sitting here, pretending to watch Nazi UFOs. Because you have a plan."

"My plan is to let it happen. I'm curious to see if he can break my security. I'm the one who trained him, so…"

He lets the rest of that thought linger in the space between us, like I'm supposed to nod my head and smile in understanding.

"If he breaks in to your penthouse…" I grind my teeth, irritated with these fucking games. "What comes next?"

"His unmanageable temper, followed by some bruised knuckles and blood." He slides me a humorless smile. "*His* blood."

Yeah, that's not going to happen. I lurch off the bed and race toward the bathroom while quickly typing out a text. Trace chases me, but I manage to lock the door and finish the message before he starts banging on the other side.

"Open the damn door," he says calmly. Too calm.

I press send on the text.

Trace: I know why Danni is so tired. We're too

overbearing and angry and it's messing with her harmony. We just need to hug it out and make up. I want to hang out with you again. And get matching tattoos. What's the symbol for BFF?

"Danni." Trace's voice muffles through the door, unnervingly composed. "Let me in."

"Are you mad?" A smile dances through my question.

The handle wriggles, and something metal scrapes against it. *Uh oh.* He must have a key. As he works the lock, I send another text to Cole for the hell of it.

Trace: I really want to kiss you. Passionately. While Danni watches.

The door bursts open just as the phone vibrates in my hand with an incoming call. Cole's ID flashes across the screen, and I bite back my grin.

"It's for you." I offer the phone to the scowling man in front of me.

"What did you text to him?"

"It's top-secret."

His scowl deepens, doing dirty things to my libido. He grabs the phone and paces into the bedroom. I trail behind him as he accepts the call.

"Whatever message you just received—" He tilts his head, listening. "What?" He turns and shoots me an appalled look.

I hide my amusement behind pinched lips and hold out a hand for the phone. He tosses it to me, like he can't get rid of it fast enough.

The device bounces off my fingers and clatters to

the wood floor. I stare at it for a second, wondering why I didn't catch it. My coordination is off.

Trace's brows pull in, probably thinking the same thing.

"I must be coming down with something?" I bend to pick it up, swaying against a sudden wave of dizziness.

He catches my arm and snags the phone, handing it over. "Make it quick. I want you back in bed."

I nod and lift it to my ear. "Hey."

"He wants you back in bed?" Cole growls.

I guess my texts didn't lighten the mood. "Were you really going to break into the king's castle?"

"Danni." He grunts. "I'll take down God himself to get to you."

"Somewhere, lightning just struck."

"How are you feeling?" The hostility drains from his voice, leaving raspy concern. "I've been worried about you."

"I'm just tired. Probably picked up a bug."

Trace perches on the bed, his arresting eyes firing with threats, the kind that promise if I don't hang up soon, he'll bend me over his knee and pommel my ass.

I lower beside him, giving him an innocent look as I speak into the phone. "I have a question."

"If it's about my heart, don't worry," Cole says. "It's still yours."

My chest rises, filling with warmth. "Are you off work tomorrow?"

"Yes. I aligned my schedule with yours, so I'm off when you're off. When are you coming home?"

I reach over and clutch Trace's hand on his lap. "I'll

be there tomorrow."

As expected, Trace tenses, and I squeeze his fingers. I've spent twice as much time with him as I have with Cole, not that I'm keeping track.

"We'll see how you're feeling," Cole says. "But if you're up for it, I have something planned."

"That sounds great." Now comes the hard part, and my insides twist. "I'll see you tomorrow."

He's going to say the words, and I'm going to repeat them back. While Trace sits next to me. If I leave the room to say it, it'll be obvious, and it's too late anyway, because Cole just sighed, which means...

"I love you." His voice reverberates through me, full of commitment and honesty—the only way to love.

I close my eyes as the potency of three syllables swells the chambers of my heart. Then I turn my head and meet Trace's gaze, speaking to both of them. "I love you, too."

seventeen

The next day, Trace takes me to brunch in his Maserati GranTurismo, with its metallic charcoal paint and Italian leather seats. I don't give a shit about sports cars, but I'd have to be dead to not appreciate the view of him driving it.

With a hand draped over the steering wheel, he works the gear shift with sleek confidence. His blond hair combs back in a textured style that somehow looks both windblown and photo-shoot ready. A brown suede jacket hugs his upper body in all the right places, and fitted black slacks accentuate the bulge of his groin so distractingly I can't stop myself from reaching over to feel the shape.

His fingers capture my wrist before I make contact. "I'll pull this car over right now." His hand tightens, twinging my bones. "And fuck you on the hood, on the side of the road, in front of God and everyone." He releases my arm. "Try me."

I click my tongue. "That sounds illegal."

"What you're doing to me should be illegal."

A swallow hangs in my throat. "What am I doing to you?"

"There are a lot of ways to hurt someone." He trains his ice blue eyes on the road. "Only you can inflict pain and make me crave every minute of it."

"I…I'm hurting you?" My chest collapses, stuttering my breaths. "I don't mean to, Trace. I'm so sorry."

"Never apologize for this." He rests a palm over the thick outline in his pants. "No matter how painful, it's worth the relief I'll find with you in the end."

I sense he isn't referring to sex, but rather something deeper, stronger in the indefinite future. It's moments like this that break me. I'm running from the most important question of my life, while falling victim to the greatest irony.

Because I'm not looking for an answer.

I already have two.

Lifting an arm over the back of his seat, I stroke the soft hairs on his nape. "I hate this."

"I love you, and I'll wait. Rest on that assurance."

"Thank you." I lean my head on his shoulder and try to absorb his strength for the remainder of the drive.

We eat at a quaint little bistro, where we whisper and smile and share lingering glances while enjoying locally-grown foods and strong coffee. Then he takes me home and walks me to the front door.

I left my car at the casino, but Cole's motorcycle

sits in the driveway. I wonder if he's in the basement or waiting just inside the door.

"You want to come inside and say hello to an old friend?" I run my hands across the front of Trace's suede jacket, shivering in the chilly air.

"I'll pass." He wraps his arms around me, warming me.

"I miss you already."

His scowl twitches, and he stares at my mouth.

Lifting on my toes, I cup my hands around the back of his neck and kiss him.

He cradles my face and kisses me back, inhaling hard and deep as he swallows my breaths, my whimpers, and the whole of my heart.

Then he steps back and licks his lips. "I'll be waiting."

eighteen

Trace's kiss lingers like a fever as I enter the house. I desperately need a moment to cool down before seeing Cole. One look at my puffy lips and pink cheeks and he'll know. I don't want to hide from him, but guilt sends me darting to my bedroom.

When I reach the hallway, music blares from the basement, cluing me in on his whereabouts. I sigh with relief and slip into my room.

The sheets on my bed tangle around a six-foot-long expanse of empty mattress. He sleeps on my side when I'm not here?

The urge to curl up in his scent pulls me onto the bed. I remove my heeled boots and bury my nose in the bedding. Oh God, I love his manly, woodsy smell. I want to sleep in it.

I assured Trace a hundred and one times today that I feel fully rested. But as I lay my head on the pillow and pull the covers around me, my limbs grow heavy. Maybe I'll just close my eyes for a second.

I pass out instantly and sleep like the dead. When I wake, the sky beyond the window has faded to a muted gray. And I'm not alone.

A wall of heat covers my back, and bands of muscle wrap around my body, enfolding me in a tight embrace from behind.

"How long have you been in here with me?" I turn my head and kiss Cole's bare bicep.

"A couple hours." He kisses my neck, tickling my skin with his whiskers.

We lie on our sides, legs bent together, both in jeans. He's shirtless, making me wish I was, too, so I could feel more of him. Hell, I wish we were naked, like we were in the shower only two days ago.

It's only been two days since I've seen him.

"It feels like a lifetime." I turn over and touch his face, his rugged, stunning, chiseled face.

"A lifetime?" His breaths fan against my mouth.

"Since I did this."

I lean in slowly and angle for a kiss, tilting my head, parting my lips, and savoring the anticipation lining his expression. Right before I make contact, I swoop down and scrape my teeth against his nipple.

"Danni!" He jerks back, pushing against my forehead and warding me off. "What the fuck?"

I shift to my knees and anchor my hands on my hips. "How can a tough guy like you have such sensitive nipples?"

"I just…do." He falls to his back and flattens a

palm over the imaginary pain. "You know I don't like it."

"I didn't even leave a mark."

He lifts his hand to sneak a peek then reclaims my eyes, looking all kinds of butthurt.

"Let me try again." I can't hide my grin. "You'll like it."

"Hell no. I'd rather lick the floor."

"Big baby."

"Get off my nuts." He narrows his eyes, scanning my face. "I take it you're feeling better?"

"Much." I reach my arms over my head and bend side to side, stretching my waist. "What are we doing tonight?"

"You've been sick—"

"I'm not sick. I just ran myself into the ground. I'm all better."

It's true. I feel renewed and ready to rock.

"We should stay in bed." His forehead grooves, and he sits up, inching toward me.

"Was that your big plan?"

"No." He tucks my hair behind my ear, letting his touch linger on my neck. "My plan requires physical activity." He raises a brow. "Outside of the house."

"Count me in." I move to climb off the bed, but his hand catches my arm, stopping me.

Kneeling on the bed, he yanks me against his chest and curls his fingers around my neck.

"I should probably..." He kisses the corner of my mouth. "Give you..." His lips brush the other corner. "A full body checkup." He breathes against my lips. "Just to be sure you're healthy."

"I bet your checkup includes a rectal exam." I bite

his bottom lip. "Am I right?"

"Christ." He grips my butt painfully hard, driving his fingers against the seam of my jeans. "I want to pound your fucking ass."

"As lovely as that sounds, how about you tell me where we're going instead?"

"It's a surprise."

"What should I wear?"

"What you have on." He smacks my backside and slides off the bed. "We'll grab something to eat on the way."

Two hours later, I'm standing in the last place I ever expected—a locker room. Wearing something I never thought I'd wear on a date in November—a string bikini.

Cole hasn't explained shit since he rolled his motorcycle into the empty parking lot of the scuba dive shop. He ushered me into the locker room, told me to change, and handed me the white bikini from his bag—a bikini he stole from my closet. Then he left.

I adjust the strings on my hips, double-knotting the double-knots.

Who am I kidding? He only has to flash his dimples and these itty-bitty bottoms will fall right off.

Deep breath, shoulders back, I head into the pool area to see what he has in store for me.

The fume of chlorine stings my lungs as I stroll along the indoor Olympic-sized pool. *15 ft* decals mark the edges all the way around, but it looks a lot deeper than that.

It must be after business hours, because there isn't a soul here.

I take that back. A man stands on the far side near

the entrance to the store, gripping Cole in a one-armed hug. They smile and launch into an animated conversation, full of arm gestures and laughter.

About twenty-paces away, I round the final corner of the pool. The men turn their heads and fall silent.

Cole's acquaintance has the deepest tan I've ever seen, and he's stacked with so much brawn his shirt and jeans strain at the seams. His round head is shaved bald, but his face is youthful. He's probably a couple years older than me. Around thirty? That would make him the same age as Cole and Trace.

He carries himself the way they do, exuding that heavy-handed, macho, alpha vibe. Maybe they're all somehow connected through the military?

His eyes seem friendly. And interested. Oh man, he's really staring at me.

I shift my attention to Cole and the single piece of clothing he's wearing. Spandex dive shorts stretch across his thighs and sit low on his hips. They're so tight they look painted on, and I feel a little lightheaded and winded in the presence of all that nude skin and ripped muscle. He's only been home for a couple weeks, and he already appears bigger, bulkier, healthier. And hotter than hell.

As I close the final few feet, his focus fastens on my face. It's a heated, captivated focus that hitches my breath and wobbles my balance.

His head turns toward the other man, but his eyes stay on mine, as if he intends to resume his conversation but he just can't look away.

"Are you going to introduce me?" I touch his arm.

He blinks and scraps a hand through his hair.

"Yeah, uh…this is the owner of the scuba shop. He's—"

"Richard Hickey." The man wipes a big paw on his shirt and holds it out to me, grinning.

I shake his hand. "Hi, Rich— Wait. Did you say, Richard Hickey?"

His grin falls. "Yes."

"As in *Dick* Hickey?"

"As in *Richard* Hickey." He narrows his eyes.

"But Dick is short for—"

"Leave the poor guy alone." Cole shakes his head. "He's heard that shit his entire life."

I'm sure he has. "I'm Danni, and now my name sounds so boring and forgettable."

"I suspect there's nothing forgettable about you." Richard gives me a friendly once-over.

"Careful." Cole's expression tightens.

"Roger that." Richard holds his hands in the air and backs up. "I'll show you the equipment."

"So…" I follow them toward a storage room. "I assume we'll be scuba diving in that huge-ass pool?"

"Yes." Cole reaches back and grabs my hand.

"I don't know how."

"I'll teach you."

In the storage room, Richard leads us through a maze of shelving stacked with fins and tanks and other things I can't name.

"Where did you learn how to dive?" I ask Cole.

Richard stops and casts a confused look over his shoulder.

"What?" I glance between them.

They exchange a tense moment of eye contact before Richard cracks.

"Shit, man." He grimaces. "I assumed she knew."

"Assumed I knew what?" I release Cole's hand and step in front of him with a fist on my hip and anger heating my face.

"My background in..." He gestures at the surrounding scuba equipment and studies my expression. "You're pissed."

"How can you tell?" I grind my teeth.

"Richard." Cole slides a hand over my shoulder. "Tell Danni how we met."

The bald man folds his arms across his chest. "BUD/S training."

"I've heard that term before." I furrow my brow. "It's a military thing."

"Basic Underwater Demolition / SEAL training." Richard huffs a pained laugh. "Seven months of hell."

"You were Navy SEALs together?" I take in the scuba gear with new eyes.

"No, actually." Richard leans against a metal shelf. "I got my ass handed to me in the third phase of training. Crashed and burned. So here I am, running a dive shop."

"And you?" I squint at Cole. "You passed the training?"

Richard bursts into laughter. "He blew through it with his eyes closed. Hell, he could've taught it."

"You and your damn mouth." Cole glares at the other man. "This is why you didn't meet her five years ago."

I turn to Richard, since he seems to be a well of helpful information. "So Cole was a SEAL and—"

"No, sweetheart." He rests a hand beneath his chin, studying Cole. "He was assigned to a team, but someone plucked him from the force and poof! He disappeared. I don't know anything beyond that. It was above my pay-grade."

"I see." I shift back to Cole, unable to keep the suspicion from leaking into my voice. "Why didn't you tell me about the SEAL thing? That isn't classified information."

"Because I was never a SEAL." He brushes a thumb along my jaw. "But I brought you here to share a piece of my training with you. Do you want to learn?"

He doesn't offer an apology or any further explanation. He just looks at me with dimpled affection, as if sharing this experience with me means so much more to him than bragging about his SEAL training.

"Yeah." I release a breath and just like that, I let go of my anger. "Lead the way."

Richard hauls out the *good stuff* from a locker in the corner of the storage room, explaining that even his best equipment doesn't compare to the gear Cole used in training and on the job. He stacks everything on a long table, naming them off. Masks, BCD vests, air cylinders…

I hover beside Cole as Richard brings out more gear. The shit on the table piles chest-high, and I pick through it, a little overwhelmed. I hope Cole doesn't expect me to learn all this tonight.

Drifting closer to my side, he ghosts his fingers across the front of my thigh. My gaze darts to Richard, who stands on the opposite side of the table, rambling on about his miserable time during BUD/S.

"All these years and you're still fucking whining." Cole grins at Richard, and his touch grows bolder, skirting to the edge of my bikini between my leg and groin. "I'll tell you the same thing now that I told you then. You need to get laid."

"Some of us aren't as lucky as you, motherfucker." Richard grunts, cutting his eyes to me.

With equipment stacked on the table, I'm certain he can't see below my waist from his position. But he has a direct view of my eyes, which are currently trying to roll back in my head as Cole's fingers slip beneath the crotch of my bikini.

I steal a peek at Cole, watching his eyes close when he finds me wet. He presses inside me, and his mouth parts with a sigh on his lips.

"Cole is never without a beautiful woman in his bed," Richard says.

"Is that right?" I grip Cole's immovable arm, trembling against the curl of the fingers inside me.

While I don't like hearing about all his conquests, I know it's in the past. I'm over it.

I keep my head turned away from those dark brown eyes, but I feel them burning the side of my face. I bet he's wearing a sexy, shit-eating smile, too, and damn if my nipples don't harden beneath the bikini top.

"You're the prettiest one, though." Richard cocks his head. "If he's smart, he'll hang onto you."

Oh, he has me, exactly where he wants me—squirming and at his mercy.

"Thanks for letting me use the shop tonight." Cole sinks his finger deeper, thrusting a whimper past my lips. "I'll take it from here."

"Let me show you how to lock up." Richard gives me a chin lift. "Nice to finally meet you, Danni."

"You, too." I gasp as Cole removes his hand and follows the other man out.

When he returns a few minutes later, I'm still

flushed and trembling.

"That was cruel." I cross my arms and jut my chin.

"I'm going to fuck the shit out of that sassy little attitude."

"You think so?" My pussy clenches.

"I know so." He grabs a BCD vest and holds it out. "This controls your buoyancy in the water."

He spends the next thirty minutes walking me through Scuba 101. Each instruction adds another piece of equipment on my body. By the time he's finished, I can barely stand up beneath the weight.

"You expect me to walk to the pool like this?" I lean against him for support.

"It's like ten yards away." He adjusts the tank on his back and grins. "I've jumped out of airplanes wearing more than that."

"Good for you, you smug shit. You're also twice my size."

"Alright. Gimme a second." He hooks *more* gear onto my body, grabs two sets of fins, and bends to wrap an arm around the backs of my legs. "Hold on."

My hands fly to his shoulders as he lifts me off the floor. I must weight five-hundred pounds with all the equipment, and he's carrying me with one arm. I'm impressed. And a little turned-on.

"Someone's been working out." I kiss his cheek.

"Thanks for noticing." He strides into the pool area and sets me on a large rubber mat beside the water's edge. "Your phone's in the bag there, if you want some music. We'll have our heads above water for a while, until you get comfortable."

Moving at the speed of a snail, I remove my phone and swipe through the playlist while he messes with his equipment.

I select *This Town* by Niall Horan. The song reminds me of us—the yearning for an old flame, the lost love, and nostalgia of home.

"Ready, baby?" He tilts his head, grinning.

I'm ready to relieve some of this weight. "Throw me in or lose me forever."

He does just that, a scoop and a toss that shoots me a couple feet beneath the surface. The heated water swirls around me, and when I come up for air, I have the best view.

Standing on the pool ledge above me, he moves his fingers over the scuba computer on his wrist, with his eye mask dangling from the strap between the bite of his teeth. I can't take my eyes off him—the ridged terrace of his abs, the long outline of his cock in the spandex shorts, and the wide stance of a man comfortable in his own skin.

"You're fucking hot, you know that?" I lick my lips.

His brown eyes flash to mine, and the entire world sighs as the greatest smile ever born illuminates his gorgeous face.

Then he pushes off the edge with his legs and darts feet first into the water, piercing the surface like a soundless arrow.

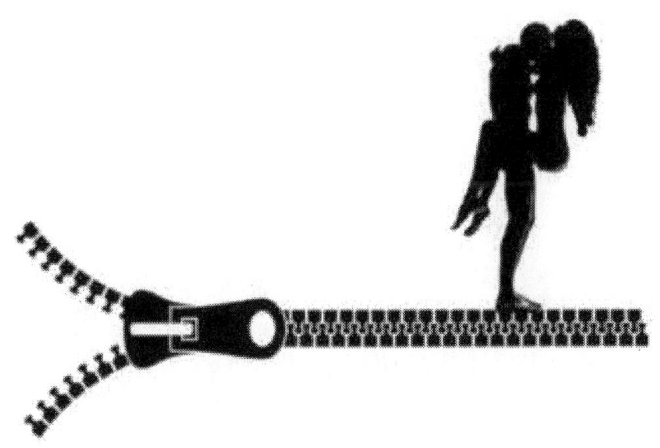

nineteen

“I think I have the hang of it.” I swim over to Cole, smiling hugely.

Granted, I haven’t actually dived to the bottom of the fifteen-foot pool, but I know how to adjust my buoyancy and clear my mask underwater.

While I practiced, he tried to put the fins on my feet, but they felt bulky and cumbersome, so I made him toss them out.

He checks my valves and adjusts the mask on my face. Then he turns to his own, his hands moving efficiently, mindlessly, like he’s done this a million times.

“Did you dive on missions?” I touch the sharp angle of his jawline.

His eyes lift to mine. “The ocean is usually the best path of escape, especially for someone trained in combat dives." His gaze turns cloudy behind the fog-less mask, and he blinks it clear. "Go slow on the descent. Steady your breathing. I'll do the rest."

I'm greedy for more details about his career, but this isn't the time. So I nod and slip the regulator into my mouth.

It takes a few minutes to get my buoyancy right. I sink too quickly, my ears popping like crazy. But when Cole removes my weight belt, I'm flipping and darting and holy shit, breathing underwater.

The thirty-pound air cylinder on my back feels like nothing in the water. I swim aimlessly, limitlessly, without a sense of the ground or the sky as my hair swirls around me in rippling waves. I feel like a mermaid.

It's liberating, like dancing, but different. There's no gravity, no weight, no pressure. Like an out-of-body experience or floating in outer space. Boundless and serene. Absolute freedom.

Cole hovers at the bottom of the pool, seemingly content with watching me swoop and dive around him. Tiny bubbles rise from his aeriform figure, the outline of his hard body fuzzy in the weak light of the water. But I know the instant his contentment morphs into something darker, hungrier. His head tips slightly, and he drifts closer. His forearms flex as he glides slowly through the water, circling, stalking, closing in.

I twist around, keeping him in my line of sight. A few feet away, his eyes glint like a shark. Then he shoots past me, cutting close enough to caress his fingers across my stomach.

He corrals me again and guns for another pass. This time, I feel a slight pull on my hip. My breathing accelerates, increasing the froth of bubbles around my face. When the water clears, I glance down and find the string on my hip untied, leaving my bottoms hanging on by a thread. That sneaky, flirty fucker. Where is he?

I turn in a circle, scanning the underwater horizon. He's nowhere in sight, which means he must be hovering behind me, moving when I move.

I crane my neck, which is a challenge with the equipment on my back. A fizz of air surges beside my head just as the knot on my other hip pulls free.

The swimsuit bottoms fall off, and I reach for them, rolling through the water and grabbing at nothing. What the hell?

I feel him before I see him. His hands sliding up the backs of my thighs. His hair brushing between my legs. Then his mouth, his lips, his exhale covering my pussy. I moan through the regulator, making it vibrate.

Floating face up between my thighs with his legs behind me, he grips my hips and licks me with vicious strokes. My spine bows, and I suck harder on the apparatus. Sweet lord, it feels so good I'm going to use up all my air.

The scuba mask encloses his eyes and nose, preventing water from entering those parts of his face. But he removed the regulator from his mouth.

He's holding his breath. For how long?

Panic rises amid the swelling pleasure. But I push it down, reminding myself he's trained for this. He probably endured all sorts of inhumane drills that forced him to go without air for extended periods.

My fingers tangle in the silken strands of his hair as I grind against his mouth, weightless and drifting. I take care not to bump his face mask while the hands on my hips hold me in place.

I don't think I can come like this. I'm too worried about sinking or shooting to the surface. Not to mention the fact that he still hasn't taken a breath. It feels unbelievably sinful, though. Without a doubt, the best sexual experience I've ever had.

He curls his tongue inside me, his lips sucking with delicious pressure while tingling my flesh with each exhalation of air.

When he finally moves his mouth to take a breath from the apparatus, he releases a barrage of bubbles that caress and slide along my skin on the way to the surface. Fucking amazing.

He swims through the *V* of my legs and skims up the front of my body. A fold of white material peeks out of his vest. *My swimsuit bottoms.*

I bet he planned every detail of this date. The easy removal of a string bikini. The rubber piece in my mouth, preventing my protests. And the exquisite seduction of naked, tangled bodies underwater.

The regulator conceals his expression, but the hunger in his eyes burns behind the mask. It's the same hunger that rages through my blood and trembles my insides.

I'm in trouble. I know this as soon as his hands fall to the buckles on my BCD vest. He unlatches it and slides it off my arms, taking the tank with it. Alarm spikes through me, widening my eyes. He's taking my air!

He taps my jaw and shakes his head, telling me not to panic.

After a few steady breaths, I rest my trust on his shoulders. And my hands. There's no way I'm letting go.

My vest tries to sail to the surface, but he holds onto it. His other hand unhooks the emergency regulator from his vest—every diver has a backup. I understand his intentions when he holds it up to my face.

He wants me to swap mouthpieces and breathe from his tank. If we were a hundred-feet deep in the ocean, I might've hesitated. But we're in a pool, and he won't let anything happen to me. Worst case, I'll hold my breath and swim the fifteen feet to the surface.

I open my mouth and hold my breath as my regulator slips free. He removes his own, and we float toward each other instinctively, our mouths colliding in a wickedly hard kiss. He angles to deepen it, but I don't know how to engage my tongue without swallowing water. I'm awkward as all hell, but the kiss? It's fucking thrilling.

It's not completely silent underwater. The pressure against the ears puts a different perspective on sound. Everything is louder, deeper, resounding in the chest. Like the flow of air through the tubes, the swish of the water around us, and the groans of our voices as our lips move together.

When I pull back, he slides his backup regulator between my lips and pops his own breather in his mouth. Somewhere above us, my tank and vest bob away.

Since we're sharing an air cylinder, we'll use up the oxygen in half the time. But I know that's not the reason for the urgency in his eyes. He stares at me with ravenous need. To claim me. To fuck me. And he illustrates the direction of his thoughts by gliding his hands up my back and untying the strings on my bikini top.

This is happening. I'm going to have sex with Cole.

The moment I'm naked, Trace's handsome scowl flashes through my mind. But I stop myself from analyzing and dreading and tripping into guilt. Instead, I focus on Bree's words.

For once in your life, you're going to put yourself first.

Cole swims around me, his biceps bunching with the slicing movements of his arms, his physique strong and chiseled beneath the vest and tank. I turn with him, physically connected by an air hose and emotionally attached to every beat of his heart.

We glide toward each other, our bodies sliding and tumbling together, our hands roaming, gripping, nails scratching across skin. His palms cover my breasts as I feather my fingers down the bumps of his abs, over the waistband of his dive shorts, and stroke the outline of his swollen cock.

I try to temper my breaths, but they come fast and hard with the fire roaring inside me. My nipples go taut, and my pussy throbs with the need to be filled by him.

He releases me and descends, sliding down my body until my thighs rest on his shoulders. Droplets of air fizzle upwards, blurring my view of him. What is he doing?

Something moves in the corner of my eye. I turn my neck just as his abandoned shorts waft by.

My pulse pounds through my veins. *He's naked.* I wave away the effervescence of air and look down, trying to see him beneath me.

The water clears a millisecond before he slides up my chest and positions my legs around his waist.

I grip his shoulders, and the underside of his erection rubs hard and hot between my legs. Nothing separates us, not even doubt. I love him. I want him. If I don't take him into my body right now, in this magical subaquatic moment, I'll regret it for the rest of my life.

He studies me from behind his mask, communicating more with his eyes than he could with words. He loves me, too. And if I don't let him fuck me, he might die from the bluest balls in the history of blue balls.

It's been over four years.

Four fucking years since he's had sex.

His fingers curl around my wrist, lifting my hand beside my face. Then he taps my palm. He wants me to give my consent, using the underwater hand signals he taught me.

Without hesitation, I shape my fingers into the universal sign for *okay* and give him a nod for good measure.

His lips part, and the regulator floats from his mouth. Tiny beads of air trickle from the curved-up corners of his mouth, and he yanks me tight against him. With an arm locked behind my back, he lines himself up with my center and slams me down on his cock.

I suck huge gulps of oxygen and clench my inner muscles around his thick girth, whimpering at the shocking bliss. Even more arresting is the sight of his head falling back on his shoulders, his eyes squeezing shut, the cords lengthening in his neck, and the spume of air escaping his clenched teeth.

But it makes my chest hurt when he's not breathing from the tank. So I grab his regulator and press it against his lips. He pulls in a deep inhale, meets my eyes. Then he fucks me.

Kicking his hips into a voracious rhythm, he

strokes his cock from tip to root, stretching me, using me, owning me, body and soul. If I were a screamer, I would've drowned already. As it is, I'm draining the air tank with every panting heave of my chest.

He pauses briefly to the check the gauges. As he shifts a leg backward, I realize he's standing on the pool floor, using his strength or weight, maybe both, to keep us stable.

With a hand on the back of my head, he holds our face masks together and drives me down on his cock. I moan and writhe and lose all sense of time and space. Chained to the pleasure, I bask in the reunion, running my hands through his hair, riding the thrusts of his hips, sharing his air, and clinging to the powerful flex of his body.

Cole's body.

My first love.

The connection feels every bit as intimate and real as the day I met him.

Too soon, he pauses again to check the gauges. His eyes tip toward the surface.

Time's up.

We make a slow ascent, letting our lungs acclimate to the change in atmospheric pressure. He doesn't pull out of me. But he doesn't thrust, either, as he keeps us level and buoyant with adjustments to the valves on his BCD vest.

The moment our heads emerge above water, he removes my mask and tears off his own. Then he pins me with the full force of his eyes, his lungs panting, and his expression shocked, overwhelmed, consumed. He feels it, too. The invisible, soul-stirring bond that connects so deeply.

The kiss that follows is carnal and uncontrolled, full of teeth and animalistic desire. Still buried inside me, he thrusts inside me, but he doesn't have leverage and keeps falling out. With a growl, he releases me to remove his weight belt. The vest and fins come off next, leaving us both completely naked and free of gear.

In the background, my playlist streams from my phone, echoing the sexy, thumping beats of *Now Or Never* by Halsey.

He raises a brow, followed by a cocky smirk. Then he's on me, attacking my mouth, his tongue a starving whip of swooping, licking need. I rub and grind against him, stroking his cock and gripping his rock-hard ass. I can't get enough. I want… I need…

"Right now." I hold his face in my hands, eating at his mouth. "I need you."

"I know, baby." He kisses me hard and deep, groaning. "Fuck, I know."

He pushes me against the wall of the pool, stroking his length along my clit. "I have to taste you again."

I moan against his lips. "I want your cock, Cole."

"Patience." He grins, bites my lip, and clutches my waist.

With a powerful heave of strength, he lifts me out of the water, over his head, and perches me on the ledge of the pool. "Spread your legs."

I lean back on my arms and expose myself to him, curling my feet around the concrete edge.

"Jesus." He stares at my pussy and traces a finger around the opening. "Fucking perfect and pink and swollen. This view… Goddamn, you make me hard as fuck."

With the water lapping around his shoulders and his chest pressed against the pool wall, he's eye-level with the apex of my legs. He slides his arms beneath my thighs and slowly leans in, holding my eyes, licking his lips, and teasing us both.

When his mouth finally makes contact with my flesh, my butt flies off the ground.

"Ahhh, God!" I pant, trembling. "Don't stop."

He holds me down, buries his face, and devours me. Sucking and nibbling, rolling his tongue and adding his fingers, he ravages me without pause or mercy. His teeth pull on my piercing, and his hand thrusts in sync with his lashing tongue. I fall to my back, twisting and moaning beneath his assault. My arousal coats his lips and gathers inside me like an electric charge, humming and crackling and overrunning my nerve-endings.

"I'm not going to last." My entire body clenches, gripped by sudden violent waves of ecstasy. "I'm coming. I'm coming. Don't stop."

He groans against my clit, shooting vibrations to my core and drawing out the orgasm. I sag on the ground, shaking beneath the flux of his stroking tongue, gasping, and pulling at his hair.

"Okay, okay." I twitch away from his mouth, overstimulated and out of breath. "Damn, Cole. That was…awesome."

He grips the concrete edge between my thighs and pushes up with his arms, lifting himself out. Water pours off his body, soaking my chest in warm ploppy drops. As he leans over me, the look on his face stops my heart.

His pupils are dilated, his teeth clenched, and his expression feral with predatory hunger. No words are exchanged. No tender kisses. Just the sharp sound of his hissing breath as he lowers on top of me, stabs his cock between my legs, and sinks to the root.

He snakes an arm beneath my hips and twists us around until I'm lying on the rubber mat, putting a softer surface against my back. As worked up and unhinged as he looks, I'm going to need it.

"This first time…" He lowers his head and bites my neck with a rumbling growl. "It's going to be hard and quick. Hang on tight, baby."

I fold my arms around his neck, splaying my fingers against the back of his head as I whisper at his ear, "I want it hard, Cole."

With a deep groan, he slowly pulls out. "You're my filthy little fuck doll."

Then he thrusts, powerfully, ruthlessly, hammering his hips and pounding me into the mat. My hands slip from his hair with the impact, my insides jarring and squeezing against the pleasure-pain.

He's a fucking machine, his skin soft and tight over steely muscle and endless stamina. But his unwavering eye contact is wholly human. Warm and hooded and dense with emotion, his gaze holds me close and pulls me deep.

We're connected by something precious, something bigger than ourselves. It's led us through a million miles of separation and death and unimaginable pain. Where it takes us next, I don't know. I can only focus on the present and the unshakable love I feel for him.

Pushing up on his arms, he widens his legs and forces mine to spread around his thighs. His urgency is palpable, reverberating through his grunts and the erratic thrusts of his hips.

"I'm close." He twists his fingers in my hair. "I want to see your eyes."

I haven't looked away, and I won't. Clutching his neck with both hands, I hold our faces inches apart and tighten my inner muscles. "Come in me, Cole."

He chokes, gasps. Then he comes long and hard, groaning, panting, and spilling into my body as love spills from his eyes.

Moments later, we lie on our sides in a tangle of exhaustion, touching, kissing, and catching our breaths. The electronic melody of *Latch* by Disclosure thrums from my phone, injecting the atmosphere with mellow sensuality.

"Have you done that before?" I burrow against his chest and wrap a leg over his hip.

"Hmm?" He stares at my mouth with hooded eyes.

"Scuba sex?"

"No." His gaze lifts to mine. "But we'll definitely be doing it again."

"Tonight?" My voice squeaks.

His recovery rate is unparalleled, and since he's gone without for so long, I'm certain it'll be a sleepless night. I just hope I have the energy to keep up with him.

"Not tonight." He touches my face and kisses me tenderly. "Physical activity during a dive impacts decompression safety. You need to take it easy for the rest of the night." He skims a palm down my back and slaps a stinging whack against my ass. Then his lips twist impishly. "You can just lie there while I do all the work."

By letting him into my body, I didn't just open the door. I ripped it off the hinges. There's no turning back now. He'll fuck me as often as he can, in as many positions as possible, until neither of us can walk.

I expect him to roll on top of me and take me again immediately. But he doesn't. He climbs to his feet, all hard and naked and fully erect, and dives into the pool, entering the water like an aerodynamic bullet.

We spend the next hour gathering and storing equipment, cleaning up the area, and changing into warm clothes. As he leads me into the dark parking lot behind the building, there's a chill in the air that seeps beneath my coat and shivers my bones.

I bend over the saddle of his motorcycle to unhook our helmets, and his hands catch my wrists. He stands behind me, his groin pressed against my ass as he wrenches my arms behind my back.

"Cole?" My whisper echoes in the dark silence, and my pulse accelerates.

"I thought I could wait until we got home." He leans over my bent position with his breath ragged and hot on my neck. "But I'm done waiting."

My gasp shivers the air with white plumes, my chest rising and falling against the bike seat. The parking lot is empty, and we're tucked in the shadows behind the shop, surrounded by tree cover. But it's a commercial property. There would be some kind of security in place.

I turn my head, straining to scan the perimeter. "Cameras—"

"We're out of view of the lens." He folds my hands together against my tailbone, his voice gruff. "Lock your fingers. Yeah, like that. Now rest your weight on the seat."

I relax my chest against the bike and close my eyes. He unclasps the button on my jeans and yanks the denim and panties to my thighs with an impatient tug. Then he fumbles with his own fly, and the sound of his zipper spikes a jolt of heat to my pussy.

There, in the hush of a dark parking lot, he caresses me, fingers me, and sinks into my body with a hissing groan. The strokes of his cock are unhurried, the hands on my skin firm yet soft with devotion.

He rides me to orgasm before finding his own release. Then he takes me home and fucks me again and again.

Hours later, I curl up against his warm body in my bed and sink into a satiated sleep.

It's still dark outside when I wake. I roll to my back and squint in the pitch-black of my bedroom. Sliding an arm across the mattress, I reach for him only to find the space beside me cold and empty.

I lift on an elbow and glance at the clock. *3:12 AM.*

Where did he go?

As I shift toward the edge of the bed, my attention catches on the shadow in the corner of the room.

"Cole?"

The dark outline of his head lifts. I can't see his eyes, but I can make out his slumped posture where he sits on the floor with his arms resting on his bent knees.

"What's wrong?" I crawl across the mattress, closing the distance.

His inky eyes hold mine for an elusive moment before he rests his head back against the wall and stares at the ceiling.

Dread slithers up my spine. I slide off the bed and kneel beside him.

"Hey." I trail my fingers along the tense muscles in his face. "Talk to me."

His nostrils widen with a heavy inhale, and he clasps his hands in front of him, pressing his palms together, fidgeting. Then he finds my gaze in the dark.

"I'm just..." A swallow bounces in his throat. "I'm dealing with some shit in my head."

I run a hand through his hair, my whisper shaking with nerves. "Like what? Why do you look so scared?"

He releases a sharp breath. "I'm terrified that one day I'm going to watch you walk away with the one who stole my dance." His eyes cut away before shifting back. "You won't even glance back at me, because you'll be so absorbed by the life he gives you. A stable future, your career, his philanthropy. And the breathtaking smile on your face... I won't be the one giving you that, either. That's when I'll know, when I'll really truly know just how badly I fucked up the best thing I ever had."

"You didn't fuck anything up."

"I left you!" He leaps to his feet, knocking into the dresser in his distress. "I deserted you, chasing some bullshit career—"

"It wasn't bullshit." My heart hammers as I stand to face him. "It meant something to you."

"You meant more. Then and now. But that fucking realization is too little, too late."

"It's not—" Uncertainty fists my throat, choking my words. "You're not too late."

"Then marry me. Tomorrow. Be my life, Danni."

My breaths grow shallow and panicky, and my eyes burn with moisture. I want to say *yes*. I want to scream it, because I can't bear the pain contorting his face.

You're trying to determine who will be less heartbroken.

"Cole, I…" I press a hand against my mouth, silencing the tears in my voice.

"Dammit." He rushes toward me and envelopes me in a constricting embrace. "I'm sorry. I'm not pushing you. I'm just…"

"Scared."

"Yeah." He kisses my head, my temple, then my lips. "I'm afraid to close my eyes. Afraid that when I open them, you'll be gone."

"I'm here." I press my mouth to the corner of his. "I'll be here when you wake. I promise."

"Okay." He nods, and nods again, as if assuring himself.

With my hand in his, I guide him back into bed and pull the blankets around us. Eventually, his chest relaxes against my back, and his breaths even out. Only then do I let myself fall back asleep.

Just as I slip out of awareness, his hand clenches around mine, snapping my eyes open in the dark.

"You have my heart," he whispers against my nape. "Please don't hurt me."

twenty

The next morning, I hang my head over the toilet and vomit for the third time in two hours. My guts cramp through each wretched heave. My body shakes and chills, and sweat saturates every pore.

"This is my fault." Cole crouches behind me, holding my hair and rubbing my back.

"Shut up," I say weakly and drop my brow to the toilet seat. "Just let me die already."

"I should've made you stay in bed last night."

"We were in bed." I wobble my head, sliding him a look. "A lot."

"You know what I mean." Worry creases his face. "Are you done?"

"I think so." I push away from the toilet and lower the lid. "I don't have anything left in my stomach."

He hits the flusher and pulls me to a teetering stand. "Easy."

"Need to brush my teeth."

He helps me, supporting my weight while I scrub the icky taste from my mouth. Then he lifts me in his arms.

As he carries me out of the bathroom, the doorbell rings.

I groan and rest my cheek on his shoulder.

"Expecting someone?" He heads to the bedroom and eases me onto the mattress.

"I messaged Trace an hour ago. Told him I was throwing up."

"Fuck." Cole sets his jaw.

"I told him not to come over."

"And you expected him to listen?" He drags a hand down his face and takes in my thin tank top and panties. "I'll get you something to wear."

"I'm burning up." I kick the sheet off my legs as an inferno blazes beneath my skin. "Just…please, go let him in and try not to kill each other."

I feel a little delirious, because one second, Cole is glaring down at me. Then I blink, and it's Trace's blue eyes sweeping over me.

"Did you swap bodies?" My mumble sounds logical, but I don't really know what I'm saying.

"You've been asleep for a while." Trace touches a hand to my forehead then my cheek. "Fever's still high. Think you can keep down some fluids?"

He holds up a bottle of clear fruit juice.

I nod. "Where's Cole?"

The instant the question leaves my mouth, my insides contract for reasons unrelated with nausea.

I had sex with Cole, and guilt stabs painfully hard as I look at Trace. Can he see the shame in my eyes? Smell the betrayal on my body?

"I'm right here." Cole's voice rumbles from behind me.

I turn my neck and find him sitting in a chair next to the bed, his disgruntled gaze locked on Trace. If Cole loses his temper, I'm in no condition to intervene. I can't even work up the strength to worry about it.

Trace slides a hand beneath my head and helps me sit up.

"Just a few sips." He holds the juice to my lips.

The cherry flavor trickles down my throat, cool and refreshing. I grab his wrist, wanting more, but he sets it out of reach.

"I talked to the pharmacy." He lifts a plastic bag from the floor and places it on the bed. "There's a stomach bug going around."

"I hope I don't get you guys sick." I rub my head, swaying with dizziness. "You should probably fumigate or something."

"I'm not concerned about that." Trace reaches into the bag and looks at Cole, hesitating. "I also picked up this."

He removes a rectangular package and drops it on my lap.

A pregnancy test.

Denial slams into me, tightening my shoulders. I have an IUD, and it doesn't expire for years.

Cole surges from the chair, his features twisted in pain and horror. He paces a tight circle beside the bed, his hands raking through his hair and shoulders bunching. Then he stops at the window and stares outside.

"I'm not pregnant," I say to his back.

If I were, the baby wouldn't be his. I got sick before last night, and he knows that.

"Take the test." Trace straightens and clasps his hands behind his back. "We need to know for sure."

He looks unruffled and indifferent in his fitted navy suit and pinstripe button-up. His wide stance and natural scowl emanates intimidation and sternness, but I see beneath it. The brightness in his blue eyes, the twitch in his clean-shaved cheek, and the way his body leans slightly toward me—all of it radiates emotion. Eagerness. *Hope.*

I don't know if he wants to be a father, but if I were carrying his child, that would certainly give him the fate he's waiting for. It would tie us together forever.

"Let's get this over with." I slide off the bed, waving them away when they move to help me.

I'm not going to pee on a stick while they glare and growl at each other. The bathroom isn't big enough for the three of us anyway.

My legs shake, and the floor spins as I trudge toward the toilet and take the test. I'm so certain it'll be negative, I don't wait for the results before returning to the bedroom.

Trace plucks the stick from my hand while Cole tucks me in. Then we wait.

The tension in the room is so thick it's hard to breathe. Cole and Trace want different results from the test, and one of them will be disappointed. I wish I can say or do something to make it easier for them, but I'm struggling just to keep my eyes open.

Trace doesn't take his focus off the plastic stick. Another minute passes before creases bracket his scowl and his shoulders fall.

"It's negative." He tosses it in the wastebasket, staring at it with unblinking eyes.

My heart hurts for him, but he must know that a baby would've put a terrible wrench in an already confusing situation.

Cole releases a heavy breath and lowers into the chair beside the bed. He doesn't smile or shout for joy, but relief is evident in his soft expression.

Since he returned, he's mentioned numerous times he wants a family. I don't know how I feel about that, and this is probably the worst time to bring it up, but it's on my mind.

"Can we talk about this?" I lean back on the pillow.

Two pairs of eyes turn to me and widen.

"Don't freak out." I pull the sheet over me and instantly feel too hot. I kick it off. "What I need to say has to do with both of you."

"You need to sleep." Trace sits on the edge of the bed.

"I will." I pull in a breath and slowly release it. "Cole, you said you want a family."

"Yes."

I peer at Trace. "What about you?"

He considers the question, staring at his hands before meeting my eyes. "I find that my love for you is ever-expanding. If you give me children, I'll love them and protect them with my life. If you don't, I'll still be the happiest man in the world. As long as I have you."

A shiver sweeps over me. From his words. And the

fever.

"Motherhood has never been an aspiration for me." I close my eyes and speak into the silence. "Maybe I'll change my mind as I get older, but right now, I'm not in a place where I even want to think about it. So if that's a deal breaker for either of you, I understand."

I open my eyes and lock onto Cole's.

His eyebrows gather, and he chews on his lip. Then he slides into a casual recline and rests a foot on his other knee. "I'm not going anywhere."

Trace leans his arms on his thighs, bending toward me. "You know where I stand."

Right here. That's where they both stand. Stubborn till the end.

twenty-one

I have the stomach flu. Trace called in a doctor—an elderly man with a grumpy disposition—who helpfully advised, "It's utterly miserable, and there's no cure."

Oh, and avoid coffee. *Fuck me.*

The flu persists for the next forty-eight hours, rendering me nonfunctional and completely useless. Trace and Cole force fluids like drill sergeants and restrict my menu to bananas, applesauce, toast, and sleep. Lots and lots of sleep.

Trace spends the days at my house, but I make him leave when Cole gets home from work. He's gracious enough to not argue that point, but I see the hurt in his eyes when he kisses me goodbye on my forehead.

Maybe it's selfish on my part, but I hear his heated whispers with Cole in the other room and feel the constant tension vibrating between them. I need to recover, and I can't do that with all the damn negativity in the house.

Cole carries his own share of disappointment, since I won't let him sleep in my bed. They've both been exposed to my cooties, but letting him roll around in my sickly, sweaty sheets? That's just gross.

By the third day, I feel well enough to putter around the house, disinfecting and doing laundry. But I hold off on going to work.

The morning of the fourth day, I'm back to one-hundred-percent health. The severe aches and muscle pain that plagued me for almost a week are gone. Energy buzzes through my blood as I shower and drink coffee and ponder how I'm going to spend the day.

Oddly, neither Trace nor Cole are here. The motorcycle's gone, and Trace hasn't stopped by to check on me.

I have the house to myself.

With a grin, I head to the spare room that serves as my closet and change into a black beaded bra and bikini dance bottoms. Then I run through a stretch routine in the dance studio.

Bouncing on my toes, I scroll through my song selection on the stereo. I should work on the ballroom dance Nikolai and I will be performing at the mayor's Christmas party in a couple weeks. But the dance pole in the corner draws my attention.

I haven't touched it since Cole left almost five years ago. Chewing my thumbnail, I eye it with longing.

It's time.

I select a song, put it on repeat, and approach the pole. My freestyle moves will be rusty as hell, but I already feel the adrenaline speeding up my pulse and quickening my pace.

As the electronic pulse of *Undisclosed Desires* by Muse bounces through the room, I walk around the pole, grasping it lightly above my head. My feet cross, one in front of the other in an exaggerated fashion, and I let my toes drag the floor behind me while pushing out my hip.

On the next rotation, I slide my back down the pole, kicking a leg high as my butt descends to the floor. Climbing back up, I swing upside down into a chopper position with legs straight and spread above my head. My core muscles engage, my fingers clenching hard around the pole as I suspend my inverted weight.

I transition through all the standard moves, splaying my legs open, arching my back, and setting my underused muscles on fire. By the time the song restarts for the third time, I'm swinging my head, rolling my hips, and working up a delicious sweat.

When I climb the pole again, I focus on my spins, full-turns and U-turns, while flipping, leaning back, and stretching into horizontal variations of the superman and the slingshot.

Oh man, I missed this—the sensual movements, the coordination and muscular exertion, and the liberation in hanging from the ceiling by one leg.

Once my feet return to the floor, I close my eyes and swing with the hypnotic beats of the song. With a hand on the pole, I circle my hips and bend my knees, dipping down and sliding back up while flipping my hair round and round.

It's been so long I probably look like a fumbling amateur, but the movements feel second-nature. Pole dance is rooted in belly dance, after all. In the era of traveling sideshows, belly dancers undulated on the tent poles to draw crowds for the shows. And like belly dance, I find it impossible to dance on a pole and not feel sexy doing it. Every movement fosters a carnal emotion that can turn an innocent girl into a seductive temptress.

The temptress in me has definitely been unleashed. I push my butt out as I climb, splitting my legs open and arching into a deep back bend that inverts my body and gives me an upside-down view of the kitchen doorway.

And the two pairs of legs standing on either side of it.

My breath hitches, and my grip slips. I quickly tighten my fingers, stopping myself from plunging face first to the floor.

Slowly flipping back to my feet, I grip the pole for balance and look between Trace and Cole. "How long have you been here?"

Trace stands ramrod straight, hands behind his back and head angled down, taking in my half-naked body with a scowl in his brow.

"A couple minutes." Cole rubs the back of his neck, his voice low and thick as he peruses me from head to toe. "How are you feeling?"

"Fantastic." Rags of air heave from my exerted lungs. "Thank you, both of you, for taking care of me."

It's strange that they're both here, when they weren't a few minutes ago.

"Did you guys just happen to arrive at the same time?" I rub my sweaty hands on my thighs. "Or were you together somewhere this morning?"

"We had a meeting," Trace says at the same time Cole blurts, "We grabbed breakfast."

"A breakfast meeting." Trace glares at Cole and returns to me. "Why?"

"You had breakfast together?" I cross my arms. "For what reason?"

Did Cole tell Trace we had sex? A spike of fear chills my skin. I don't want to keep secrets, but it's…delicate. I need to be the one to tell him.

"We're trying to figure this out." Cole gestures from me to Trace to himself, drawing an invisible triangle.

"Really?" My tone is dry as I fidget with the beaded bra to ensure my chest is covered. "What did you figure out?"

"That you should pole dance," Cole says. "Every day. Just for me."

I wing up my brows and pinch my lips together.

"I think…" Trace breathes in slowly. "*We* think this situation is making you sick. Your health is a concern. If we push you for a decision, it'll likely make you sicker."

"But I'm dragging this out." I clutch my throat. "I can't—"

"It's only been a couple weeks, Danni." Cole rests his hands on his hips. "You've been sick half that time. Give yourself a break."

"I'm trying." I lift my fingers to the pole and walk a circle around it while working up the nerve to ask them about the holidays. "Thanksgiving is next week."

Neither of them have families. No one to spend Thanksgiving and Christmas with.

They watch me steadily, their expressions giving nothing away.

"Bree's having turkey dinner at her house." I

release the pole and hug my waist. "Would it be weird if I invited you both?"

"I'd love to go." Cole, impulsive as always, offers me an eager smile. Then he pushes off the wall and disappears beyond the doorway of the spare bedroom.

I share a look with Trace, taking in the sculpted lines of his face.

He rolls his lips, reading my eyes, and nods. "I'll be there for dinner."

"Thank you." I smile. "Our first Thanksgiving together."

A second later, Cole returns with my seven-inch platform stilettos dangling from a finger by the ankle straps.

Oh shit. He wasn't joking about wanting me to dance for him.

I shoot another look at Trace. "I don't think this is a good—"

"I'm not asking." Cole squats at my feet and holds out his palm, waiting.

Trace rests his fingers in his pockets and holds up the wall with his back. He would never complain about me dancing. Hell, he put me on a stage in his casino in a glowing beam of light.

I blow out a breath, ruffling the hair away from my face. Then I give in and place a foot in Cole's hand.

He slides on the stiletto, buckling the strap around my ankle. As he moves to the other foot, his fingers trail softly up the back of my calf.

An exquisite shiver races up my leg, and my eyes flutter closed. He does it again, and I have to gulp down a moan. I can't let him do this. Not with Trace watching.

"That's enough." Trace's voice cuts through the air,

cold and sharp.

I wobble in the heels, and my hand flies to Cole's head for balance. His hair slips through my fingers, soft and silky. I linger there for a heartbeat before forcing myself to pull back.

"I'll finish this one." I crouch beside him and buckle the second shoe.

He leaves me to it and prowls toward the stereo. I rise to my full height, seven-awesome-inches taller, just as *Physical* by Nine Inch Nails starts playing.

It's the song Cole chose the first time I pole danced for him over five years ago. Unbidden, memories of that night heat my face and shorten my breaths. He fucked me half-way through that dance, right up against the pole. Then he spanked me for making him so horny and fucked me again.

The speakers crackle with the staticky screech of a guitar, pulling me back to the present.

"Dance, Danni." Cole grabs a folding chair and flips it around to straddle the seat with his arms resting on the back.

Trace doesn't move from his stance across the room. Tall, dark, and arrogant, he watches. And he waits.

I begin the pole walk, crossing one stiletto before the other and pushing out my hip. When the grungy vocals kick in, I swing my hair and climb the pole.

My dance outfit is exactly that. A two-piece ensemble designed to not interfere with my movements. But as I writhe before them in the beaded bra and panties, I feel like I'm wearing lingerie. I might as well not be wearing anything at all.

They're so attuned to my movements, they seem to

have forgotten each other. I try to keep it sexy and alluring without being a tease, exaggerating hip circles and leg kicks sparingly, like an exclamation point.

I slowly, sensually, slide to the floor, let my head and hair fall back, and close my eyes. This is what defines me. The emotion in movement. The anatomy of art and music. I might be performing for them, but I dance like I'm alone. This is my space, my outlet, my meditation. My time to think.

And I have a decision to make.

I need to dig deeper, beneath the footwork and the melody, and really figure out who I am and where I want to go.

Maybe then I'll know who I'm meant to be with.

twenty-two

Inviting two men to a family dinner might've been my worst idea ever.

On the surface, the atmosphere in my sister's dining room is cozy and warm. We've eaten our fill of Thanksgiving turkey and settled into easy conversation around the table. Bree sits on one side with her husband, David, and my four-year-old niece, Angel. I'm across from her, hemmed in by Cole and Trace.

She and David fill Cole in on everything he missed over the years—their lives pretty much revolve around soccer—while Trace engages in a silent, oddly sweet stare-down with Angel.

Beneath all the smiles and content expressions, however, simmers a sense of discomfort. Bree chitchats and laughs as she talks with Cole, but her eyes keep flitting to me, then to the men on either side of me, and back again.

Yeah, it's awkward. I'm here with two dates who haven't said a word to each other since we arrived. Every adult in the room feels the tension lurking underneath the conversations yet no one's willing to give it a voice.

Not even me.

I spent the last six nights hopping between beds. My time with Trace is filled with cuddling, kissing, stroking embraces without sex. Then I go home and let Cole ravage and plunder every hole in my body.

And Trace doesn't know.

Because I'm a cowardly dickhead with a backbone made of jelly and shame.

I'm sick with guilt over it, and this godawful feeling isn't going away until I tell him.

I rode here on the back of Cole's bike, but I intend to leave with Trace. I'm going to confess everything tonight, and I'm scared shitless.

I broke my no-sex rule with one of them, but not with the other. That's what scares me the most, because it feels like I made a choice without consciously doing so, and the choice doesn't sit well with me. Not that I think Cole isn't the one. It's just… It'd been years since we had sex, and dammit, he seduced me. That's not a reason to choose him over Trace.

It's just Cole's mode of operation. He charms and tempts, ensnares and claims, and I'll never get enough of it. If Trace pushed half as hard as Cole does, I'd cave with him, too.

Christ, I'm so fucking weak I annoy myself. The worst part is I'm not the one who will pay the price. When I tell Trace, it's going to hurt him terribly.

Dread coils in my stomach, and I wrap my arms around myself.

Bree breaks away from the conversation with Cole and David and sets her perceptive gray eyes on me.

"I'm glad you're feeling better." She sips her wine, regarding me. "I would've come over to take care of you, but you seemed to be in good hands."

One of those hands touches my knee under the table. I glance at the man attached to it, but Trace keeps his gaze trained on Bree.

"They're lucky they didn't come down with the flu." My breath catches as his fingers slide beneath the skirt of my dress. "They fed and cleaned up after me better than Mom would've done."

Bree laughs. "Mom isn't very good at the nurturing stuff."

I love my mother, but I'm not close to her. She's reserved and introverted, and since she and Dad moved to Florida eight years ago, the distance hasn't helped. A deeper relationship with my parents would require me to reach out to them more, which I don't do, because I have Bree.

"It's nice to see both of you here tonight." Bree nods at Cole while speaking to Trace. "It must be uncomfortable for you."

Leave it to my sister to finally address the elephant in the room. But since she thinks Cole and Trace met for the first time a couple weeks ago, she doesn't know the extent of the bad blood between them.

"When I'm with your sister…" Trace caresses a path up my inner thigh and strokes a finger along the crotch of my panties. "It's never uncomfortable."

My thighs clench together, trapping his hand. He seems perfectly at ease fingering me under the table while talking to Bree. Meanwhile, I'm so tense I probably look constipated as I try to keep my hips from rocking against his touch. My face burns, and I clench my fingers against the tablecloth.

Thankfully, Cole's still discussing soccer with David and doesn't look in my direction. If I push Trace's hand away, it'll draw attention, so I try to relax and temper my breathing.

"You know, this isn't their first meal together." I cough into my fist as Trace presses a firm finger against my clit. "They had breakfast together last week without me."

"Really?" Bree arches a brow.

"Yeah. I have no idea what they talked about—"

"I told you." Trace wickedly circles that finger, making my toes curl. "We discussed your health and our impact on it."

"Hmm." Bree leans in, studying me closely. "I will say, you never get sick. God, how long has it been? The last time you didn't feel well enough to dance was…" Her eyes drift to Cole, and her complexion pales.

When he died. That's the last time I was sick. And it was an ugly sick—inside and out, front to back, and dead all over. I didn't get out of bed for weeks.

Trace watches Cole talk to David then shifts his intelligent gaze to me. "You might've had the flu, but you were already rundown. Physically and emotionally. Your health is more important than anything else going on in your life."

"I like you." Angel, who's been quiet all night, directs her big brown eyes at Trace.

The hand between my legs retreats to my knee, and he scowls at the four-year-old. "That's good, because I like your aunt."

"I don't like him." She points at Cole and narrows her eyes. "I'm going to rip his spine out."

Angel just met Cole for the first time tonight. Evidently, she's quicker at making decisions than I am.

"Angel!" Bree angles toward her daughter, glaring. "I don't want to ever hear that again.

"So put your fingers in your ears." Angel blinks, expressionless.

"Oh my God," Bree mouths to me behind the concealment of her hand.

As laughter bubbles up my throat, Bree shakes her head at me. I guess she doesn't want me to encourage the little demon. So I arrange my face into a disapproving expression.

Bree pushes Angel's mostly empty plate toward her. "Finish your dinner."

My niece stares at her green beans and frowns. "Vegetables are ruining my life."

I can't stop my laughter this time, and even Trace smiles.

After dessert, we clear the table, and the men step out on the deck with beers in hand. It's warm for November. Jacket weather. Maybe I'll join them while Bree gives Angel a bath. But first, I need to pee.

The three-bedroom house is average-sized, appropriate for Bree and David's teacher salaries. I amble down the hall, bypassing the main bathroom, since it's currently occupied by Bree and Angel.

I slip into the master bedroom and use the facilities

in the tiny en suite. Hands washed and hair finger-combed, I open the bathroom door to step out. And slam into a hot steel wall with a startled *oomph.*

Cole pushes his way in, forcing me backward and locking the door behind him.

"What are you doing?" My pulse races at the hungry expression on his face.

Eyes hooded and roving up and down my body, he isn't here to use the bathroom.

"You let him play with your pussy at the table." His gaze snaps to mine and narrows.

"What?" *Shit. Fuck.* I don't want to have this conversation right now. Or ever.

"Don't pull that innocent act with me." He grips my hips and lifts me to sit on the edge of the vanity. "Did he put his fingers inside you?"

I shove at his immobile chest. "I'm not answering that."

Jesus. He was involved in a conversation with my brother-in-law at the time. How does he know where Trace put his hand?

"I'm always watching you." He cups my face and leans in, his eyes sooty and heavy with desire. "You look so damn beautiful in this dress."

Since my tight black sheath dress and strappy stilettos couldn't be worn on the motorcycle, I didn't put them on until we got here.

"Thank you." I slide my hands over the front of his white Henley shirt. "We should go back—"

"You're coming home with me tonight." He runs his nose alongside mine, heating my lips with his breath.

"No, I'm not," I say gently. "I was with you last night." And I rode his cock for hours.

I don't know what his reaction would be if he knew I was going home with Trace to confess what I've been doing. I'm afraid he'll talk me out of it.

He rubs his hands up my thighs and nudges me wider to spread around his hips. There's no bossy demands or heated *I-need-you* whispers. He just grasps the back of my head and stares at me, his bottom lip pouting slightly and begging to be licked.

It's a look that precedes a kiss, and as our mouths touch, we sigh together. Easing closer, reaching deeper, he brushes his tongue against mine. Each caress urges me to pull him tighter. Every rasping breath paves the way for more. More tasting. More touching. More Cole.

The wet smacking sounds of our lips echo in the tiny bathroom. Then his hands are moving, down my body, circling and caressing my breasts, and lower, pulling on the hem of my dress and yanking it to my hips.

I groan a sound of protest against his mouth and hunch back. "We can't."

"We can." He cradles my face in his hands, his lips wet and swollen. "We can do anything *you* want to do. What do you want, baby?"

I want him and me in this stolen moment.

Collecting heartbeats.

Falling in love for the millionth time.

Moving slow.

Breathing fast.

Clinging and kissing and connecting in every way.

Because it feels so damn good to be with him.

He reads my eyes and knows what I'm thinking. His exhales fall sharp and swift, and he kisses me, touches my face, his fingers shaking and flexing against my jaw.

"Danni." A pained whisper. He shoves the crotch of my panties to the side and slides a finger through my wet heat. "So damn sexy."

Each caress trembles through me, awakening an achy throb between my legs. I grip his shoulders and bite back a moan.

His breaths shorten as he unzips his jeans and frees his long, thick erection, holding my gaze.

I brace for a ruthless thrust. But instead of ramming inside me, he glides the underside of his cock along the slit of my soaked flesh. Over and over, he strokes his length against my pussy, teasing me, staring into my eyes, and running his tongue across my lips.

My feelings for this man are so absolute it's impossible to not get lost in him. But he's not the only one who dominates my mind.

I cut my gaze to the locked door and stiffen.

"He's outside with David." Cole grips the hair on the back of my head and forces my eyes to his. "Watch us, baby."

He tips my chin down and grasps my hand, positioning my fingers around the base of him.

His skin burns to the touch, stretched tight and silky over rigid steel. He continues to work the underside of his length against my folds, slipping through the wetness and rubbing against my piercing. With each pass over my clit, he presses his fingers down on the flared tip to create a delicious grinding sensation against my sensitive nerves.

Pleasure sweeps through me, trembling my legs as we watch the movement of his beautiful cock. I don't think I've ever been so captivated, so insanely turned on.

"I'm utterly consumed." His labored breaths churn the air between us, and he rubs himself harder against me. Then he slips lower, presses against my opening. "I've been waiting my entire life for you."

He seals his words with the push of his hips, sinking inside me with aching slowness. His fingers dig against my hipbone, and his mouth devours mine, kissing me until we're both breathless.

He swallows my gasps, rocking into me at a hypnotically slow pace. "Every time you let me into your body, it feels like redemption. You're my faith, Danni. My religion."

There goes my heart, swooping and thumping and gobbling up every word. He makes me greedy and thirsty. I suck on his lips, sipping and drinking, unable to quench this craving. "I'm crazy in love with you, Cole Hartman."

With a deep groan, he holds my gaze and slides his hands around my breasts, massaging, caressing, his touch like velvet magic.

"Feel me inside you? You're as far as I go." He buries himself to the root and grinds while tasting my lips. "Now until forever, you have all of me."

I have his heart, his breaths, and every hard inch that pulses against my inner walls. It's more than I deserve, and I can't let go.

I glide my hands down the lines of his back, following the hard-sloping curve of his ass and slipping beneath his jeans where they hang low on his hips. And that's where I hold on, gripping handfuls of solid muscle as he rides me languorously into orgasm.

When I fall, he chases me over the edge with a muffled grunt against my mouth. Connected in ecstasy, lips fastened, and hearts roaring as one, we reach for each other, lost in the rhythm of our breaths.

It's only after I come down from the blissful high that I start to panic.

"Was I loud?" I glance at the door and wonder if it's hollow or insulated. "Oh God, I moaned, didn't I?"

"Shh." He kisses my lips and steps back, tucking himself away. "No one heard us, and we've only been gone ten minutes."

Knowing Trace, he started a search party thirty seconds after he lost sight of me. I slide off the vanity, straighten my clothes, and slap cold water on my flushed cheeks. I should probably try to clean the come from between my legs, but every second I dally is a risk.

"I'm going out first," I whisper, reaching for the door. "Give me a few-minutes head start."

He narrows his eyes, and his mouth curves downward. I lean up and kiss that pout. Then I hit the light switch, blanketing the bathroom in blackness.

With a deep breath, I swing open the door and stride into my sister's *L*-shaped bedroom. As I round the corner, Trace enters from the hall, and dammit, I freeze up like bugged-eyed, guilty-as-fuck deer in headlights.

"Where have you been?" His head tilts, seeing too much in his millisecond glance over my body.

"Bathroom." I walk past him, head high and heart thundering. "I'm ready to go. *To your place.*"

I expect him to jump on that suggestion and follow me. Instead, he continues into the bedroom and leans around the corner, staring in the direction of the bathroom.

Panic, fear, shame—all of it crashes through me in breath-shaking waves. I'm going to confess everything about Cole, but not like this. Not here. Bree and her family don't need my selfish drama unraveling in their home and spoiling their Thanksgiving.

Trace straightens and folds his hands behind his back, his head angled down and brows pulled in. Then he paces back to me and laces his fingers through mine. "Let's go."

Composed as ever, he leads me into the hall with confident, relaxed strides.

I'm not relieved. If anything, his unflappable dispassion makes me nervous as hell.

As we say our goodbyes in the kitchen, Cole enters with my coat, slipping it over my shoulders and pressing a lingering kiss on my brow.

If Trace saw Cole in the shadows of the tiny bathroom, he doesn't mention it on the drive to the casino. Doesn't say a word as we enter the penthouse. Doesn't stop me when I head to his master bathroom and take a shower.

I dress in the button-up shirt he left on the vanity. By the time I step into his bedroom, I've worked myself into a gutless fog of misery and guilt.

He sits on the foot of the bed, still clad in his handsome suit. Knees spread and head down, he's bent over his lap, staring at his hands. In the background, the mournful vocals of *Say Something* by A Great Big World croon about giving up.

It's not a song in my playlist. He chose it deliberately, knowing that music is one of the ways I communicate. His expression is blank. His mouth doesn't move, yet he's telling me exactly how he feels through the heartbreaking lyrics.

The sad piano melody shivers through me, raising the hairs on my neck. It's an end-of-the-rope song. A last-chance, this-is-goodbye, I'm-walking-away song.

He's done with me.

My knees buckle, and my hand flies to my quivering lips.

No, Trace. Please, no.

Tears rise hard and fast, blurring my vision. Dread twists my stomach, and I can't breathe. Can't find my voice.

Say something. Say something. Say something.

Cold, emotionless, he lifts his arctic eyes to mine. "Say what you came here to tell me."

He already knows.

twenty-three

"Trace?" I force my feet to move toward him as overwhelming shame streaks down my face in salty rivers.

"Say it." His tone is calm, so deadly composed it stops me in my tracks.

The song he chose, *Say Something,* shudders through the room, and the haunting piano notes bang through me. *Bang. Bang. Bang.* I close my eyes, draw in a shredded gulp, and meet his gaze head-on.

"I had sex with Cole." My confession stumbles on a choked sob.

He doesn't move, doesn't blink. "How many times?"

My chest caves in. I cry harder and shake my head jerkily, over and over, pinning my lips together to muzzle the helpless noise clawing from my chest.

"You don't know?" His jaw twitches. "Or you don't want to say?"

"I don't know," I whisper, clutching at my neck, my throat swollen with grief.

He shoots from the bed, his movements graceful yet lightning fast. Prowling toward me, he rests his hands in his pockets.

My shoulders hunch as he circles me, his hulking frame edging close enough to brush against me. But he doesn't reach out, doesn't try to soothe me. Why would he? I'm spineless and selfish, and I don't deserve either one of them.

"You fucked him tonight." He steps into my space, towering over me, his eyes aglow with unfathomable self-control. "In the bathroom."

My face crumples, my tears thick and ugly as they roll down my face.

"You chose him." His voice breaks, forming a crack in his coldness.

"No." Tears strangle my whisper. "Trace, I didn't! Please, believe me." I sob and rub the heels of my hands against my temples, curling my fingers and fighting the need to cling to him, to hold him. "I don't know what I'm doing. I'm trying…I'm trying to do the right thing, but I'm stuck. I can't let go of him, and I can't…" Wracking cries garble my voice, and I grip the lapels of his suit jacket. "I can't lose you."

"You're a fucking mess." He pries off my hands and sets me away, glaring at me with disgust.

"Don't quit me." I wrap my arms around my waist, tormented and shaking violently. "Please."

"Is this regret?" He touches a thumb to my

cheekbone and catches a tear, staring at it with unblinking eyes. "Do you regret fucking him?"

If I slept with any other man—any man at all—I'd regret it till my dying breath. But I was with the one I never stopped loving, the man I never moved on from. As complicated and painful as that is, there's nothing confusing about my feelings for Cole.

The song ends, and deafening silence moves in, slithering and strangling and ticking down the seconds. Every breath carries me closer to the end—a finality I'm not ready for.

Trace studies my eyes, his scowl lined with a sadness I've never seen there before. His heartache is palpable in the stiff line of his shoulders, in the way he holds himself rigidly still, and in the very air coiled around him, keeping me at an agonizing distance.

I hate myself for hurting him. Doesn't matter how much he lied or deceived me, I'm the one who delivered the most painful blow.

"I regret..." I feel cold, defeated, worthless, as I stare up at him. "I regret hurting you."

He closes his eyes and tips his head back, his expression...lost. Then something crosses over his features, tightening the muscles in his face.

"Prove it." He lowers his head and tunnels his gaze into mine.

My breath stammers, and my mind races to understand. Does he want me to choose between them? Right this minute? I grasp the sides of my neck, swaying and dizzy with bubbling panic.

His eyes dip to my borrowed shirt, and realization stops my heart.

"You want me to...?" I touch the placket of buttons on my chest.

"Take it off."

He turns toward the couch in front of the fireplace, slides off his suit jacket with meticulous movements, and folds it over the arm rest.

He's going to fuck me. He's going to take my body while he's hurting and probably far more pissed than he's letting on. I'm willing to do almost anything to make this right, but I'm not sure sex is what he needs.

Or maybe that's exactly what he needs.

Reassurance.

When he shifts back to me, his eyes narrow at my still-clothed body.

"Your no-sex rule is fucked to hell." He stalks toward me, loosening his tie. "Remove. The shirt."

The cut of his voice makes me jump, but the heated promise beneath his gruff tone sends my fingers to the buttons. Maybe he just wants to pound all his loathing and bitterness into me, make me feel how badly I hurt him, and purge it from his system.

I can give him that. And more.

"I'm committed to this." Clutching the shirt, I push a button through the hole. "I'm not giving up." I release another one. "I love you, Trace."

His eyes don't stray from mine as I free each button and whisper determined words. When the shirt slips to the floor, it leaves me completely nude and trembling. Neither of us move.

The hush in the room presses against me, straining the few feet of space between us. He makes me suffer through it, taking his time scanning every exposed line and shadowed crease of my body.

"Bend over the bed." He adjusts the cuff of his sleeve. "Feet on the floor. Ass in the air."

I shiver and push myself into motion. He's going to fuck me face down in the least intimate position possible. And I'll let him. I'll let him use my body however he wants as long as he doesn't let go.

Sliding my hands over the mattress, I bend at the waist, legs straight and ass up, with my chest and cheek against the bedding.

His sharp breath sounds behind me, followed by his approaching footfalls. I tense in anticipation of his masculine heat, his expert touch, his satin lips…

"I don't resent you or think any less of you for fucking him." His palm ghosts across my backside, prickling my skin. "The rage burning inside me will never be directed at you." He kicks my legs apart, belying his words. "*You* are the only reason that son of a bitch is still alive."

My spine chills. "Trace, you can't—"

"Shut up." He caresses my bottom and softens his tone. "I'm punishing you for waiting ten days to tell me."

Ten days?

I started sleeping with Cole the night before I took the pregnancy test. Then I was sick for four days. Then six days of bed-hopping…

Ten days.

How does Trace know that?

"You were puking and sick as hell that morning." He bends over my back and speaks against the pounding din in my ear. "But I saw the guilt in your eyes the moment you looked at me."

My lashes flutter against my cheeks, my guilt

unbearable. He knew all this time and never said anything, never so much as looked at me differently.

"Do you know what it's like to watch your dreams come true?" He curves a hand around my waist. "To hold the end of your story tight in your grip, only to have it unravel from your fingers and slip away?"

An icy jolt spikes through me, quaking my body with memories of Cole's death.

"Yeah." I crane my neck and meet his flinty eyes. "I know exactly what that's like."

"Then you know…" He leans in, bracing a hand beside my head. "What I've been feeling for the last ten days."

I swallow thickly, choking on my tears. "Why didn't you tell me?"

"I was waiting for you to come to me, to say something, to *choose me*."

The hand on the bed moves in, wrapping around my throat. His fingers press against my windpipe, not hard enough to cut my air, but it's a vulnerable position. With his other hand stroking my bare backside, my legs spread, body naked, and butt perched in the air, I know what's coming before he rears back his arm.

He lets his hand hover above his shoulder, building dread in my stomach. But the moment I look into the shelter of his eyes, I swallow my doubts. I trust him to know my limits.

My breath leaves me right before his palm slams down. I wheeze with shock, lifting on my toes as white-hot pain blazes across my skin. Then he whaps me again, and again, every strike hitting harder, deeper into muscle and tissue, jarring my bones.

The hand collaring my throat doesn't tighten or

loosen. He's fully aware of his grip and the force of his hits against my backside, measuring every twitch, balancing pleasure with pain. Always in control.

Except his breathing. His chest heaves with the exertion of his lungs, rotating the air with the sounds of his hunger.

Spanking, choking, dominating—all of it makes him hard as a rock, and I feed on it, on his arousal, the rasp of his grunts, and the heat of his powerful hand colliding against my ass.

My nipples tighten. My pussy clenches, and I ache for a deeper connection. I need his confident, unwavering eye contact.

Fisting the sheets, I strain my neck against the fingers around my throat and peer back at him.

His gaze lifts, and his hand comes down, softly, tenderly, stroking my burning flesh and caressing the hurt. He holds me in the lull of his eyes for an aching moment before straightening and looking down at my fiery red bottom.

I miss his grip on my neck instantly and touch the skin there as I angle my head to follow his movements.

He steps behind me, the crisp fabric of his pants brushing the backs of my thighs. His tongue peeks out, wetting his lip as he stares at the exposed apex of my legs.

Mouth parted, chin angled down, and shoulders curled forward, he unlatches his belt. His fingers move quickly over the zipper, sliding it down. Then he shoves a hand into his boxers.

He doesn't look at me when he pulls himself out. Doesn't test my wetness as he pushes the broad head against my pussy. Doesn't hold back as he shoves roughly, ruthlessly inside me.

My mouth hangs open in a soundless gasp, and I claw at the bedding, clenching and writhing around him.

He thrusts without mercy, hammering against the back of my pussy vigorously, angrily, while hissing past his teeth. Every drive rubs the scratchy fabric of his shirt against my raw backside, reigniting the burn from his spanking.

His hand twists in my hair, wrapping it around his wrist and sparking pain through the roots. His other hand presses against my tailbone, restraining my movements as he spears me repeatedly.

I stiffen against the force of his wrath, both hating and loving it. Desire smothers the pain, but I'm conflicted, confused about his feelings. Does he still love me? Is he going to leave me? Tears well up, sliding along my nose and wetting the sheets beneath my cheek.

The first time we had sex was like this. A hate-fuck, scathing with hurt and devastation. I feel all that hostility now in the relentless slam of his hips. So much pain and torment. He's fucking me too hard, too rough, like he's trying to brand himself deep inside me.

I can handle that, welcome it even, but not while he's behind me. Not when he's avoiding my eyes.

Reaching back, I shove him off and flip over.

He stumbles, shocked by my boldness. "What the fuck?"

His black tie hangs loosely around his neck, and I grab it, pulling him onto the bed with me as I scoot toward the headboard.

"What are you doing?" He scowls, following for a second before sitting back on his heels with his hard cock jutting from the open fly of his pants.

"I want to see your eyes, Trace." I straddle his lap and wrap a hand around his length, positioning him.

"Then take a good hard look." He grabs my waist and kicks his hips in a vicious thrust.

I lift on my knees, preventing him from ramming all the way in.

"You think you have any control here?" He grips my throat, glaring at me.

"Never. Control is *your* job." I push my neck against his hand and kiss his lips. "I'm just making a request. Slow and easy? Please?"

He regards me, searching my eyes with unnerving intuition. God knows what he's thinking, and my stomach flutters with nerves.

With a steady inhale, he releases my throat and lightly caresses my cheek, then my lips. In the next breath, his mouth replaces his fingers, and he kisses me slowly, clutching my hips and sinking me down on his cock, inch by agonizing inch.

I gulp down my moans as he makes love to me in a way I didn't think he was capable. His hands roam everywhere, soft and warm on my skin, every brush of his tongue and roll of his hips bleeding with passion. It's a slow-burn of sliding lips, clenching fingers, and grinding bodies, sparking with friction and sensuousness.

I don't want it to end. I'm terrified of what follows. So when he lifts me and tosses me on my back, I panic.

I reach for him, but he's already crawling up my body, coming for me with heat dancing in his eyes.

"Stretch your arms toward the headboard." He

kneels between my legs, watching me obey with an intimidating scowl on his face. "Good. Now hold onto the rungs and don't let go."

Spread out and naked beneath the power of his suit-clad body, I grip the bars and hold my breath.

He captures my knees and wrenches them wider. Then his hands move up my thighs and skim over my stomach. His lips join in, ghosting across my breasts, his tongue swirling and teeth catching and biting my nipples.

I arch and tremble, tightening my fingers around the rungs. "Trace, please…"

His mouth moves to my neck, nibbling and nuzzling, as he delves a hand between my legs.

My yelp is breathless, every nerve-ending in my body on fire and charging toward release.

Bending over me, he fingers my pussy with curling strokes. I lift my head, reaching, and our mouths collide. He kisses me with total domination, and I surrender, panting, screaming, and falling headlong into a mindless orgasm.

He continues to work his fingers inside me, holding my gaze as I catch my breath.

"You're the song I'd never heard." He touches his lips to my breastbone. "The universe that didn't exist. You're every little thing that used to be empty."

My chest swells, lifting with a deep intake of air. "I love you so much."

His expression darkens, and he grips his erection, holding it against my opening. "Did you say those words to him when he was inside you tonight?"

My heart slams into my throat, and I clamp my legs around his hips. "Trace…"

He pushes my knees away and slides off the bed, tucking his swollen length into his pants.

"What are you doing?" I crawl after him, my stomach tumbling with dread.

He didn't come.

He fixes his tie and slides on the suit jacket, yanking and straightening his clothes without looking at me. Then he grabs his keys from the bureau.

My blood runs cold. "Where are you going?"

"Out." He steps into the hall and vanishes around the corner without a backward glance.

I scramble to my feet and snatch the shirt from the floor. Holding the wadded material to my chest, I race after him.

When I reach the elevator at the entrance of the penthouse, he's already inside, staring at the floor with a hard, unflinching expression.

"Trace." I sprint toward him, my voice shrilling with desperation and fear. "Don't leave."

His gaze lifts to mine, his features empty of emotion. The elevator closes shut.

"Please, don't leave!" I slam against the doors, too late, and burst into sobbing tears.

Sliding to the floor, I let myself think the worst. He's done with me. He's going out to find someone else, someone stronger and better, someone he doesn't have to share with another man.

My stomach cramps miserably, the tears endless and hot on my face. And I have no one to blame but myself.

I've been holding two men in a state of flux for a month. I should've made a decision by now. I shouldn't have broken my own rule about sex.

What do I do now? Does he want me to stay here or leave? If I leave, he'll think I've given up and gone home to be with Cole. If I stay and he returns with another woman…

Turnabout is fair play.

My insides constrict. He wouldn't do that. Maybe he just needs to cool off. He'll be back.

He'll come back to me.

I wait for hours, curled up in his bed.

I wait all night, texting and calling his phone like a crazy, obsessed girlfriend.

When the sun rises over the St. Louis skyline, I finally sleep, but it's restless and fretful. I wake two hours later, and it's already seven in the morning.

He never came home.

Did he stay in a room in the hotel? Did he spend the night with a woman? Maybe he slept in his office. I lean toward the last option and decide to go check for myself.

Showered and dressed thirty minutes later, I take the elevator one floor down and stride through the lobby toward his office.

I spot him immediately, his tall frame leaning against the reception desk as he speaks with his new assistant.

Marilyn is an older woman, maybe mid-sixties, with a warm disposition and a pretty smile. She glances in my direction, and a grin lights up her eyes.

Trace follows her gaze and looks at me. No, he looks *through* me. Then he turns and walks away, veering into his office and shutting the door.

I flinch, and my heart shatters on the floor.

We're strangers again.
Strangers sharing the same soul.

twenty-four

Determined and slightly hysterical, I pound on Trace's office door until security gently yet firmly escorts me to the parking garage. Livid doesn't begin to describe my state of mind as I'm shoved into the back of Trace's sedan and driven away from the casino.

My hands shake so badly I can't type out a text, which is probably a good thing. The words I want to send to him are viciously resentful and seething with *fuck you's*.

He didn't just send me away. He had me physically removed from his property.

Is this just a temporary reflex in pissedoffedness? Or has he written me off forever?

I squeeze my fingers around the phone as my heart takes a nosedive into sobbing regret.

I'm not giving up. He can be angry and hurt and shut me out all he wants. But that's not how this ends. I will not choose one of them by default. When I know who I belong with, it will be decidedly, absolutely, without doubt or fluctuation.

He's the one who told me to let the decision happen on its own. He told me he'd wait. A month ago, he sat there on my couch and agreed to date me while I dated Cole. He knew this wasn't an exclusive arrangement. And as intelligent as he is, he knew it was only a matter of time before I broke my stupid no-sex rule.

He just thinks I broke it with the wrong guy.

Did I?

Deep down, I don't feel a wrong or right answer when it comes to them. I just feel love—bottomless, devoted, undying love times two.

The driver drops me off in front of my house, and Cole greets me at the door the moment I trudge in.

I don't have to look at a mirror to know my eyes are bruised and swollen from crying and lack of sleep. My shoulders weigh a hundred pounds each, and I can't stop my chin from trembling.

Cole takes one look at me, and his demeanor shifts from friendly dimples to hard-lined tension.

"What happened?" He cups my face, probing my gaze with alarm in his eyes.

"Trace knows we slept together."

His forehead wrinkles, and a huff of air escapes his lips. "Is he being a little bitch about it?"

"Don't." I shove out of his hold and slip past him with anger burning my cheeks.

He charges after me and catches my elbow in the

hall, whirling me around. "What did he do?"

The past twelve hours knot and twist in my gut. Trace seemed angrier about me keeping a secret from him than anything else. I won't make that mistake again.

"What would you do?" I whisper, staring at the hand on my arm.

"What would I do…" Cole tightens his fingers around my bones. "If you fucked him?"

I close my eyes, nodding stiffly as fear trickles in. I can't bear the thought of one of them despising me, let alone both of them.

Lifting my chin, I give him my tearful gaze. "We had sex last night."

He yanks his touch away and shoves his hands in his hair, his voice guttural. "Why?"

"Why?" I stare at him, wide-eyed and blinking rapidly. "I love him, Cole."

With a great shuddering heave, he rubs his face, his neck, and turns to pace in the small square hall.

"You act surprised by this." I step into my bedroom and slump onto the bed. "I was going to marry him before you—"

"Do you love him more?" He stands in the doorway, gripping the frame.

"If I knew that answer, we'd be having a different conversation."

I'd be saying goodbye.

He hangs his head, his chest rising and falling. "Look, I know this is more than you can handle."

"More than I can handle? Don't say it like that, like I'm a naive little girl playing in a big man's world." I grind my teeth. "Let's not forget that I waited for you. I waited two lonely, miserable, goddamn years after you died before I even looked at another man. Meanwhile, you're off fighting wars that don't exist with the expectation that I'll run into your arms—celibate and alone—when you miraculously return from the dead."

"Danni—"

"I didn't fall in love with Trace out of spite or betrayal or selfishness. I *lost* you, Cole. I was grieving and miserable with my eyes locked on the rearview mirror. I needed to look forward, *move* forward, and Trace helped me do that. Then you came back and upended all the progress I made." I draw in a ragged breath. "You say this is more than I can handle, and I say I'm holding it together pretty fucking well."

"You're right." He pushes off the doorframe and prowls toward me. "You're the strongest person I've ever met. It's one of the million reasons why you're the only one I want, now and always."

He kneels in front of me and runs his hands up my knee-high boots, slipping beneath my denim skirt to caress my thighs.

"Cole." I grip his forearms, the rigid muscles straining beneath my fingers.

He inches closer, wedging himself between my legs, his hands creeping higher as he takes my mouth in a tender kiss.

I melt against him, needing his affection, his determination, his seduction… No, wait.

"Cole, you can't—" I scramble back, scooting across the bed and climbing off the other side. "You can't just force yourself into my space and seduce me and…and fuck me and expect everything to be alright."

His eyes sharpen, and he surges to his feet. "Isn't

that what Trace did? Last night? You told him about us, and he fucked you until I was eviscerated from your body and mind."

"No, that's not—"

"I bet you didn't think of me once while he was driving into your cunt."

His words cut, knocking the air from my lungs and welling tears in my eyes. But the torment in his voice breaks my heart. His entire body shakes with rejection and anger. And maybe even fear.

"This is why I didn't want sex involved in this." I step to the window and watch the shavings of rain pass over the neighborhood. "It turns a messy situation into a jealous war of pushing and fighting—"

"Maybe you should've only fucked one of us."

"*You*, you mean?" I spin around. "If I only had sex with you, all of this would go away?"

"Yes." He clenches his hands at his sides.

"Are you even listening to yourself? Because you sure as hell aren't listening to me. I love *both* of you. That means everything I give you, I give to him." I gentle my voice. "When I returned your engagement ring, do you remember what you said?"

"You're my heart." He steps around the bed, his gait slow and heavy. "I can't live without you."

"And now?" I sit on the edge of the mattress, following his approach out of the corner of my eye. "Has that changed?"

He lowers beside me and breathes in, out. "No. But…"

I go still, my fingers twitching between us.

"I won't share you, Danni. I can't…" He leans

forward, folding his hands together between his bent knees. "I can't sit here, alone in this house, knowing you're fucking him when you're with him."

"He kicked me out of the casino."

"What?" He jerks his head toward me, working his jaw. "Did he hurt you?"

"No. He's just… I don't know. He left last night and didn't come back. He won't talk to me."

"I'll handle him," he says with a growl.

"Don't you dare. This is between him and me."

I'll be back at the casino this afternoon, that is if I still have a job.

"You need to understand…" I rub my palms on the skirt. "As long as I'm in this place of indecision, I'm not giving up on him."

He stares at the floor, clenching his teeth and making his jaw bounce. Then he stands with his hands on his hips and directs his gaze at the doorway. "I need to think."

I don't know what I expected, but his sudden need to leave wasn't it. My shoulders fall, and I lower my head to hide the despair tightening my face. It's quite possible I'll end up with neither of them, and I'm not sure I'll survive that.

"I'm not going anywhere." He touches my chin, lifting it. "I just…"

"Need to think." I nod as worry sets in. "I'm going to take a nap until it's time to go to work."

He leaves the room, and when I wake from my nap hours later, he's already left for his job at the stadium.

I drive to the casino and dance through my eight-hour shift, scanning the dining room for any sign of Trace. He always watches me dance.

Except tonight.

Security never showed up to remove me from the stage, so I guess that's something. I still have a job.

At midnight, I hurry to the dressing room, shower and change clothes, and head to his private elevator. Punching in the access code, I wait for the doors to open.

Nothing.

I try again.

Still nothing.

My blood boils. He fucking locked me out!

Pulling the phone from my pocket, I open a text window.

Me: A) The elevator is broken, B) You're really pissed, C) This is a test to see if I'll bang my head on the doors and make an ass of myself.

Me: I need to talk to you.

Me: Please, let me upstairs.

In the seven months I've known him, he's never *not* responded to my messages instantly. I know he's reading my texts. Hell, he's probably watching me on the security feed.

My stomach feels hard, my eyes itchy and hot. If I stand here all night, the only thing it proves is that I'm a desperate, pathetic woman. Clinging to an elevator isn't fighting. It's sitting down and taking it. If Trace wants to give me the cold shoulder, I'm not going to suffer it under the watchful eyes of his cameras.

With a steeling breath, I gather what's left of my self-respect and drive home.

I'm not a wily or cunning person. I don't know how to manipulate or play games. Stalking and calculation is for people like Trace, and that leaves me at a disadvantage. If he intends to put distance between us, I can only go at him with the things I have: love and stubbornness.

That night, Cole sleeps beside me with a foot of space between us, as if I need more distance in my life. But I don't fault him for it. I rejected him this afternoon, and if he tried to seduce me tonight, I would've rejected him again. Because sex isn't helping any of us.

And so it goes for the next week. I dance at Bissara, call and text Trace every day, and make attempts to access his elevator.

I haven't heard from him once, but I see him. He watches me dance from the shadows at the restaurant. Twice, I jump off the stage in the middle of a song to confront him. But he slips away both times, fading into the crowds in the casino.

Avoiding me.

His silence hurts. It makes me feel forgettable, invisible…unwanted. I shouldn't have to beg someone to be part of my life.

But there's a difference between ignoring me and *pretending* to ignore me. I'm certain he's pretending and decide to test the theory.

At midnight, seven days after he revoked my access to him, I wrap up my shift at Bissara, shower, and change into jeans, a t-shirt, and a heavy wool coat. Instead of heading to his private elevator to perform my nightly ritual of trying my passcode and sending ignored texts, I walk through the lobby of The Regal Arch Casino and Hotel.

My Midget is in the parking garage, but that's not where I'm going. I don't glance at the countless cameras in the ceiling, don't scan the gaming area for his tall lean frame. I stride to the side entrance, where there are no bellhops or other employees who might report my location to the controlling casino owner.

Cold drizzling rain splatters my face as I step outside. A shiver races through me, and I huddle deeper into the coat. A few cars motor past, but the side street at this end of the casino is relatively quiet.

If he's watching me, he won't be…right about…now. I just stepped out of view of the exterior cameras.

Following the sidewalk, I hop over to the next street, where numerous small bars and taverns light up either side of the road. I peer into the windows as I pass, soaking up the glowy warmth of the laid-back atmosphere and cheery groups of late-night drinkers.

I chose this path because it's usually densely populated this time at night, making it safer to walk alone. But tonight, I'm the only asshole standing outside in the icy sleet.

The poltergeist-white pellets spear the calm black sky. It's neither windy nor raining hard, but every frigid drop seems to find its way beneath my clothes, biting my skin and penetrating my bones. After a few minutes of this, I'm drenched and trembling.

Just as I'm about to turn back, footsteps close in behind me, stomping the pavement at a fast pace.

I spin around and spot Trace sprinting out of the shadows a block away. My chest hitches, and I hurry toward him.

His blond hair falls in sexy sodden strands across his brow. A dark gray suit clings to his muscular frame, every thread saturated and dripping beneath the spitting rain.

Standing just out of arm's reach, he holds his shoulders back and clutches his phone at his side. "What the fuck are you doing?"

"Trying to get your attention."

His head jerks back, and he blinks against the icy drizzle. "You have my attention. Every second of every day."

"Is pretending I don't exist your special way of letting me know I'm on your mind? If so, I must be really dense and stupid." My teeth chatter against the cold. "It definitely doesn't make me want to punch you in the nuts. Not even a little. So go ahead. Keep ignoring me. It's a great approach in building trust and commitment in a relationship."

He leans in, his blue eyes glowing with anger. "Excuse me if I don't take advice on *trust and commitment* from a woman who fucks around behind my back."

My breath cements in my throat, choking my voice. "Tell me you hate me, that you don't want me. Say it, Trace. Tell me it's over. I'd rather hear it than endure your silent treatment. Being brushed off without a word, ignored like I mean nothing… It's the worst feeling."

He closes his eyes and wipes the rivers of rain from his face. Then he lifts his phone and types something on the screen.

"My driver's on the way." He glances at the entrance to a small bar across the street. "Let's go inside and—"

"Talk to me, dammit!"

His eyes harden, wide and unblinking as he glares at me. "Are you still fucking him?"

Of course, that's what this is about, and I don't hold it against him. If I were in his shoes, I would crumble, gasping and bleeding, beneath the jealousy. I could never share him with another woman. It would destroy me.

The least I can do is ease his mind.

"The last time I had sex was with you." I hug my chest, shivering.

Every night, Cole sleeps beside me. He's been uncharacteristically quiet and reserved, keeping his hands to himself. But he's still present in my life, casting glances in my direction, touching my lower back and brushing my hair behind my ear whenever he walks by. He's not ignoring me.

Trace searches my face, expressionless and unreadable. As we stare at each other in the endless rain, my lungs fill with all the words I've messaged him during our separation. *I love you. I miss you. I need you.*

There's a fine line between fighting for someone and being clingy and desperate. I've been walking that line for the past week. Trace knows how I feel. He knows I haven't given up. Whatever comes next is up to him.

He continues to scowl at me, motionless and eerily silent in the rain, and the reason becomes painfully obvious. His glare doesn't pin me down with intimidation or hold me hostage as it's known to do. He's frozen and staring because he doesn't know how to proceed.

It doesn't show in the sharp angles of his beautiful face, but for the first time since I've met him, he's standing before me without an agenda. The calculating controller of schemes and strategy has no idea what to do.

He's so lost in his head he doesn't notice the car pulling up until it stops beside us at the curb.

He blinks, straightens his spine, and steps to the side to open the door for me.

I don't hesitate to slide onto the backseat and escape the freezing rain. As I scoot to make room for him, I realize he's not following. "Trace?"

With a hand on the roof of the sedan, he leans down, dripping with icy water.

"I don't hate you." He trails cold wet fingers across my cheek. "I love you so much I want to be a better man. A man you deserve."

"Don't say that. I love you just the way you are." I clasp my hands around his neck and bring our foreheads together. "I think I have a thing for assholes because I'm the biggest asshole in existence."

"No, you're not. Not even close." He sighs against my lips. "I want to be more, Danni, and it starts with giving you what you need."

"I need *you*."

"You need space. Time to just *be*. That's the only way this will work itself out."

"Is that what you've been doing? Giving me space?"

"No, I've been…displeased."

"You mean *pissed*."

"Yes." He releases a breath. "I'm working through that."

"We can work through it together." I touch my mouth to the icy, pliable flesh of his. "Let me stay with you tonight and—"

"I'll fuck you, Danni. If I take you home, I won't be able to stop myself." He grabs my throat and breathes against my lips. "I'm seconds away from fucking you right here on the backseat of the car."

My lungs release a shivery pant, and my skin inflames beneath my wet clothes. But I don't beg, because I know he's right.

"I'll have your car delivered tomorrow." He releases my throat and steps back on the sidewalk, gripping the door. "When you're ready, I'll be waiting."

The door shuts with a deadening snick, and my heart crashes against my ribcage. The driver eases the sedan into motion, and my pulse bangs harder, louder, thrashing in my ears.

I touch my fingers to the window as Trace slides his hands in his pockets and hunches in the rain. He watches me, and I watch him, until the darkness stretches between us.

Removing my phone from my coat pocket, I send him a text.

Me: Distance doesn't separate us. We're waiting together.

I pull up my playlist and select *We Can Hurt Together* by Sia. Then I rest my head against the window, humming brokenly to the melody while trying not give into the achy burn in my eyes.

He's not ignoring me. He just wants to give me space and time. *To just be.*

Because he loves me.

But he's also sending me home to another man. What if this so-called *space* pushes me closer to Cole? Trace might not have a plan, but I know he's considered this. Still, he put aside his fears and took the risk to give me what I need.

It's a remarkable act of selflessness that only further endears me to him. Maybe that's exactly the reaction he intended. If this is all an orchestrated game, I'm playing into it beautifully.

I'm tired of the egos and rivalry and constant state of uncertainty. It makes me question every action and twist around every word. But I can't lose sight of one important thing.

I trust him.

twenty-five

Over the next week, I spend my nights off work visiting the homeless shelter and my days practicing a Waltz routine for the mayor's Christmas party with Nikolai. I'm too busy to make use of the space Trace is giving me, but that's about to change. Tonight was the mayor's party.

The performance went off without a hitch, and I don't have another gig lined up until next summer. With the stress of my second job behind me, I should be happy and relieved. But as I step inside my house after the party, carrying the sparkly gown and heels, I feel out of sorts and misplaced, like I don't know what I'm doing or where I belong.

Cole emerges from the basement as I pass through the hall, and our paths collide.

"How did it go?" He lifts the dance costume from

my arms and takes it into the spare room to hang up.

"They want us back again next year." I lean against the hallway wall, watching him through the doorway.

"That's great."

He steps into the hall and stops a few feet away, regarding me with unshakable focus. His expression is cautious, mouth slightly parted and gaze fixed on mine.

I strain to hear the words he doesn't speak. Whatever he's thinking is right there, hovering on the pillow of his kissable bottom lip.

His jaw shifts, his head angling imperceptibly to the side. His eyes, so deeply brown they appear black in the dim light, are bordered by dark lashes, giving him a sexy, sleepy look. A baseball cap sits backward on his head, making him appear younger than his thirty years. A gray shirt hangs from his slope-shouldered body, partially tucked into low-slung jeans that fray along the seams. And he's barefoot, which I find obscenely sexy.

"You've only been home a month and a half and you've put on weight." I give him another once-over and shake my head. "Not a single ounce of fat."

He glances down at his body and rubs the ridges of his chest, as if noticing his physique for the first time.

His mouth crooks up in a lopsided smirk. "I've had a lot of time on my hands."

He works out nonstop. God knows he has to expend all that sexual energy somehow. He's gorgeous and virile with an off-the-charts libido. He could have any woman he wants in his bed. He could fuck a different beauty every day or several at the same time. Instead, he lingers in this house, comes home every night after work, and waits while I relegate him to the limbo of my indecisiveness.

My fingers tingle to touch his whiskered face, to hold him against me and tell him I'm sorry. I don't know where we stand anymore. He said he needed time to think, but he hasn't told me the verdict.

I rest my hands on the backs of my hips and stare at the floor. "I'm ruining us, aren't I?"

"No." His soft timbre lifts my head.

"This is..." I gesture between us. "It's painful. Don't you feel it?"

"Attachment hurts, Danni." He inches closer, right up into my personal space, and frames my face in his hands. "It means you're human, and you love to the point of pain."

I drag in splintered breath. "Does it hurt to love me?"

"I love you so much it hurts." He leans his face against mine, his fingers curling around my neck and thumbs stroking my cheeks.

"No matter what I do, someone's going to get hurt. At the rate I'm going, we'll all be alone in the end."

"No." He clenches his teeth. "You choose him or me. Those are your only options."

What if I can't choose? It's like telling a mother she can only keep one of her children and has to let the other one go.

"I want to be your future." He kisses my bottom lip, suckling on it before moving to the top one. "But more than that, I want you to be happy."

I tilt my head up, absorbing the sincerity in his voice.

He stares back at me with the flames of dreams in his eyes. If I braved the fire and peered in, I'd see a beautiful future, *our forever*, flickering in the depths.

With a dip of his head, he kisses me again, deeper, more passionately, touching his tongue to mine as his fingers twist in my hair. We break apart long enough to move to the bathroom and strip our clothes.

Then he kisses me in the shower. He kisses me while we dry off. Then we spend the rest of the night in bed, lips locked and tongues reaching. Deep and slow. Stoking the passion that hums beneath our skin.

I close my eyes and hold him in the dark, my arms wrapped tight around his back and fingers tracing the taut muscles along his spine. His entire body vibrates with the need to touch and grind and fuck. But he doesn't.

For now, we simply cherish the moment, with our bodies pressed together, limbs entangled as our love spills into the shared rhythm of our heartbeats.

The next morning, he's up early, working out to his obnoxious music in the basement. I spend the day in the dance studio, choreographing new belly dance routines while trying to embrace Trace's advice and *just be*.

Cole leaves for work thirty minutes before I do. Our hours are the same, but I'm always running late.

I dart through the kitchen, grab my keys, and gulp down an afternoon cup of coffee. Then I'm out the door and tumbling into the Midget. Trace had my car delivered the morning after our confrontation in the rain, but I haven't seen or heard from him since.

As I shove the key in the ignition, something crinkles beneath my butt. I lift my hip and yank the offending object out from beneath me.

It's a brown 8x11-sized envelope, sealed with one of those string thingies that wrap around a paper disk. I flip the package over a few times, but there's no writing, nothing to indicate what it is or why it was left in my car.

I leave the car door unlocked. Anyone could've put it here, but I suspect Trace was involved. Last time he left me an envelope, it contained a concert ticket to see Beyoncé.

A grin steals over my lips as I unwind the tie and dump the contents onto my lap. A stack of photos spills out. Huge photos, the size of the envelope. I hold up the first one.

What the tits?

Those are some serious tits. Big, round man-eating knockers. The nude, dark-haired woman in the photo has her head tilted back, her mouth in an *O* of ecstasy, and her legs straddled around a man's body on a bed.

My heart hammers as I bring the picture closer to my face, studying the naked man. I don't have to look very closely. The instant I see the snake tattoos on his arm and neck, my stomach collapses and my airway clamps shut.

NoNoNoNoNo. Cole would never cheat on me. This isn't real. It can't be.

I shove it to the bottom of the stack, moving to the next one. It's the same bed, same lighting, same woman. Different position. And the man… My heart rate skyrockets, chilling my skin. It's undeniably Cole, his face rigid with tension as he pounds into her from behind.

Tears blur my eyes, and my hands shake violently as I flip through three more pictures.

The only thing that changes from photo to photo is the position in which he fucks her. Her on top, him on top, behind, in front, bent over…when I get to one with his face between her legs, bile hits the back of my throat. I can't breathe, can't move. I'm going to be sick.

I roll down the window, gulp down a draft of cold air, and force myself to look again. There's no time stamp on the photos or calendar on the wall in the background, nothing to place the date. He had the tattoos before he met me. As godawful as it is to see this, the woman could be one of the hundreds he was with before we were together.

This doesn't mean anything.

He's not a cheater.

Fighting down panic and nausea, I sift through several more photos before a new scene pops up.

Blood. Pools of it spread out around the gruesome body of a man laid out on the floor. A crimson gash slashes across his throat, his lifeless eyes open and staring at the ceiling.

Dread broils in my stomach as I look closer. There's another man standing at the edge of the frame with his back to the camera. My mind immediately tells me it's Cole, but that's not what I'm seeing.

The image is fuzzy and zoomed in, showing little of the surroundings. But the wood floors… the black suit on the man standing just inside the frame…

My pulse thunders as I flip to the next photo. And I gasp.

The shot is zoomed out, capturing a wider view. The man in the suit is turned to the side, his profile elegant and stern and unmistakably Trace Savoy.

I bite down so hard on my lip I taste iron. The blood-soaked, honey-wood flooring is *my* flooring. The fireplace, red velvet couch, and orange armchair… This happened in the front room of my house.

Why is Trace in my house with a man I don't recognize? A man who clearly died from a cut across the throat.

Numb, frozen, I choke on air I can't seem to pull into my lungs. Did the dead man come for *me*? Did he break into my house? When?

I skip through more photos, more shots of Trace standing over the body. Now that I'm looking closer, I see the knife clenched in Trace's fist.

He killed a man.

In my house.

I press a hand over my mouth to stifle my keening noises. No wonder Cole and Trace were always on my ass about locking my doors. They fucking knew I was in danger and never told me.

I feel myself breaking down—runaway heartbeat, erratic breathing, ice-cold skin, sobbing wretched tears. I need to pull it together.

Wiping the moisture from my eyes, I clear my vision and focus on the floor in the pictures. The purple rug isn't under the coffee table. I bought the shaggy thing at a yard sale about a year after Cole died. That means this photo was taken before I met Trace.

As that realization sinks in, my lungs wheeze, and more tears course down my cheeks.

Trace murdered someone in my house either before Cole left or while he was gone. Does Cole know? Where was I when it happened? What if I'd been home at the time?

I start to hyperventilate with fear and overwhelming paranoia. My lungs slam together, and my body rocks with my heaving gasps as I scan the surroundings and watch the rearview mirror. Am I in danger now?

Someone put this envelope in my car.

An envelope filled with incriminating evidence.

Trace committed a crime, and I'm holding the proof in my hands. Who would give this to me and why? Is there a vendetta against Cole and Trace? Is someone out for revenge? What if I'm the target?

With a sobbing breath, I turn over the ignition and shove the Midget into reverse. I plow through a bush, back over the curb, and hit the street. Then I throw it in first and slam on the gas, tearing through the gears and putting distance between me and my house.

Whoever left the envelope knows where I live. Clearly, they know my connection to Cole and Trace. Whatever this is, it's connected to their stupid secret jobs.

When I veer onto the main thoroughfare, I glance at the speedometer and yank my foot off the gas pedal. *Fuck.* If I get pulled over by a cop with these pictures on my lap, Trace would go to prison.

He might be on my shit list—*population: 2*—but I should probably hear his plea before I have him hauled off in handcuffs.

I slow down the car, keeping my speed under the limit while stuffing the photos into the envelope. Except the last two. I raced out of my driveway so fast I didn't make it through the stack.

Keeping my eyes on the road, I can't study the final two photos, but quick glances tell me they're more of Trace in my sitting room, only these are from a different camera angle. An angle that shows Cole's motorcycle parked in my dining room.

That narrows down the date. It happened

sometime after Cole left and a year before I met Trace. In that two-year time frame I was living alone and clueless as fuck.

As I put away the last two photos, the second camera angle raises more questions.

Was there a cameraman taking the pictures? Or were there multiple cameras hidden in my house? Are there cameras in my house now? If so, how did they get there?

For the next ten minutes, I keep driving, my mind spinning and my entire body painfully stiff and trembling. I have no idea where I'm going. I just can't go home, and the only two people I can talk to about this are the last two people I trust right now.

Did Cole cheat on me? Or did he fuck that woman before we met? What about Trace? Did he murder a good man? A husband and father with a family that mourns him? Or was the man there to hurt me?

No matter the answers, I've been lied to. Deceived. *Again.* How much more are they keeping from me?

I don't know where to go, but my subconscious seems to have made the decision for me. The Regal Arch Casino and Hotel looms two blocks ahead, its steel architecture glittering in the sunlight.

I'm supposed to be at work, but that won't be happening. I park the car and head straight to Trace's private elevator, hugging the envelope to my chest. I haven't tried to enter my passcode since the night I drew him out into the sleeting rain.

Hunched over and shaking uncontrollably, I enter the code.

The doors open instantly.

I'm too freaked out to feel relief. I probably look it, too, like a trembling, wild-eyed nutjob with tears splotching my face. Good thing I'm all out of fucks to give.

I hit *30* on the panel of buttons, assuming he's working. When I arrive on the office floor, I cross the lobby, turn down the hall, pass the receptionist desk, and reach for the door to his office.

"Miss Angelo, wait." Marilyn, his assistant, rises from her chair. "You can't go in there. He's on a call."

I swing open the door and shut it behind me.

Trace sits behind his desk, typing on his laptop with a phone at his ear. He looks up, scans my trembling, rigid posture, and meets my eyes.

"I'll call you back." He hangs up the phone and continues to stare at me, his scowl creasing with worry.

If I open my mouth, I'm going to burst into tears. So I drag my feet across the room and drop the envelope on his desk.

He glares at it like it's going to bite him. Then his gaze returns to mine, questioning, sharpening. A muscle twitches in his cheek, his hand hesitant as he reaches for the envelope. After an agonizing moment, he lifts it and slides out the photos.

The pictures of Cole are on top. Trace examines each one, his scowl emotionless. But he lifts his eyes repeatedly, checking my reaction. When he flips to the images of the dead man, he stiffens, and his nostrils go wide.

His gaze snaps to mine, and he presses a finger to his lips, wordlessly telling me not to talk.

His entire demeanor changes in a blink. His breaths come hard and fast as he snatches his phone and types something on the screen.

Who is he texting?

Without speaking, he gathers the photos, stacking them and returning them to the envelope.

Is he worried about someone listening? The FBI? He committed a crime, and now I'm wondering if by coming here, it makes me an accomplice.

Or is a different threat putting him on alert? Whoever delivered those pictures is probably not working on the right side of the law.

My scalp tingles, and my muscles are so stiff I struggle to unlock my joints. He darts around the desk, grips my shaking fingers, and guides me toward the door.

He touches his lips again, reminding me to remain silent. Then he leads me out with a hand on my back.

Where are we going? Maybe I shouldn't follow him. He's a killer and a liar and hell knows what else? My trust in him is shattered. Except I know, without a shadow of a doubt, if I'm in danger, he'll protect me.

He ushers me into the elevator and presses the button for his penthouse. Maybe it's safe to talk there?

When we arrive on the 31st floor, he clasps my hand and pulls me into the open kitchen. Shoulders stiff and back straight with tension, he scans my body with narrowed hawk eyes.

I wrap my arms around myself. "What are—?"

His hand flies to my mouth, his fingers pressing hard as he shakes his head.

Still no talking? What the unholy fuck? I glance around at the kitchen and living room. Does he think his penthouse is bugged?

He reaches for my coat, and I watch in frozen horror as he slides his fingers along the seams, checking the pockets and freeing the buttons to examine the liner.

He thinks I'm bugged.

The gravity of that realization crushes the air from my lungs, and all that remains is the strangling death of a breath.

twenty-six

Layer by layer, Trace removes the clothes from my quivering body. I hold still, paralyzed, as he inspects every garment, searching for listening devices. I don't know if he thinks I went to the police and had a wire put on me or if there's another threat causing his hands to shake. One that endangers both of us.

Neither of us has spoken.

My clothes scatter the floor around my feet, and all that's left to remove is my panties. After examining every seam and stitch from my bra to my boots, he hasn't found anything suspicious.

Crouched before me, he rests his hands on my hips and hooks his thumbs beneath the waistband of my bikini briefs. Then he gives me his eyes, the pale blue depths glowing with intention.

I hug my bare chest and widen my stance with a nod.

My skin prickles with goosebumps as he slides the lacy material down my legs. His fingers, warm and familiar, slowly skim my thighs. I shiver.

He cut a man's throat with those hands, and I'm standing in his domain completely nude and vulnerable.

Closing my eyes, I focus on breathing.

Over the past six weeks, I've made assumptions about Cole's job, including the likelihood that he's killed people. I justify his actions by telling myself they were bad people, people who tried to hurt him. The same rationalization grips me now.

I have no doubt Trace killed that man to protect me. But that doesn't excuse the fact that he kept it from me. I don't give a shit about the restrictions on sharing classified information. There was a fucking murder in my house, and I didn't know about it.

He softly touches my thigh, and I snap my eyes open. My phone sits in his hand. He must've found it in my coat pocket. The cover has been removed, exposing the electronic insides.

"You're not bugged." He offers the phone to me.

I leave his hand hovering there in lieu of grabbing my underwear.

"Who's the dead man in the photo?" I drag on my panties and reach for the bra.

He rises to his full height with his hands behind him, watching me from beneath dark brows. The intensity in his expression makes me nervous, but he seems more relaxed now that he knows I'm not bugged. He also hasn't taken his eyes off my body.

"Stop staring and answer my question." I reach

behind me and clasp the bra hooks with trembling hands.

His jaw flexes as he glares at me for another irritating moment. Then he lifts the envelope from the floor and empties it on the kitchen island. "Come here."

I step beside him, gripping the edge of the counter while he straightens the photos, side by side, grouping his and Cole's separately.

The images of Cole with that woman stirs so much poisonous jealousy in my gut I can't look at them.

"This man"—Trace points at the dead body—"broke into your house with a gun concealed in his waistband and a knife sheathed beneath the leg of his pants."

"He meant to kill me?" My face turns cold, bloodless.

"Yes."

"Because of Cole?"

A muscle twitches beneath his eye. "Correct."

"Do you know why or who he is?"

He flattens his hands on the counter and gives me a look that says everything and nothing. He has the answers, and they're not going to pass his lips.

"You checked my clothes for bugs." I cross my arms over my chest. "Who did you think was listening?"

"Anyone Cole made enemies with. I don't know who delivered the envelope or what their motivation is. All precautions are necessary."

My throat swells shut, and I stab a finger at the snapshots of my sitting room. "When did this happen?"

"A week after Cole cut all communication with me."

"That was nine months after he left." I run a hand

through my hair and stare at the photos. "If you knew this man was connected to Cole, you knew Cole was in trouble."

"I knew something was wrong the moment Cole stopped returning my encrypted messages. I didn't know if he was lying low or already dead."

"Did you kill or harm anyone else on my behalf?" *How many attempts have been made on my life?*

"No."

"Does Cole know about this?"

Trace's phone vibrates, and he lifts it to his ear. "Send him up."

"Send who up?" I glance down at my body, clad only in a bra and panties. "I'm not dressed."

"Nothing he hasn't seen before." He tosses the phone on the counter and turns back to the photos.

"Cole?" My pulse races. "That's who you sent a text to in your office?"

He nods stiffly without moving his eyes from the pictures.

"I don't want to see him!" I shove my hands in my hair, panicking. I'm not ready to deal with his betrayal. If I see guilt in his eyes, if he cheated on me, I know what I'll have to do, and I can't bear it. "Send him away."

Trace's gaze shifts to the photos of Cole. Then he looks me and huffs a scornful laugh. "Trust me. I don't want to see him, either. But he has answers I need."

Fuck. I spin toward the pile of clothes on the floor and grab the jeans just as the elevator opens.

Cole storms into the penthouse, clad in his black security uniform with a gun on his hip. His sharp gaze sweeps over my half-naked, hunched-over posture, flicks to Trace, and lands on the counter covered in photos.

I shove on my jeans and sweater, my breath bursting in and out, as I monitor his reaction.

His strides are strong and swift, eating up the floor in his approach to the island. He leans over the disgusting collage and examines every image without a twitch of shock on his face.

"Is it resolved?" Trace stands beside Cole, taller, sterner, more formidable, with judgment and scrutiny tapering his eyes.

There's no question who used to be the boss. For a curious moment, my turbulent emotions are diluted by fascination as they slip into their former work relationship.

"It's locked down. Physically." Cole looks at him. "Sentencing was this week."

Trace directs his gaze at the sex photos, his voice quiet. "Defector?"

Cole waits several seconds before giving a sharp nod.

"What does that mean?" I glance between them, struggling to follow the conversation. "Are you saying the woman is a defector? Like she turned against…what?"

They don't break eye contact to spare me a look or any form of acknowledgment.

"Fuck." Trace releases a breath. "*That* was the mission?"

"Yes." Cole grinds his teeth. "It was a goat fuck operation from the start, but it's wrapped up. I'm officially out. Out of all of it."

"When did you fuck her?" My eyes burn as waves of pain unfurl inside me.

"I can't disclose any—"

"Fuck you!" I turn away as a sob rips from my throat.

"Danni," Cole says firmly and grips my upper arms from behind.

"Don't touch me!" I lurch away from him, retreating backward and crying noisily against the cover of my hands.

He cheated on me. He left me and cheated on me and my heart hurts so badly I can't breathe.

Cole holds his fists at his sides, his expression stricken and posture tightly coiled.

"Tell me the status of Danni's safety." Trace's deep rumble echoes through the penthouse.

"She's safe." Cole angles toward him, leaving a foot of volatile air between them. "I wouldn't have returned to the States if she wasn't."

"Except I wasn't safe." I angrily snatch one of the photos of Trace and hold it up to Cole. "Did you know about this?"

Cole closes his eyes for a tense moment before pinning me with a resolute glare. "There was a breach. Stolen information. But it's over. The perpetrator is behind bars."

Lies. I taste them, salty and pungent, on my lips. I can't swallow anything the cheater tells me. His sour tongueless words lodge in my throat like a poisonous pill.

"You said no one knew your true identity." I pace through the kitchen. "No one knew where you lived, who you cared about. You said I wasn't connected to any of this."

The only response Cole gives me is a fixed stare.

Trace steps toward me, his gaze lingering on the tendons stretching in my tense neck. A foot away, he reaches for me, as if to hug me.

"No." I hold my hands up, warding him off. "Did you know about Cole and that woman?"

He pulls in a breath and releases it. "When I was his handler, I sent him into dozens of beds."

"Trace." Cole growls

"To retrieve information?" I wrap an arm around my cramping stomach. "That's what you told me. That sometimes information is the only goal in a mission. Is that what this was?" I look at Cole, shuddering with bitterness. "She had information, and you fucked it out of her?"

He rests his hands on his hips and lowers his head, blowing out a sound of exasperation. "I can't talk about this. Just know I'm done with that job. It's over and—"

"If that's true…" I flick a finger at the pictures. "Why was that in my car?"

"It was an event trigger." Cole collects the photos and stacks them into a pile. "Something happened that sent certain actions into motion. Actions that are supposed to end with you being served this bullshit and me losing the only thing that matters to me."

"So this is about revenge?"

"Yes." Cole crams the pictures into the envelope.

"*Her* revenge? The woman in the photos?" My stomach caves in.

"Danni, look." His voice cracks. "I'm sorry you had to see those pictures—"

"Sorry I had to see you with another woman? Had to find out you cheated on me? What a horrible inconvenient shame that I couldn't just carry on dumb and blind and fucking oblivious."

"It's not what you think, dammit."

"Is that not your dick inside that woman?"

He shoots me an unblinking glare.

I return my own. "Did you fuck her before or after I mourned your death?"

"Don't do this to yourself." Trace steps between us and brushes a knuckle against my tear-soaked cheek. "It will eat at you and ruin—"

"It's already ruined," I snarl. "The three of us? We're fucked to hell. There's no coming back from this."

"Bullshit." Cole slams a fist on the kitchen island. "I refuse to accept that."

I give Cole my back, facing Trace. "If this is a revenge scheme against Cole, why are there photos of you?"

His gaze drifts over my shoulder, locking on Cole. "I can't say."

More secrets. More shit piled on shit. My heart labors in my chest.

Trace won't disclose his involvement, but I know, at the very least, he killed that man to protect me. The question is, how did he know the man was in my house?

"Before I met you, how were you able to watch me?"

"I set up cameras before I left." Cole's voice is gentle, hesitant, against my back. "They're on the outside of your house and in your car."

Startled, I spin around to see his eyes. "*You* set them up?" I gasp. "Are there cameras in—?"

"None in the house." Cole studies me intently, like he's trying to get a pulse on my feelings.

I don't know what I'm feeling. The security measures he put in place kept me alive, but it's a horrible invasion of privacy.

"There were listening devices in your house." Trace wraps a hand around my wrist, as if to keep me from running. "That's how I knew when to show up for your date the night we met, with the Bissara deal already in motion."

"You were listening to me?" Heat blooms beneath my skin, and I yank my arm away. "You heard everything in my house after Cole left?" My mind races, and embarrassment squeezes my stomach. "You could hear my vibrator. And my bodily noises. *Oh my God.* I didn't even know you!"

Cole bends toward me. "No, that's not—"

"How did that conversation go exactly?" I can't decide who I want to castrate more, but I glare at Cole. "Did you call up your best friend and say, *Hey man, I bugged my girlfriend's house, and I need you to spy on her. She's a bit of a moaner, so just tune that part out?"*

Trace reaches for me again, and I jerk away, darting to the other side of the kitchen and putting the island between them and me.

"Is my house still bugged?" Tremors quake through me, trying to bury my voice.

"No." Trace rests his hands on the counter, leaning into the five feet of space between us. "I removed them when I started sleeping there. I never invaded your privacy more than was needed. I have software that triggers off certain sounds and words, sending me notifications to investigate."

I feel violated, deceived, and icky all over. "What

you did is illegal. So is killing a man. Are you running from the police, Trace?"

"Men like us," Cole says, "don't always work within the boundaries of the law. And we're very good at staying under the radar."

They're manipulators, liars, criminals, and I fell in love with them.

I still love them. I love them more than I will ever love anything or anyone in my life. But I've reached my limit.

Maybe it's hypocritical to resent Cole for cheating or to be angry at Trace for keeping more secrets from me. But they continued their relationships with me knowing I was dating both of them. I wasn't exclusive with either of them, and I never set out to deceive them.

They put me in this position with their untruths about their jobs and their friendship. They told me they loved me with mouths full of lies. They wrenched me back and forth between them under the pretense that the secrets were behind us. I'm a fucking fool.

Their deceit has warped my love, trailing its toxic, spineless tentacles around the trust I freely gave them. If I don't untangle myself, their lies will continue to constrict and suffocate until nothing is spared and life is strangled from my body.

Just like that, the decision I've been waiting to happen *happens.*

It surges up my throat in searing tattered sobs.

"Your death destroyed me," I say to Cole, gulping down a painful cry. "But this? This is my breaking point. I mourned a man while he was cheating on me. I trusted a man who killed someone under my roof. My privacy has been recorded and analyzed and violated by two people who supposedly love me." I lower to the floor to slide on my socks and boots. "You both know what the other has been up to and all the while I know absolutely nothing. Thanks for making me feel so fucking stupid and oblivious."

"Danni." Cole takes a step forward, expression tight. "That's not—"

"You led me to believe I knew you, but you only showed me a tiny glimpse of the men you are. It's betrayal in the cruelest form. It feels like you're taking turns killing me, only I'm still alive and breathing and feeling every goddamn second of it."

"That was never my intention." Cole closes the final distance, hard-jawed and hard-headed, with hellfire in his eyes.

"Fuck off, Cole." Anguish claws at the flesh of my heart.

"You're not leaving." He crouches beside me and extends his fingers toward my face.

"Swear to God, if you put your hands on me or try to stop me in any way, I will escalate this into screaming, punching, kicking, whatever it takes, and I'll probably end up hurting myself." I wobble to my feet and pull on my coat. "Let me walk out of here with whatever remains of my goddamn dignity."

Trace hasn't moved from the island. His arms hang at his sides, his head bent low. The shadows of something dark and purposeful rotates in his frosty eyes.

"That goes for you, too," I say to him, hating the tears plopping against my cheeks. "I'm terminating my employment at Bissara, effectively immediately." My voice fractures. "I won't be coming back."

His fingers curl into tight fists, his entire body deadly still.

I need to get out of here before I have a total meltdown. My phone sits on the counter, and that's where it'll stay. No contact. No connections. Cut all ties.

Gathering my strength with a hard-hearted breath, I walk quietly to the elevator and press the button.

It opens instantly, waiting for me, mocking me.

I can't do this.

It feels like I'm walking away from life. Everything I want and cherish, everything that I *am* is right here. There's nothing outside of this room.

"You're not a quitter." Cole's deep angry voice penetrates my spine. "Don't you fucking run away."

I push my feet into motion, step onto the threshold of the elevator, and turn to face them for the last time.

"I want you moved out in three days." I force my watery gaze to Cole, pulling stinging breaths into the ice block of my chest. "Pack up your shit. Whatever you leave behind will get sold when I return."

"Where the fuck are you going?" Cole flexes his fists at his sides, his eyes wild.

Trace lifts a hand to the counter, staring starkly at the floor.

"I put up with the secrets about your jobs, the manipulations with Marlo and Bissara, the rivalry and jealousy, the constant pushing and pulling." I back up into the elevator and press the button for the garage.

"Danni." Cole steps forward with the heel of his hand against his chest.

"I'll coast along and tolerate just about anything. Until I have to push the throttle to the floor. Then I stomp on that son of a bitch with both feet and slam a heavy hammer on it to hold it down." Tears course down my face as elevator doors slide close. "I just dropped the hammer."

twenty-seven

The elevator doors close, and the flood gates burst open. I double-over, choking on the brutality of the sobs fraying my throat. I can't catch my breath. Can't feel my heart beating.

I lost them.

I fucking lost my entire world.

It's an agonizing drive across town with my fingers clenched so tightly to the wheel my knuckles blanch. I go straight to Bree's house, and that's where I stay for three days.

She doesn't know about the photos, the cheating, or the cameras and murder. I told her I ended it with both of them because I couldn't choose. Then I left it at that.

On the third night, I lie on her couch, with my face buried in a wet pillow. I haven't stopped crying since I stepped out of the elevator.

"Cole's supposed to be gone by tonight." A thick keening noise garbles my voice. "I can go home now."

"Stay as long as you want." Bree sits beside my curled-up body and strokes my hair. "You need to give yourself time."

I'm jobless.

Loveless.

Hopeless.

Fucking pathetic.

"I'm going to sell the house." I choke on the words I've been chewing on for three days.

The dance room, the basement, the fucking street where I met Cole—it's all too much, too many memories, too much pain. I lived through loss before, and I know this wretched feeling will never go away. I also know reminders make it worse.

Since Bree was with me the first time I grieved Cole, she understands my reasons. What she doesn't know, however, is how Cole and Trace monitor, stalk, and invade my privacy. I'd be stupid to believe they let me walk away without keeping an eye on me. As long as I remain in St. Louis, they'll be watching. To completely sever ties, I have to leave town.

"Where will you go?" she asks.

"I called Mom this afternoon." I lift my heavy head and meet her eyes. "I'm moving to Florida. Going to live with them for a while. I'm starting over."

Her chin trembles, and she wraps her arms around me. "Dammit, Danni, I don't want you to go. But I get it. Whatever you need to do, I'm here for you."

"Thank you." I hug her back. "I'm going to miss you."

I drive home the next morning. The motorcycle's gone. The house is quiet. I force myself down the stairs and linger on the last step, unable to go farther.

Everything's gone. The futon, weight equipment, punk rock posters… He even took the wedding gown. Why? It's not like I'll ever wear it. I would've sold it.

That's why he took it.

My tears come back with a vengeance, shaking my shoulders and chopping my breaths. I turn back up the stairs and shut the door behind me, leaning against it to support the trembling weight of my stupid broken heart.

Do they feel like this? Like nothing exists but unbearable, inconsolable loss?

At least they still have each other. I hate them a little for that. I hate them for forcing me to do this alone. For making me find the strength to overcome this when all I want to do is lie down and be a doormat for their lies.

But I can't do that. I won't.

That afternoon, I purchase a new cell phone.

Then I call a real estate agent.

twenty-eight

Five weeks later, I wander through my house, finishing up a final walk-through. My boots click along the wood floors, every step echoing with a hollow thud in the empty rooms.

I'm doing this. I'm moving on, and I fucking hate it.

I haven't heard from Cole or Trace since that day in the penthouse. But several times a week, the rumble of a motorcycle passes down the street. Always early in the morning. Always the same slow speed.

The day after Cole moved out, I scoured every crack and cranny in my house, searching for cameras or something that doesn't belong. I found nothing. If Trace is watching me, I don't know how he's doing it.

I think about them. With every breath. Every tear.

Every miserable beat of my heart. I miss them so fucking much.

Christmas was the worst. I spent the holiday with Bree and felt utterly and completely alone.

Because I *am* alone. I tell myself I'm moving on, but I never will. Still, I have to try.

I walk into the dance studio, and a surge of misery fires behind my eyes. With my phone in hand, I pull up my song selection and play *Moving On* by Kodaline.

I'm going to Florida to start over.

It's a new year. A new beginning. I can do this.

With a deep breath, I say goodbye to my house, my dance studio, the beautiful memories, the darkest hours. Then I whisper goodbye to Cole and Trace.

I open the back door, move forward, and pause mid-step on the threshold.

Sitting on the sidewalk just outside the door is a tall paper cup with a plastic lid. The logo on the side advertises my favorite coffee from the small coffee shop down the street.

I lift it, smell it, and confirm it's my favorite blend. Peeking under the lid, I find it prepared exactly the way I like it. There's no note. Nothing to indicate who it's from. But I can narrow it down to two people.

My heart pounds as I scan the driveway, the street, searching for them, hoping, needing to see them with every aching breath.

The world around me is empty.

Silent.

I'm alone.

With a trembling hand, I bring the cup to my mouth and sip. *Still warm.*

My stomach sinks. I *just* missed him. Cole, Trace,

whoever it was. I would give anything to see one of their faces again.

The song streams from my phone, reminding me what I'm supposed to be doing.

Move on, Danni. One foot in front of the other.

I slip the phone into my coat pocket and lock up. All my belongings are in storage. Once I find a place of my own, I'll have my things shipped to Florida.

I still have the Midget, and as I lower behind the steering wheel, I'm glad it's going with me. I love this car.

Except it won't start.

I crank the engine over and over. It doesn't make a sound. *Fucking fuck fuck!*

Why did I think this car would get me all the way to Florida? I can't even get it out of my driveway.

Shivering in the cold January temperatures, I drink the coffee, savor the warm rich taste, and consider my options.

I need to go back inside and call a tow truck. I can stay with Bree until the car is fixed.

Opening the door, I climb back out, and the pall of vertigo hits me sideways. Jesus, I don't feel good all of a sudden. I attempt another step and sway. What the hell?

A loud rushing sound roars in my ears. Dizziness grips me hard, spinning the ground and splotching my vision. I need to sit down. I need to…

My knees buckle, and the pavement rises up, slamming against my chest. The coffee tumbles from my grip, and darkness creeps in around me.

Unable to lift my cheek from the cold ground, I stare in a daze at the paper cup where it rolls on its side beside my limp arm. Rolling… Slowing… Stopping.

The last thing I see before the world goes black is three words written in unfamiliar handwriting on the bottom of the cup.

It's not over.

up next

The Danni-Trace-Cole love triangle concludes with:

THREE IS A WAR

three

is a war

Three means war.
Three sides vying for forever.

Cole.
My first love.
The bad boy with the dangerous smile and passionate temper draws attention like a lit fuse on dynamite. But his dark molten eyes spark only for me.

Trace.
My second chance.
Over six feet of Norse god in a tailored suit, he calculates every move and seizes my hungry breaths with an iron fist.

Me.
The free-spirited dancer, torn between two men with no resolution in sight.
I tried leaving, staying, refusing, and surrendering.
What options do I have left?

I love two men, and I do the only thing I can. I fight.

books by pam godwin

DARK COWBOY ROMANCE

TRAILS OF SIN SERIES

Knotted #1

Buckled #2

Booted #3

DARK PARANORMAL ROMANCE

TRILOGY OF EVE

Heart of Eve

Dead of Eve #1

Blood of Eve #2

Dawn of Eve #3

DARK ROMANCE
DELIVER SERIES
Deliver #1
Vanquish #2
Disclaim #3
Devastate #4
Take #5
Manipulate #6
Unshackle #7
Dominate #8
Complicate #9

STUDENT-TEACHER / PRIEST
Lessons In Sin

STUDENT-TEACHER ROMANCE
Dark Notes

ROCK-STAR DARK ROMANCE
Beneath the Burn

ROMANTIC SUSPENSE
Dirty Ties

EROTIC ROMANCE
Incentive

DARK HISTORICAL PIRATE ROMANCE
King of Libertines
Sea of Ruin

playlist

Issues by Julia Michaels
Uptown Funk by Mark Ronson
Lust For Life by Lana Del Rey
Beautiful Liar by Beyoncé and Shakira
Don't Let Me Down by The Chainsmokers
Pillowtalk by Zayn
I Hate U I Love U by Gnash
This Town by Niall Horan
Now Or Never by Halsey
Latch by Disclosure
Undisclosed Desires by Muse
Physical by Nine Inch Nails
Say Something by A Great Big World
We Can Hurt Together by Sia
Moving On by Kodaline

pam godwin

New York Times and USA Today Bestselling author, Pam Godwin, lives in the Midwest with her husband, their two children, and a foulmouthed parrot. When she ran away, she traveled fourteen countries across five continents, attended three universities, and married the vocalist of her favorite rock band.

Java, tobacco, and dark romance novels are her favorite indulgences, and might be considered more unhealthy than her aversion to sleeping, eating meat, and dolls with blinking eyes.

pamgodwinauthor@gmail.com